AN
HOUR
TO
KILL

AN
HOUR
TO
KILL

[a n o v e l]

KARIN YAPALATER

WILLIAM MORROW
An Imprint of HarperCollinsPublishers

Grateful acknowledgment is given for permission to reprint the following:

Aleksandr Pushkin poem "Little Bird" as translated by Vladimir Nabokov by arrangement with the Estate of Vladimir Nabokov.

"Medusa" from *Ariel* by Sylvia Plath. Copyright © 1965 by Ted Hughes and HarperCollins Publishers.

FIRST EDITION

Designed by Kris Tobiassen

Printed on acid-free paper

Library of Congress Cataloging-in-Publication Data

Yapalater, Karin.
    An hour to kill : a novel / Karin Yapalater.— 1st ed.
      p. cm.
    ISBN 0-688-16599-0
    1. Police—New York (State)—New York—Fiction. 2. Central Park (New York, N.Y.)—Fiction. 3. Undercover operations—Fiction. 4. New York (N.Y.)—Fiction. 5. Police murders—Fiction. 6. Policewomen—Fiction. I. Title.

PS3625.A69 H6   2003
813'.6—dc21

                              2002043239

03 04 05 06 07 WBC/RRD 10 9 8 7 6 5 4 3 2 1

FOR GREG
. . . entre chien et loup

Strip his clothes off, then he'll heal us,
If he doesn't, kill him dead!

. . . .

O be joyful, all you patients
The doctor's laid with you in bed. . . .

— from Franz Kafka, "A Country Doctor"

In this treacherous world
Nothing is the truth or a lie
Everything depends on the color
Of the crystal in which one perceives it. . . .

—Calderón de la Barca

ACKNOWLEDGMENTS

It all started with a little murder. I needed a lawyer and a cop fast. Over coffee on the Great South Bay, I consulted my brilliant friend and judicial advisor, Toby Pilsner, to whom I am deeply indebted. She introduced me to the venerable Daniel McCarthy, Chief Trial Counsel for the Bronx District Attorney's Office. Dan showed up carrying two Bloomingdale's bags filled with a rather gruesome load of documentation that served as my entrée into the world of homicide. After firing off numerous questions, Dan smiled and said, "You gotta meet Frank." Frank turned out to be none other than the highly esteemed Frank Viggiano, Detective Sergeant, New York City Police Department, former Squad Commander of the 47th Precinct Detective Squad, and Chief Investigator of the Bronx District Attorney's Office. I was a rookie, making up a murder, asking two titans to go along for the ride. They jumped into my fictional landscape with boundless enthusiasm and dedication. No questions were too ridiculous, no requests ever turned down. They shared their experience, knowledge, and singular sense of humor with me, and I am so deeply grateful to them both for their friendship and generosity. I could not have pulled this off without them.

Equally invaluable was Vernon J. Geberth's book *Practical Homicide Investigation* (of the CRC Press, 1996). Mr. Geberth is a retired Lieutenant

Commander of the NYPD, and I greatly appreciate his kind permission to use his extensive, voluminous, and thoroughly well-documented book to learn the ropes. In addition, books that were helpful in my research include *The Freud/Jung Letters*, edited by William McGuire (Princeton University Press, 1974) and *Joel-Peter Witkin: A Retrospective* (Scalo, 1995).

For support over the long haul, I'm deeply grateful to my extraordinary agent, Beth Vesel. When times got tough, she rolled up her sleeves, pulled rabbits out of hats, and stayed the course. Many thanks to her hardworking assistants Carol Chase and Emilie Stewart. For keeping the faith and helping me get to the heart of the matter, infinite thanks to my astute editor, Claire Wachtel at William Morrow. Thanks too to her assistant, Jennifer Pooley, for keeping on top of the details. For keen editorial insights, overall brilliance and dedication thanks to Susan Bell, who taught me the subtle art of becoming the lotus. For early editorial support and encouragement thanks to Ann Darby, Patricia Haas, Maureen Howard, Jenny McPhee, Rick Moody, Helen Schulman, and Bill Roorbach. A special toast to Pat and Gloria and unforgettable thanks to Professors Henry Larom and Dan Masterson.

For stimulating psychoanalytic dialogue and enlightenment, thank you Dr. Alvin Yapalater and the New York Psychoanalytic Library.

For welcoming me into the Central Park Precinct and giving me the generosity of their time, sincere thanks to P. J. Maroney, Detective Sergeant, NYPD, and Adrienne Jones, Detective, NYPD.

Heartfelt appreciation and gratitude to my family and friends who have been there from the start, cheering me on before anyone else knew I was even trying. Dad, Mom, Leslie . . . Greg, Sophia, Tristan . . . this one is for you.

Prologue

The hood of night slips on to drape the park in the dreary dreadful gray of winter. I skulk along desolate, tangled pathways and creep within the shadows of looming boulders. Leaving the lights of the city far behind. Broken bottles, dog shit, stubs of cigarettes.

Going to the private wood. Crawling close to the ground, hiding behind bushes. Silent, stealthy. Creature of the forest. My black Lycra a slick body glove, camouflaged head to toe. Only my eyes, holding no expression at all, exposed to track movement in the darkness.

Snowfall. Perfect for a short walk in the woods, or a screw in a car . . . roll the windows up, release stale heat from slatted vents, tune the radio to something slow.

Perched on the heavy limb of a black oak, waiting, for show time.

And then, by the light of a full moon, watching, as she strikes a bargain with another three-minute lover. On her knees, head bobbing, in synchronized rhythm. His taut legs spread, back arched. Urgent moans rising as he grips her head to home base, far too eager to finish this cheap love song.

Rinsing her mouth with dirty snow, she laughs to herself, relieved that the chore is over. Her hands tremble as she reaches into her bag for a cigarette, the light of the flame faintly reveals her lips. She walks up over the hill to meet another.

The one all the waiting has been for.

Inhale, life. Exhale, death.

Who am I?

I am Fire.

Burning . . . burning . . . burning.

[1]

Final Release

"I'm uncomfortable talking about it."

"All the more reason to talk about it."

"I don't know."

"Go on."

She tilted her head to the right, shifted in her chair, uncrossed her legs. She wore a tight button-down blouse, black, a short wool skirt to match. Her jet black hair, flecked with auburn highlights, tousled on her shoulders. "If you think it matters."

He looked at her, felt the saliva well up under his tongue.

She brazenly met his gaze, then looked right past him, over at the cat on the windowsill. She laughed. "Looks like your cat's gonna kill himself."

The cat was not the point.

He focused his eyes on the tip of her nose. Then her lips. Cherry red. She was young, too young for the life she'd led. "Notice how you've just changed the subject?"

She brushed a hair from her face, then slouched back. She rubbed her palms up and down her thighs, offering a view of one black garter.

"Tell me how you've been." He crossed his arms, his rolled-up shirt-sleeves revealing the muscular forearms of an avid sportsman.

She fingered the gold pendant that rested like an amulet between her breasts. She arched her back. She stared up at him, then looked down at her hands. She exhaled loudly. "There's that look on your face again. You're losing patience with me."

They'd been at it for six months now. This was no ingénue from Kansas seeking the talking cure. In need of a fix, she was blurring boundaries, again. An accomplished tease who had tempted him out of his chair. It had begun with a reassuring caress. An empathetic gesture extended after a particularly intense exchange. A gut-wrenching outpour about incest with her dear father. He could remember wiping her tears. Then, their bodies in close contact. Her lips on his. A mistake? An indulgence.

Subsequent episodes followed. Fondling. Prolonged good-byes. The brush of a hand making contact with the contour of a breast, a thigh, her ass. Regular meetings took place. In the park. In his car. Couldn't resist the game of taboo.

"No smoking, huh?" She huffed.

He usually discouraged smoking, anything that would take a patient away from the self, away from dealing with their truth. But with her, the rules did not apply.

"Go on." He wanted out, out of this mind-set, out of the room. The heels on her boots just high enough, her skirt just short enough.

"One?" Her look was coy, well rehearsed. She fiddled with the buttons on her blouse as she'd done so many times before, nonchalantly opening one more, the curve of each bare breast summoning his cock to attention. She smiled when he nodded his approval. She reached into her well-worn leather jacket, got the pack and shook one out. She offered him one.

At first, he refused. Joining in a smoke was her idea of connection.

But then he lit up, and she let go—a stream of smoke propelling her to carry on. "I keep having the same dream. You know the one. I'm with my father. Front seat of his car. He passes me a bottle, tells me to drink up. He has me strapped in. He's laughing. Like it's all some big joke. And then he's between my legs, sucking there . . . like a baby. And it's bad, you know, I want it to stop. And then I look down, and . . ."

"Yes." He lifted his chin, his eyes caught the light.

"And then I look down. And . . . it's . . . you."

He offered his best impression of neutrality. His self-control was a hard thing to shake, but she had a way of making him spin. He let the silence moderate.

"I wake up, but then I'm back to sleep . . . I can see the car . . . doors all locked, and the car . . . the car's on fire." She paused. "You're in there . . . and I'm watching you burn up and die."

If he had a gold coin for every one of his patients' fantasies. To be him, to fuck him, to kill him. "Tell me how you feel."

At first she looked disappointed. Her eyes so vacant, he wondered if she had heard him. "About the dream or about you?" She probably could have convinced anyone but him that she'd forgotten.

He rubbed his chin. "Both."

She looked away, toward the wall. Framed diplomas and citations. Yale. Prestigious psychoanalytic societies. Outside, the winter wind howled, but here, inside these walls, it was hot as hell. "I don't like this. You know everything about me and I know nothing about you."

"I'm here to listen. That *is* what you said you wanted?"

She said something under her breath, coughed it away.

"What is it you want to know?" He pursed his lips, furled his brow.

"Will you tell me the truth?" She smiled.

"I am prepared to accept whatever you tell me as truth."

"I said, will *you* tell *me* the truth?"

He nodded yes.

She twisted in her chair. "I mean, don't you think we should talk about us . . ."

He glanced at the clock on the wall. Quarter past four. He heard a faint ringing in his ears. A day's worth of stale air and an invisible force field stood between them. "I'm afraid we haven't . . ."

"Time."

"No. It would be better to . . ."

"Deny it?"

He looked at her mouth, could imagine himself kissing her. He cleared his throat, stayed the course. "It would be better to discuss your dream."

"I want something to stop these dreams."

In his mind's eye she had her mouth around his cock now. He clenched and unclenched his fists. Imagined his hands cupping each of her breasts. Her tongue communicating in ways absolutely forbidden here. He took a deep breath, exhaled, blew the image away. "How about going to detox?"

"Don't want to go back." She rubbed the back of her neck. Her legs spread. "That shit they gave me last time made me sick."

He stood, went to his desk, opened a drawer. Thinking that he was about to write a prescription, she smiled.

Instead, he handed her a card.

Disappointed, she frowned. "What's this?"

"They're experimenting with a new cure. I hear it's effective. Completely painless. And it wouldn't cost you a thing."

"Nothing's free, Doc."

"I could give them a call, set something up for you." He placed his hand on the phone.

"I don't know." She squirmed a bit in her chair.

He picked up the phone and watched her as he dialed. Within a few minutes, he had arranged an appointment. When he hung up, he wrote down a time and date and handed it to her. "Now, it's your choice whether to show up."

Reluctantly, she took the slip of paper. "Monday, March 23rd. Ten A.M. Shit." She frowned. Gave her all weekend to get wasted.

"That gives you all weekend to think about it."

"I don't want to talk about detox. I want to talk about us. About *you*—"

"We've been working together for over six months now—"

"Working." She smiled.

"You know that the way I feel is not the issue here," he continued.

"What is the issue here, Doc?" Her voice was low, breathless.

He wanted her. The ache he felt between his legs impossible to ignore. He had tried, initially, to manage the desire within himself and yet allow for the nuances of countertransference. The books that lined the walls behind him were filled with lengthy discourse on the subject— cautionary words of narrow-minded traditionalists, uncomfortable in the arena of the erotic. So-called pioneers of psychoanalysis.

She had come to him emoting the ills of a nomadic childhood. Young, but far from naive. Spilled into his already complicated life. But then, what was life without complication? He surveyed the stacks of papers piled on his desk. She was his last patient for the day. He could relax. Forget the clock, the self-imposed confinements of time. Friday. End of a long work week. Some inner process was at work. Time to abandon old principles . . . challenge the dated textbook point of view.

His look was all the invitation she needed. He swiveled in his chair and began to rise, but was pushed back down as she knelt between his legs, her beautiful cleavage resting in his lap. His fingers began to knead her nipples until they were hard and stiff. She unzipped his fly and played with his cock, teasing with her tongue, taking him in with exquisite ease and agility.

"No . . . not here . . ." He wasn't whining, but it sounded like a plea nonetheless.

"Shhh." She sat on his lap, played with herself, coaxed him to find his way inside her.

"Not here." He stopped her.

"Later, then . . ." she eagerly demanded.

"In the park, then . . . usual place and time."

This was his trip. He got off on clandestine outings. Tempting fate, under the night sky.

Could have sworn he heard a door open. "Shhh . . ." He lifted her off his lap and leaned away from her. "Please. We have to . . . stop." He eased away, his hard-on quickly deflating. He zipped up his trousers, tightened his tie.

Cautiously, she wiped her mouth with the back of her hand and then adjusted her clothes. Her coat provided a layer of distance. Right arm in the right hole, left arm in the left hole. She walked herself out backwards, not taking her eyes off him, not saying a word.

Once she'd gone, he reached for her file, scratched his beard with the end of his pen, and began writing. Wish fulfillment. Car. Fire. The cat leapt off the sill and came over to him, curling around his ankles and purring loudly for his attention. The cat's long, black tail waved hypnotically against his leg. Mid-thought, the door opened, then closed shut.

He was about to call her name. But this next visitor moved in too fast, took a seat on his lap and planted her mouth on his. He responded in kind, began to unbutton her dress, fingered her black lace bra. He encircled each nipple gently while she unzipped his pants. He was already hard. Before hiking up the hem of her blue gabardine, he reached in a drawer and extracted a condom. She attempted to distract him, have him enter her bare. But to her dismay, he remained doggedly focused, completing this task before permitting penetration.

The chair rocked, tilting and then righting itself with the rhythmic sway of their weight. Then, locked in place, he took her down to the carpeted floor, repositioning her on all fours. She tried to slow him down. But in an orgiastic frenzy, he tightened his grip. She came, ass in the air, one hand massaging her clit, one eye on her watch. He followed, a look that could have been mistaken for pain on his face; the image of his previous patient providing the unexpected backdrop for his final release.

[2]

Better Late Than Dead

James Gurson had requested the transfer out of the three four. Last-ditch attempt to save his marriage. Came through a year too late. Based on an impressive clearance rate, they wanted to stick him someplace upscale, a place like the one nine. Cut him a slice of the Upper East Side. But he wasn't looking for high-profile action, he was looking for a place to lighten his load awhile. Be home before dawn. Something to make the wife happy. Figured he'd do six months in Central Park. Watch his kid and the grass grow. Go to work in a playground, better known to cops as the dump.

Unfortunately, by the time the request came through, his wife had already filed papers. He'd gone a bit bonkers losing her. Had a brush with Internal Affairs when she called to report that he was harassing her. Harassing her. All he was doing was keeping an eye on her from afar, making sure she was okay. IAB ordered him to keep his distance. Gave him his transfer now that he didn't need it and told him to make the best of it. Tagged it "temporary." CP precinct needed a brain, they told him. And Gurson was it.

Place didn't even have a permanent sergeant. Revolved a boss in and out every six months. Sergeant presently on duty, Vincent Bianchi, was his old boss from the three four. Burnt out and close to retirement. Probably the one to thank for arranging this gratuitous move for Gurson.

Gurson was second-generation blue. His father had worn a licensed NYPD revolver. Proudly. Until he blew away a punk dealer who just so happened to be the nephew of a well-placed district judge. Old man said the kid had pulled a piece. But it turned out the kid was packing plastic. Seventeen good years on the force and they put him up on charges, said he violated the dealer's civil rights. Prosecution threatened to put him away for life. Might have too, if he hadn't decided to pull a final exit in the family garage. In full uniform, behind the wheel of his black Eldorado. Closed all the windows and doors and let her run.

Reluctantly, Gurson stepped into his old man's black shoes. Three years in, he traded in his street uniform for a shiny gold shield. The promotion was pure overtime. Helped push Gurson's marriage right over the edge. Every step he took, they measured him against his old man. Old man. His father wasn't even forty when he checked out. Gurson was thirty-four now. Two steps forward, three steps back.

He was called into the park to replace a bad seed by the name of Charlene Leone. Hispanic undercover narc now enjoying an extended vacation without pay for taking her work home with her. Namely, a base pipe and enough blow to waste a small cartel. While Leone continued futile appeals for full reinstatement, Gurson was called in to ride shotgun with her old partner. A black cop named Didi Kane, who looked more like the monthly pinup than the precinct's purported badass.

Seven A.M. Saturday morning. He'd worked a double shift to clear a string of muggings down by the Boat Basin. Pack of j.d.'s wilding in the snow. Pop fly. Three out. Time to leave the ballpark.

"Anybody want this?" Bianchi entered the precinct, holding up an old Walkman.

Gurson took hold of the headphones. "Does it work?"

"Would I be giving it away if it worked?"

Gurson flipped it over, rattled it around.

"Hey, take it easy."

"Thing's broken, boss."

"So fix it. You want it?"

"I'll give it to my kid." He slipped the player and phones in his jacket pocket and followed Bianchi into his office.

Bianchi marked the day off on his wall calendar.

"Bit premature, don't you think?" said Gurson. "I mean, day's just starting."

It was the final month of Bianchi's six-month stint. Soon he'd be lounging back, collecting half pay. He twirled his number 2 pencil and looked at the calendar. "What do you know. March 21st. First day of spring."

"Not from this window," said Gurson.

"Ought to have someone check your pulse, Gurson. Looks like you're dying of boredom."

Gurson tried opening the window next to Bianchi's desk, but it wouldn't budge. He looked at his soot-stained fingers and frowned.

"Where's Kane?"

"Personal day."

"Makes three this month," said Bianchi. "Do her a favor. Tell her I'm counting her personal days."

Gurson took a sip of cold coffee. According to Kane, Leone had been set up, her dismissal a case of gender discrimination. An opinion she held alone, begrudgingly. Just Gurson's luck. To be coupled with a stunning grudge. Kind of like his ex-wife, come to think of it. Teed off, too often, their arms wrapped around them, like the yellow tape running across a crime scene.

Bianchi turned on his radio. A scratchy Sinatra. The sergeant shook his head. "Go home, Gurson. You've been here too long. Get some sleep. You're starting to look pasty."

"Must be all this fresh air." Gurson took a deep breath and looked out the dirty window. Flurries were still falling. "Feel like I'm working in a freaking snow globe."

First day of spring? From the looks of things, winter wasn't planning any quick defrost. Instead of taking the 85th transverse cross-town, Gurson decided to walk the scenic route through the Rambles. Fresh air smacked his face. Felt good. Cleared his head, fuzzy from overtime. He planned to catch a subway to Sty Town, his old neighborhood, to pick up his kid for a sleepover. A visit they were both looking forward to. He checked his watch. Despite the slight detour, he'd be there just as the kid was waking up. The kind of thing he hadn't realized the importance of while he was married. He climbed the incline and started walking. Snow blanketed the 843 acres of the park. Each cubic yard a potential crime scene. Mayor claimed the park was the safest place in the city. All relative, Einstein. Nobody lived here full-time. No houses to rob, no cars to jack. Street-smart New Yorkers took the high road after dark. Unless they were in pursuit of nature's illegal gifts—prostitution, hawking, nickel and diming. Take back the night? Take it where? To touch the New York night deep in this wood was suicide.

He was enjoying the early morning solitude, watching one foot and then the other, kicking up drifts of white snow. Park in all its winter glory. Pine trees edged with frost, the sky a cloudy silkscreen. Crystal quiet. The only sound a plane buzzing overhead. Just before taking a left out of the grove, leading east, he stopped. Off at a distance he saw a car stuck in the snowy brush.

Instinctively, he picked up speed. When he reached the car, he peered in. He could see a man in the driver's seat, his head tipped back on the headrest. Skin crimson.

Gurson walked around the car. A wad of filthy cloth wedged into the tailpipe. The car was low to the ground. Foreign. More than half its face sitting pretty in the woods, covered by snow. Still running but going nowhere. Three-pointed silver emblem. Old Mercedes. Odd color. No color really, dull gray. With his gloved hand, Gurson reached for the door handle. A tug popped it open, but instead of swinging out, the portal swung up and nearly knocked him over, arching overhead like the wing of a bird.

A rush of gas choked the air. The car's unique construction made it impossible for him to slide in. High-caliber cockpit custom fit with bucket seats. He leaned on the doorsill and looked inside. Ivory interior, immaculate. He snuffed the motor.

"Buddy, can you hear me? What happened?" Gurson loosened the guy's dark paisley tie. The guy moaned, a low gurgle. No blood, but that thick head of hair could easily stash a bullet. He looked around the car. Freaking guy's zipper was open. Tip of his goddamned johnson peeking out through his skivs. Didn't look like he'd been in any kind of struggle, probably just out here playing with himself before biting the big one. Caught a glimpse of himself in the rearview mirror, which was turned toward the driver's seat, positioned so the guy could see his own face. Gurson put his hand to the guy's throat and felt for a pulse. Guy might not make it waiting for the medics. He opened the guy's shirt, eased his head back. Still breathing. Gurson frisked the guy's pockets. Empty wallet. If he'd been robbed, the asshole missed the Rolex. Gurson noticed a piece of paper peeking out of the visor. Typed words. He took hold of it and read:

I have become accessible to consolation . . .

He placed the note inside the empty sleeve of the wallet and slid it into his own jacket pocket. Then he flicked open his cellular. "Detective James Gurson to 911, CP squad, off duty, scene of possible suicide. Get a 10-85 with a unit and send me a bus."

On the passenger seat lay the carcass of a small dead bird, its wings missing. Neatly sliced off. He took a closer look. Sparrow.

"He dead?" A homeless bum appeared out of nowhere and began pissing in the snow. He walked toward the car, shaking his last drops inches from Gurson's shoes.

"Whoa, watch the shoes. Back it up. I need room, here."

"Wha'choo?" The man weaved toward Gurson. "You the he-ro?"

Gurson shook his head. He reached into his front pocket and found his shield. "No," he said, "are you?"

"Hah." The bum backed off.

"You see what happened here?"

The bum's weathered face was flat, his bloodshot eyes swollen. He laughed. "See? Man, I can't see nothing." The man ambled back into the woods.

Gurson put a second call into 911. "Detective Gurson. . . . Put a rush on that bus, victim still alive, possible gunshot wounds. . . ."

Guy probably wouldn't make it. Mouth to mouth? In this infectious city, most cops would wait for the medics. Gurson put his mouth to the guy's mouth and started breathing.

As Orrin Gretz slipped in and out of consciousness and took the last labored breaths that would become his final sleep, one thought consumed him. Nobody would be left behind. No heir, no living legacy.

A siren. A sea of strange faces.

Could he remember his own name?

Orrin Gaylord Gretz. Psychiatrist. Emotional translator. Here to interpret pain. But he couldn't speak. Could only imagine opening his mouth to form the words. Words that might explain how his life had come to this.

His mind rambled on, short-circuiting. He had not imagined death quite this way. Imagined there'd be something more. Death would take a thinking man by the hand, lead him from this life to a deeper knowing. He'd imagined a stairway to higher consciousness.

All he felt was numb. Helpless. He could no longer feel his legs, tried to, tried to move them, but the paralysis was complete. He wanted to come up for air, like a swimmer down in the deep too long. Wanted to stand up, take it on his feet, this final blow, but the ground seemed to be pulling him down, down into darkness.

Inside the park, the police marked the area off. They canvassed for possible witnesses—joggers, vagrants, kids walking dogs. But the place was deserted. Crime scene techs conducted a preliminary photo shoot. Had to handle it like a crime scene, pending investigation. Tow was on its way to take the car to the precinct garage. Fresh snow was quickly covering the ground. Soon it would look like nothing ever happened.

Gurson opened the glove. A flashlight, a few maps, and an old catalog with a picture of the car on its cover. Mercedes. 300 SL. Gullwing. 1957. He took a look under the seats. Something shiny under the passenger side caught his eye. Silver. Mini guillotine. Size of a credit card. Used to cut cigars. He looked in the back. No trunk to speak of. Just a shelf with a small leather duffel sitting on top. He unzipped the bag hoping to find some ID, but it was just filled with old rags.

The precinct detective squad arrived just moments before the ambulance took off. Gurson left them with the rig. The guy was still breathing, which meant he had to go along for the ride. Try to make contact. Chaotic scene. Med tech stuffing tubes down the guy's throat and rigging IV; siren blaring and the ambulance dipping and swerving like a cyclone all over the road. Didn't look like the guy would make it to the hospital. Nice if he could get some dying declaration.

"Talk to me. Was anyone with you? Come on . . ."

"The . . . car . . . the . . ." Incoherent.

The ambulance sped on, the deafening shrill of the siren bouncing off concrete.

"Car? What about the car?" Gurson shouted.

"Car-diac arrest." The med tech checked the guy's vitals. "Dammit. We're losing him. He's going."

The guy went into spasm, vomiting up bile and blood. The med tech furiously pumped his chest. Then he slumped back. "Shit. That's it, man. Gone."

"Gone?"

"Gone."

Gurson's ears started to burn. He took a deep drag of cool air. Felt like he was filled with helium, hovering over the scene. Dizzy. Just tired, yeah, that must be it. Hell, he'd seen plenty of nasty things. Dead and dying, rotting corpses. *But not like this one, only saw this once before.*

Thoughts of his original destination came back to him. His son. Jack. Shit. What time was it? Almost ten o'clock. Christ.

As soon as the ambulance reached the hospital, the medics marked the chart DOA. They'd ship the body off to the morgue. Squad would track down next of kin, file necessary papers. Suicide, open, shut. He'd check in first thing in the morning.

No time for mass transit, so he hailed a cab. Would have to explain why Daddy wasn't there when his boy woke up, as promised. Val's green eyes angry, the way they were when he let her down, which had been all too often. Hell, she'd married a cop, knew what that meant. Of course, he'd managed to make it worse, always working overtime when he should have been home. Did he still love her? Sure. But what good was that? A lot of regret a little too late. Kicked his ass out a year ago. Already hot and heavy with someone new. Some office schmo. Kind of guy that didn't need to wear a bulletproof vest to work.

The city passed him by from inside the car. He'd quit smoking a year ago, but seeing Val always gave him the urge. She'd be tapping her foot at the door right about now, checking the time. He patted himself down, in search of a phantom pack, and felt some bulk in his left jacket pocket. The stiff's wallet. Shit, thought he'd passed it to the squad. Swing around first thing in the morning, drop it off. Daddy's on his way, Jack. Two hours late for his little boy. But hey, better late than dead.

[3]

Gavotte

This was one of Ren's favorite calls. Rich couple on the Upper East Side, dabblers in voyeuristic sex. A regular engagement that had helped pay the rent for a number of years. It had been a predictable gig, courteous and civilized. Like fucking friends. But as with most ménage à trois, it had turned into a rather competitive triangle. Sensing her waning interest, hubbie upped the ante. One hour of her time now commanded a cool two fifty. He was a far cry from her usual sleazoid patrons. On the high end, she worked her ass off to pocket a twenty for lap dances at a downtown burlesque club. Hard work, and too much contact with dirty old men who slobbered and tipped her with meager generosity. Hubbie was a helluva lot classier than the three-dollar blow jobs that had marked her early beginnings on the street at the ripe old age of twelve. From three-dollar blow jobs to three-hundred-dollar snow jobs. On her own, or in the hands of pimps, men trashed her while promising love and protection.

Hubbie's deep pockets made it hard to say no.

It all began as his private gig when the wife was not around. A cross-dresser, he liked to watch. Into dungeons and dragons, slipknots and rubber. Liked to indulge her with expensive champagne and killer pot. She figured he was somebody important. Kind of guy you hired to keep you out of the can. In his spare time, he sported lacy garters and stockings under his conservative three piece. He'd gotten so looped on one occasion, Ren had actually managed to snap a few shots of him decked in his finest drag. Along with mace and a .22, a loaded pocket Instamatic was a girl's best friend. Never knew when a girl might need to call in a favor.

He had introduced her to the wife on some special occasion. On her birthday . . . or was it an anniversary? One snowy evening, he had presented her to the wife, wrapped in silk and ribbons. Called her "a precious gift."

Wife was no slouch either, a professional too. Knew how to spend hubbie's extra cash, which made them, if nothing else, a symbiotic pair. The wife really took to her. Feeling was mutual. She liked the wife best. Perky tits and the prettiest mouth. Gentle touch. Closet Sappho.

It wasn't long after that first celebratory eve that the wife asked for her own secret arrangement. Each of them making her promise never to let the other one know. Wife liked to see her for companionship, mostly. Wasn't into sex. Preferred tea parties at posh hotels. Long walks in the park. Interested in Ren's hard and bitter life. Something about her fascination with human behavior.

Hubbie was none the wiser. Continued their own routine and let him arrange another regular, high-paying tryst for her. Some very hush-hush transaction he said he absolutely didn't want the wife to ever know about. No problem. Their pact had given her some independence from her pimp, and she kind of got off on playing both ends against the middle.

When it was "à trois," hubbie was content to stay on the sidelines.

Sitting on the sofa, nursing his scotch and an unimpressive hard-on, he'd get off just watching. Worked out at the gym, Ren suspected. No potbelly stove on this one. Pumped abs, sculpted pecs. Not bad for a middle-aged silver fox, despite the set of saggy balls. But his desire was obviously more than his poor limp dick could ever hope to manage. Sometimes he'd pull out a little blow to really frustrate himself. Pass the straw. And then the party would officially begin.

Tonight the aphrodisiac of choice was some expensive imported vodka, though she guessed they'd both popped something before she got there to cut the edge. Hubbie lavishly poured the icy Grey Goose into three heavy tumblers. They sat around and drank awhile, until their knees and their inhibitions went numb. Then the husband flicked on the projection TV and pulled out a DVD from his impressive library of lesbo flicks, well concealed behind a set of slick wooden doors on their floor-to-ceiling mahogany bookcases. Music, please. Ren's signal. Rise and start dancing, slowly undressing down to her corset and gartered stockings. Wife joined in, a slow erotic gavotte. Caressing, body to body.

Ren knew the wife was somewhere else in her head. In the room, but not there physically. It was a mind game that Ren herself was well acquainted with. A kind of mental blindness. Like Ren, the wife was fully able to disconnect—from the act of sex or the act of living life itself. They worked this gig *together*. In his mind, of course, hubbie was the ringmaster, in charge of the show. But in truth . . . to them? He was just a john, insignificant. The money, honey. The big easy. The schmuck.

In essence, the wife was a whore. This gave her and Ren their special connection from the start.

Ren began humming the wife's dildo along the lips of her own sex, her eyes slightly open to take the wife in. The wife wore her beautiful pout, remotely intrigued. Ren leaned forward, gently applying the moistened toy between the wife's thighs. A low satisfactory moan encouraged Ren to continue. In this way, they conspired. Music pumped loud, bodies on the big screen writhed and moaned, and in less than fifteen minutes, it was all over. Like clockwork, the husband left to regain composure. TV off, music down. Money had already changed hands.

The wife walked Ren to the front door. "You cut your hair," the wife noted. "I hardly recognized you."

"Feel it." Ren ran her own hand over her closely cropped mane. "I'm a boy. Like it?"

Missus felt the short, thick locks, letting her hand drop to Ren's neck. She frowned.

"What's up with you?" Ren reached for the wife.

"Don't."

Ren rubbed her own nose and smiled.

The wife escorted her to the front door.

Ren sucked in her breath, puffed it out, like she was smoking. "You're pissed off, right, 'cause I haven't called?"

The wife looked away. "Where've you been?"

"Here and there."

The wife raised her brows in a show of concern.

Ren slowly ran her right index finger between the wife's breasts. The wife stopped the hand and wrapped her own around it. "I've been so worried about you. All this trouble you said you're in."

"All in a day's work, I guess." Ren shrugged.

"I've left you messages. You could have called me, let me know you were okay." She was intent on making a point now, her energy high. "You look pale."

Ren shook her dark bangs out of her eyes. The wife was acting like a protective den mother again. Too needy for Ren's taste. Ren took a step back, then a step forward. Having the wife's empathy felt good and bad. She liked the attention but didn't dig the pressure. The wife suddenly wanted to fix her, had some dream of changing her life. It was a big fat juicy worm. When she was hungry, Ren would take a bite, but she had no intentions of getting hooked.

"Trying to stay off the shit, you know," Ren lied. The wife loved to hear that she was trying to kick drugs. Ren liked to lie, hated it too.

The wife smiled. "I told him not to pull out anything tonight."

Ren was disappointed, had been hoping for a little blow, but pretended to appreciate the wife's concern.

"It's good you're trying."

Ren dropped her head. "Feels like shit."

The wife stared at her disapprovingly. "That trouble you wouldn't give me details about, are you still involved in that?"

Ren paused, took a deep breath. "I got bills to pay just like anybody."

The wife reached into her pocket and pulled out a hundred-dollar bill and handed it to Ren. She was always giving her money, things. Expensive trinkets. Usually, Ren would hock gifts from clients. But the ones the wife gave her she kept. She fingered the solid, smooth pendant around her neck now, the first gift. A gold Tibetan mandala, the size of a nickel, engraved with a small lotus flower.

Ren looked at the money in her hands now. "Thanks."

Seeing the pendant, the wife smiled. She opened the door and spoke cryptically. "You're the lotus, remember . . . rise above."

Ren shuffled her feet. The lotus. With her roots stuck in muddy water. She looked up at the wife. The wife put her hand to her own lips, then touched Ren's cheek. She smiled a sad, lonely smile. "Take care of yourself. If you need help . . . call me."

The door closed before Ren had a chance to say more. Ren walked toward the street. At the corner, she looked up at the cold, exclusive buildings. She looked both ways and thought, *I am the lotus*. I am the walrus, cukoo-cachoo.

Must be dandy to be the wife, Ren thought. Warm and cozy in her townhouse. Marble bathtubs. Fireplace. Credit cards, checking accounts. Something that resembled real life. But then, what made a life real? Stashed in the back of closets across the country, you wouldn't find pictures of the wife and kids. In the dark, you'd find every man's pornographic dream. From the Bible Belt to Wall Street. Four-color spreads offering a variety of takes on the Kama Sutra. Why not get paid for it? When it all came down to it, they all wanted what she had for sale—anything to take them out of their homey reality.

Almost April. It would be wise to pay bills, cover overdue March rent. But who was in the mood to be wise? She was in the mood to be wasted. Ride that train one more time. Then she had other plans.

She ought to call Tommy. Her main man. She was due to check in. But Tommy hadn't set up this score, so why courtesy call? The pimp would only hassle her, want to know where she'd been, weasel a cut. Once out on the street, she looked in her bag. Ripe with cash. She held the crumpled bills to her nose and smelled the dirty wad. Beautiful. She turned the corner and walked into the park. Tommy could wait. The whole fucking world could wait.

ANOTHER FALLING DREAM. WICKED COLD. HIS FATHER TWENTY stories high this time, friends and enemies from the force beckoning below. And he's right there beside him. Just a small boy, unable to abort this takeoff. On the ledge with his old man, the ground below barely visible, a cluster of black dots in the snow, people pleading, specks of dirt. But not even the look on his own kid's face can call him back. Not even the hope locked in his boy's blue eyes, eyes just like his own, can call him back from the edge.

Ready . . . set . . . go . . .

And his father's face as he falls, full of fear and despair. His son falling with him now, holding fast, as if he can hold him back, as if he can get their feet back on solid ground. But there is nothing to stand on.

They soar in a kind of slow motion, the pavement drawing near. Flying through thin air and clouds, as if launched from a cannon, plummeting, heavy, heavier. He is on the bottom now, perfectly placed to break his father's fall. He is imagining the end, reworking the outcome. On the ground, he braces himself, his arms open wide for this moment that matters, this moment, when he may hold his father, safe in his arms.

Gurson woke before dawn. Lying in bed, eyes open but unseeing. An empty, hollow ache in his gut. The room dark and cold. The pillow soaked with sweat. The sound of bus brakes. The building vibrating with the throttle of traffic rolling over asphalt. Heat banging through rusted pipes. Muffled voices. All there to remind him that he was only a slab of concrete away from sleeping in his neighbor's bed.

He would have liked to have died with his father in the garage that day, their lives irrevocably linked. To have slid right in beside him, a passenger in that front seat, inhaling the noxious fumes deep into his young pink lungs. Breathe the toxic vapors and let the world go to hell.

How had it come to this? His wife in someone else's arms, his kid a case of custody. Living in a furnished fourth-floor walk-up in Hell's Kitchen. Wanting and wishing. His life fractured.

His ex talked about new beginnings, how she was starting over, getting herself a real life. And he wondered, lying there, staring at his boy sleeping, just where it was written that he should get the flip side.

When the sun finally lit the morning sky, he got up and looked out the window. The city and all its garbage temporarily undercover. Snow day.

Just as he began enjoying the thought of a day off, the phone rang.

"Where the hell are you, Gurson?" asked Bianchi. "I got my hands full down here this morning. Guys calling in from all over crying they can't make it in 'cause they live in bumfuck upstate New York. Rockland, Orange, who the hell tells them to move up there?"

"Supposed to have the day off, boss. I got my kid," Gurson began.

"Call his mother, Gurson. Nobody's showing up today. You're my city man. Get your ass to Sector 7. We got a stiff."

"Stiff?"

"Crispy critter. Over in the Brambles." Bianchi huffed. "D.A.'s henchman is on the way."

"Which one?"

"Tucker Norville," said Bianchi.

"My luck," Gurson grumbled, clearing his scratchy throat. "Where's Kane?"

"Covering your ass for a change." Bianchi huffed. "And Hernandez tells me you left the scene yesterday with a wallet. Then you don't come back here. What's with you?"

"Who caught that case?"

"I'll tell you who caught it, Gurson. You caught it. You leave the goddamn scene with the freaking guy's purse and you ask me who caught the case. His jalopy's parked in my spot in the garage. I want it out of here. Today."

"Meant to pass it. No ID, figured I'd swing by this morning—"

"Put your ass in your pants," Bianchi snapped. "Sector 7."

Gurson looked over at his son just opening his eyes in bed. He crawled back in beside him. "Hey, wait till you look outside."

Jack crept out of bed holding a blanket. Seven and a half, full of energy and expectation. "Let's go out and play."

A familiar lump whirled in Gurson's throat. "Tell you what. I'm going to call Mom and you guys can hang out this morning. I'll pick you up later this afternoon and we'll go sledding in the park."

"No."

"No?"

"How come *we* can't go out and play *now?*"

"Because Daddy has to go to work."

The boy looked around the room for a place to hide. He leapt back into bed and huddled under the covers. "I'm not going."

Gurson looked at his watch. If he took the boy with him, Bianchi would have a fit. What did he think the precinct was? Goddamned day care?

"Hey, I got something for you." Gurson walked to the chair where his leather jacket was hanging and reached into the pocket. Instead of finding the Walkman, he felt the stiff's wallet.

"What, Daddy, what is it?"

Gurson put his hand in the other pocket and retrieved the Walkman. He'd fixed it up the night before, good as new. The boy took hold of the gadget and became preoccupied with the buttons. Gurson took the wallet and went into the kitchen, staring down at it. He took out the note that he'd slipped inside and read it again as if it were some kind of a summons.

I have become accessible to consolation. . . .

[4]

A Little Snow

SUNDAY, MARCH 22

Out the window it seemed deceptively warm, the sun glinting off mounds of new snow. The flurries had drifted on the breeze like pollen, like baby's breath, slow, dreamlike, in crisscrossing diagonals. Soft and small, the flakes gathered in clusters, increasing in force around midnight, then finally letting up just before dawn. The sun crept up over an icy Hudson River, lighting the way for the weary retirees of the night shift and the first yawn of early risers.

An unnatural hush engulfed the street, interrupted occasionally by a row of garbage trucks doubling as snowplows. Another six inches. For New Yorkers, this was either cause for childlike celebration—get out the sled and cross-country skis—or a majestic pain in the ass—*I told you we should have parked the car in a garage. . . .*

Wished he could stay in bed all day. Order in. Read the *Times*, cover to cover, for a little drama. Fat chance. In rain or sleet or snow, murder kept the Manhattan D.A.'s office open for business.

As usual, Tucker Norville awoke hungover. Smell of caffeine in the air. Television humming in the den. He made his way down the steep staircase of the three-story townhouse and then navigated the long indigo hall toward the den on the main floor. He could hear his wife, at the piano, playing a somber overture.

He stood in the entrance of the large room and recalled the night before. This very room had served as the backdrop for their sexual play. Everything appeared different now, bathed in sunlight. The butter yellow walls reflected a warmth that only served to exacerbate his already outstanding headache. He squinted at the light sneaking in between oak slats. He cupped a hand over his eyes and made his way to the window, looked out onto the quiet tree-lined street, Seventy-fifth off Park, and then methodically closed each blind with a loud flick.

The little woman was wearing jeans and a pale turquoise turtleneck that accentuated the blue of her eyes. Sitting at the Steinway, her back to him. The music a bit too somber, even for his head. He glanced at the television. Tuned to *Sesame Street*, again. Dreaming of some lost baby. A suckling that would never nurse at her breast. A center of gravity that would never fill her bottomless void. Constantly waking in the night, wandering the halls. Something, she said, about the sound of a baby crying.

L-M-N-O-P.

Sesame Street said it was so.

Theodora stopped her playing, closed the door on the keys, and turned to find Tucker staring at her.

"Handel?" Tucker stood a few feet away, close enough to enjoy catching her off guard.

"Bach. 'Badinerie.'" Theodora's eyes were red. She rubbed her temples, wincing.

"Gloomy." Tucker looked over at the television. Muted sound. "Learning the alphabet?"

"Siggy's beginning to understand the possibilities of the letter P," she said flippantly, without looking up. Her long auburn hair gathered haphazardly in a loose knot. She got up from the piano and stroked the dog, with all the tender affection she no longer bestowed upon him.

Watching her gently pet the dog, he was reminded of her early affection for him. She had married him hoping for a child, but turning the corner on yet another year of wedlock, eight to be exact, their cupboard was still bare. She'd had one early miscarriage, not too far along, about four years back. And then nothing. He would have been content to have her all to himself.

He was no guinea pig. Hardly the type to lend himself over for the trials of lab work. Jerking off into plastic cups in clinical bathrooms stocked with soft porn under the sink was low on his list of heroic gestures. The sexual novelty of timed coital interludes had quickly worn thin. But he was under no illusions. He knew an empty nest would not keep Theodora home. So he made halfhearted attempts. Let them sort and count his flotsam and jetsam. When they found it was his problem, his willingness to pursue the matter medically hit a brick wall. Theodora's physical interest in him promptly did the same.

He took to buying her suggestive talismans. Phallic figurines of Indian fertility gods, precious stones and erotic aphrodisiacs. When that failed to amuse, he began to drink heavily. Their occasional trysts, all too often the result of drug-induced passion, were not enough to satisfy either of them. And their antics outside the bedroom, antagonistic and brimming with contempt, did little to enhance their already dwindling libidos. Perhaps if he were kinder, she'd fuck him more. Perhaps if she fucked him more, he'd be kinder.

"The letter P," said Tucker, taking a step nearer. "Prostitution . . ."

Theodora rolled her eyes. The dog got up and walked toward the kitchen. Theodora rose on cue. "Siggy hungry?" She cooed in that singsong way mothers speak to their young children.

P is for Princess, thought Tucker. Past prime. Soon, Theodora would crack forty, her eggs all rotting in a row. Which had come first? The infertile rooster or the frigid hen? He glanced at the dog and then at Theodora as the two left the room. Destined to raise a canine instead of *kinder.*

"Have you looked out the window?" Theodora called out.

"Precipitation," said Tucker, gazing out the tall living room window with its view of Central Park, a winter wonderland. The trappings of old family money. His grandfather's cache earned after the crash of '29. A now dwindling portfolio, strictly doled out on a monthly basis by anonymous accountants to the last remaining heir, Tucker Norville.

"*P is for potato,*" said an animated tuber. Tucker took the remote and switched channels. He needed news. He caught the tail end of the weather.

"*. . . wet, frosty, and cold . . .*"

He glanced at his watch. The tiny window beneath the glass revealed the number 22. Sunday, the twenty-second of March. "Not sending anyone home from Rikers today." He continued to channel surf. "Goddamn city falls to pieces just because of a little snow."

Theodora sat at the kitchen table and began reading the newspaper. "Will you be gone all day?"

"Yes . . ." Then Tucker whispered inaudibly, "lucky girl," as he strolled into the kitchen and poured himself a cup of coffee. "Burnt carcass in the park."

"Thanks for sharing that."

He sipped his coffee from a mug bought for him by his coworkers, bearing the imprint of iron bars and a greeting that read, "Welcome to Rikers. Have a nice stay." He opened a wooden cabinet, found a bottle of extra strength Excedrin and downed three.

Theodora got up to leave. He stopped her as she passed him and bent to smell the nape of her neck. Nectar of pear and cassis. He could feel her resistance. "You smell good. Working on a Sunday?"

"Paperwork." She looked into his eyes.

Tucker held her gaze for a moment, then let her go. He leaned against the wall and watched as she walked down the long hall to the bathroom.

He noticed her black winter coat hanging over the arm of a chair. Impulsively he went to it, held the collar to his nose, and inhaled. Obsessively, he picked her pockets in search of clues, but found only crumpled Kleenex and a blank book of matches.

She was planning her exit. Didn't need to be a goddamned detective to figure that out. She couldn't possibly expect him to make leaving easy. Hadn't married him, after all, for his calm demeanor, or his passive, laissez-faire ways. Besides, marriage had its entanglements, the albatross of shared history. Change required tenacity. Reclaiming one's life must take its toll.

THEY FOUND HER UP IN THE BRAMBLES. NAME GIVEN TO THE deserted wasteland at the far north end of Central Park. Black Rambles. The Playing Fields, the Loch. 105th and nowhere. Nice spot. Isolated, quiet. Tailor-made for murder.

Tucker Norville stood on a mound of snowy earth and looked uptown. He then joined Bianchi, a few paces away, the rubber soles of his shoes crunching downhill through the ankle-high snow.

"Walking to a crime scene always gives me the willies, how 'bout you, Norville?" Bianchi stopped walking and caught his breath.

"Yeah. Never know what you might step in."

They arrived at the scene, where Bianchi checked in with the cops who were scanning the site. He walked back to Norville, observing an unofficial moment of silence. The forensic squad was busy documenting the scene. Norville took a quick glance at the roasted remains. "Nasty. Did the freak take a souvenir?"

"Hard to tell. Most of the flesh was burned to the bone. Kane," Bianchi called out. Kane joined them. "Can you fill in here?" Bianchi asked.

Didi Kane looked out over the wintry landscape. Her face a beautiful black canvas. Her long, thick dreads pulled back and twisted in a knot. The soft features belied her tough edge. Working undercover, this came in handy. She didn't look like the kick-ass cop she was. The only clue at the moment: a gold shield hanging from the pocket of her navy peacoat. She looked at her boots. "We don't know if the killing took place here, or if it was done elsewhere and the body just burned here."

"We talking X or Y chromosomes?" asked Norville.

"Can't tell," said Kane.

"Only thing crawling around this slum is reckless," said Norville.

Kane shot Norville a dirty look. "You saying somebody *deserved* this?"

Norville looked at the sergeant. The day they let women become cops, the force went to hell. "I'm saying this ain't exactly the lobby of The Plaza, honey."

"Honey?" Kane planted herself firmly on the ground and gave Norville a nasty glare. "Who's he calling honey?"

Bianchi intervened. He was a cop's cop for the most part, but Kane had yet to earn his full respect. She'd been a rising star at the two eight, but like her old partner Charlene Leone, she had a little problem with authority. Transferred to the park two years ago for rubbing her commander the wrong way. Going to night school now, earning a degree in something esoteric. Always scribbling in little spiral notebooks. Poetic nonsense. Had a hefty volume on her desk the other day on botany, said she was decoding the park's indigenous flora. They called her Britannica, precinct bookworm. Small-print category. As good at using the Queen's English as she was at pitching street slang.

"Boss fighter?" Norville leaned into Bianchi's ear but spoke loud enough for Kane to hear.

Kane shot Norville a look. She'd expected no less. Norville's fine reputation had preceded him too. He'd been a prosecutor for the Manhattan D.A.'s office for over twenty years. It was rumored that he didn't really have to work. Family money. According to his opponents, he was a pit bull. He was as smart as he was tough. Damn smart. Skipped like a stone over high school, cutting out senior year to plunge into prelaw studies. Flew through Columbia Law, one of their youngest grads at twenty-three. Family connections landed his ass at a cushy desk assisting the D.A. Early on in his climb, a series of difficult wins suggested he might have a shot at a political career. But his pomposity got him skewered in the press and killed that dream. Now he was pushing fifty, and the blind ambition of his youth was tinged with resentment and bitterness. He still had the drive but lacked the promise. Unable to turn back time, his edge, which should have been dulled by disappointment, was edgier. Tall, dark, and fiercesome, in and out of the courtroom, Norville was known for his dominant presence. Without speaking a word, he could transform an arena. In this instance, a sloping stretch of Central Park. In his wake, the air seemed sharper, acrid.

Bianchi knew that Norville was fond of prosecuting high-profile killers and far less fond of cops. He took Norville aside. "Kane has some of the best informants this side of the river, Norville. She's good one on one, but not the greatest at team sports, if you know what I'm saying."

Norville turned back toward Kane. "So, what else we got?"

"Not much," said Kane.

Norville furrowed his brow. "Isn't it possible we're talking self-immolation?"

Kane folded her arms across her chest. "What do you mean?"

Norville pursed his lips and used his hands to help him along. "I mean, say our faceless friend here was homeless. Out here in the cold night, cops some crack, lights up, wham! Maybe starts a fire to keep warm. I've heard of it happening. The shit they cut that stuff with is pretty combustible. Those handheld butanes can backfire."

"Self-immolation?" Kane's tone was sarcastic, cool. "I say this is *corpus delicti*, Counselor."

Just another fancy word for murder. Norville was unimpressed. "What if J. Doe here was already dead by the time our terminator happened by, Detective?" He was about to go on when his beeper went off. He reached into his jacket pocket and checked the code.

"We'll just be another five minutes," said Bianchi.

Norville put the pager back in his jacket.

Bianchi walked Norville a short distance away from the scene. "Looks like this one knew what he was doing."

"Sick bastard." Norville shook his head.

Kane distanced herself from the two men but remained within earshot of their conversation.

"Who else you got on it?" Norville asked Bianchi.

Bianchi scanned the scene. He watched the pathology team sketch the baseline of the clearing. He looked at the sky. Clouds moving in. "Putting my best man on. James Gurson. Worked with him over at the three four. Kid's got a remarkable clearance rate. Third eye. Arson's right up his alley." Bianchi tapped the wrinkle between his thick brows.

"Gurson? Wasn't his old man a cop?"

"That's the one."

"Snuffed some kid . . ."

"I remember that case."

"So do I," said Norville.

"Weren't you the one who was on line to prosecute?" asked Bianchi.

"One of my first." Norville rubbed his gloved hands together, recollecting. He'd been twenty-five at the time; the cop had been a seasoned vet, in his late thirties. "Trigger-happy bastard checked out before we could haul his ass to trial. Killed himself."

"Well, his kid's all right. Ivy cop. College grad, straight A's. Psych major."

Norville looked around. "So, where is he now?"

Bianchi waved his hand. "Damn storm's slowing us down this morning. He's Kane's partner, they'll work up a psychological profile. Rule out the obvious. Narrow the odds."

"All that psychobabble's a lot of nonsense." Tucker gnawed on an unlit cigar.

"Yeah, but it's not like the old days, Norville, huh? When we had to sniff things out by ourselves with nothing more than a good nose." Bianchi pulled on his own large snout and glanced downhill.

"Hear you were just wrapping up," Norville said, smiling. "Too bad. Once the press gets a hold of this, you'll be sitting in the dump another six months."

Bianchi took off his cap and rubbed the bald spot on the top of his head. "Found one like this about a year ago. Remember? Up here in the Brambles. Never tagged her or the killer."

"Sore point for the mayor," said Norville. "This park's his treasure."

"I figure he'll back us up."

"Nix that. Word is, mayor wants lockjaw."

"Lockjaw." Bianchi laughed, looking around half expecting a news team to leap from the bushes. "Press hounds will be camping outside my window."

"No information to the press, pending investigation," insisted Norville. "Orders straight from the mayor. D.A.'s office has already prepared a statement. Homeless vagrant . . . too close to the fire trying to keep warm, blizzard got the poor schlub disoriented. If I were you, I'd find this pyro's matches before the snow thaws."

"You mean before the bastard strays across town and takes a shit on the mayor's front lawn?" Bianchi scowled. "No press, huh. Too bad, Norville. We all know how much you like getting your mug on the front page."

Norville gave Bianchi a pat on the back. "You ought to be happy, Bianchi. This gives you and your understudies something to do." Norville looked up at the gray sky. He thought of the park with all its murky caves, all its damp, dark nooks and crannies. He thought of all the other bodies they'd found there, year after year, how long it usually took to clear those cases. The unsolved and unsolvable. Dementos, junkies, born-again freaks. Mindless wanderers strolling the jungle at the crack of dawn and after dusk. Living in some kind of dreamland. Wrong place, wrong time. All of them, asking for it.

[5]

Disneyland

Gurson picked up his pace as he entered the park. The air was brisk and cool. He dashed beneath the sloping pines, cutting a fresh path across the snow. His feet keeping time with a tune playing in his head, something his son had been singing, something about turtles. His green eyes surveyed the lay of no-man's-land.

The crime scene came into view. Stable of cops standing guard. He flashed his shield and made his way to the body lying covered on the ground. Kane was there waiting for him. "Gurson. Where the heck have you been?"

"Had to drop my kid."

She put a hand on his shoulder. "How's it hanging?"

"Fine now that we've touched." The corners of his mouth curled up in a boyish grin. "Blue plate special?" Gurson lifted the sheet, took a look.

"Bar-b-qued ribs."

"Well done." He blew out a deep breath.

"Cooked, then frozen."

What had once been a face was now a seared landscape. The nose was melted down to the bone, the eyelids and eyeballs gone. The scalp was scorched and what was left of the hair was fried. Limbs were grossly distorted, twisted and gnarled. Ten fingertips, gone. More than three quarters of the body was badly blistered. Like an alien life form, nothing resembling a life once human.

"Looks like sulfuric acid was used on the face," said Gurson.

"Same for the fingers." Kane took out a small Instamatic camera from her breast pocket to snap a picture of the crime scene.

"What are you doing?" asked Gurson.

"Documenting the scene," said Kane, snapping another shot of the black stumps that ended at the victim's knuckles.

"What's the matter, you don't trust the forensic squad?" asked Gurson.

Kane shrugged the question off and focused her camera. "Whatever was used burned the clothes, face, and fingers right off."

"He or she?" Gurson tilted his head for a better view of the torso.

Kane put her camera away. "No idea. Autopsy will tell for sure."

"M.E.'s gonna have a helluva time figuring out how long the body's been here," said Gurson. "Anybody move anything?"

"Scene's been fully documented. About to ship the remains to the morgue."

"Where's Bianchi?"

"Just missed him. Escorted the ADA the hell out of here."

"Who found the body?"

"Couple of kids. At the precinct for questioning."

Gurson dug his hands into his pockets. "Find anything?"

Kane crossed her arms over her chest. "The squad just uncovered a gun not far from here."

"Have you seen it?" Gurson asked.

Kane nodded.

"Don't tell me." Gurson leaned forward on the balls of his feet.

"Shaved numbers."

Gurson ran a hand over his chin. "They calling in a special unit?"

"They're marching a shitload of uniforms around, putting a task force together just in case it turns out it's some politician's girlfriend. But according to the A.D.A., the mayor wants it cleared."

"How's that?"

Kane shrugged. "Racial profiling's my guess. If we're talking about dark meat, they'll bag the bones and call it a day."

"In that case, we ought to save the city money. Dig a hole and bury the kill right here." Gurson rocked in place. "Arson investigation's a pain in the ass. Any backup?"

Kane filled her cheeks with air. "Looks like we're it." She paused, looking down at the ground. "Boss told the A.D.A you have a third eye." She looked curiously at the space between his eyebrows.

Gurson kicked up a drift of snow. "He said that to Norville? I can just imagine what the prick said back."

"You know him?"

"You could say I know *of* him."

"I hear he carves his guests up at the dinner table."

Gurson's breath curled in a frosty mist. "Well, business as usual." He knelt down beside the charred body and had a closer look. He found himself simultaneously exhilarated and revolted. He'd seen this kind of thing before. Burning bodies was a popular device for masking evidence. But flesh burned slower than most people thought. There was usually something left over to tag. Most often, the victim was dead of other causes before any flesh started to burn. Inhalation of smoke and gases created by the fire killed them. "Could be my own mother and I wouldn't recognize her. Jesus."

"Jesus? He ain't here. But Hay-seus, he's around the corner, can fix you up real nice with a dirty needle." Kane turned up her collar. "Go on and say your prayers, Gurson, then get off your knees. I'll give you a lift to the house."

∗   ∗   ∗

The Central Park precinct looked almost quaint with its eaves trimmed with snow. But the filthy flag and the black steel bars on the windows quickly stripped it of any such homey illusion. Gurson walked in to find the place hopping. He went straight for Bianchi's office.

Bianchi's door was open. He was sitting at his desk eating a late breakfast of cold coffee and powdered donuts. When Gurson came in, he looked up. "Fix your hair, Gurson. Press just got word. They're on the way."

"Who's running for office?" Gurson checked himself out in the dirty window glass.

"I thought you were," said Bianchi, sarcastically.

Just outside Bianchi's opened door, in the large room where all the detectives shared an office, Kane was sitting behind her desk, feet resting on a half-opened drawer, reading the newspaper.

"So what's our story?" asked Gurson, taking one of Bianchi's donuts.

"Our story is we have no story," said Bianchi. "For now, we blame the weather. Homeless vagrant got too close to the fire. . . ." Bianchi recited.

"All part of the mayor's campaign to 'glorify a complex urban issue,'" Kane read loudly from the front section of the *Times*. "We need to focus attention on the less fortunate, mayor says here, 'a segment of city life that most busy New Yorkers have learned to overlook.'"

"When's the autopsy?" asked Gurson.

"This morning," said Bianchi.

"That ought to be special." Gurson rolled his eyes.

"By the way, where's the guy's wallet?" Bianchi was looking at his clipboard.

Gurson mumbled something neither Kane nor Bianchi could make out. He took the wallet out of his pocket and laid it on Bianchi's desk.

"Nice move, Gurson."

Gurson dodged the insult. "You run the plates?"

Bianchi tossed him a print sheet. "Car's registered to a Dr. Orrin Gretz, Central Park West."

"Doctor?" said Gurson.

"Shrink," said Bianchi. "No priors. Ought to be a quick wrap. Sent a couple of uniforms around there yesterday. Nobody was around. Figured you'd clear it." Bianchi sat at his desk and spoke without looking up. "Seeing as the guy died in your arms . . ."

Gurson licked his bottom lip.

Bianchi smirked. "Go on, take a few steps out of the park back into the real world, Gurson. It'll be good for you."

"Watch out, Gurson." Kane was now standing in Bianchi's doorway. "I heard of guys turning to stone out there."

"In that case," said Bianchi, "I could use bookends. Go with him."

"Coroner find any lead in this shrink?" asked Kane.

"Not that I know of. Guy died sucking fumes." He rubbed his chin. "Left some note in the car. It's inside the wallet."

Bianchi looked accusingly at Gurson. "You lift anything else?"

Gurson clenched his teeth, trying to keep himself still. "Nah, just the wallet and that line . . . I put it inside the wallet. Could be a suicide note."

"Could be a suicide note. Won't know, will we, now that your prints are all over it." Bianchi shot Gurson one of his irritated looks. He took the slip of paper out and read aloud. "'I have become accessible to consolation. . . .'" Bianchi shrugged. "How dramatic." He looked over at Kane. "Kane, you're our resident bookworm. What's it mean?"

Kane shrugged. "Maybe you ought to analyze the writing."

Bianchi snorted, indifferent. He looked at the note. "The guy was sick and tired. Killed himself. The end. Contact next of kin and then clean it off your plate. I want his car out of here." Bianchi wiped his hands together, then reached across his cluttered desk and produced a piece of paper. He handed it to Gurson. "More important . . . we need ID on the grilled ribs they found in the Brambles. Coroner's doing us a favor. Rush job. Scanning what's left in a couple of hours. Both of you, be there."

"Snow ought to keep the press from getting too close," said Kane.

"Never stopped them before," said Gurson.

"Then consider it your job," said Bianchi, his customarily sour expression sweetened by a smile.

The garage doors were closed to keep out the damp air. Hard enough lifting prints off a car that had been outside in the snow. Took hours for the car to dry out.

Gurson walked up to the garage and opened the lock on the outside of the door. What he saw as the doors swung open was not what he was expecting. "What the hell?" He walked in, looked at the car, and started to rant to himself. "This isn't the freaking car. What's this? Where's my car? This is a goddamn Honda, am I correct? The goddamn car my guy was in was a sports car. Where is it?" Gurson stormed out of the garage and headed back into the precinct.

Gurson barged back into Bianchi's office, yelling. "Boss, I need a word with you."

Bianchi looked annoyed.

"The car—"

"What about the car?"

"The car," said Gurson. "Where's the car?"

"What car?"

"My car, the one the guy gassed himself in."

"What do you mean? It's in the garage."

"That's not the car. The car my guy aced in was a sports car, a fancy shmancy car. Had a dead bird on the passenger seat."

"What is this place? Disneyland?" The sergeant shook his head. He stormed to the front desk and asked the desk sergeant to check the auto voucher. "Department tow screwed up, Gurson. Your car's at the pound."

"The what?"

"Don't look so surprised, Gurson. This is the Central Park precinct. Things going wrong means everything's just right."

[6]

Corpus Delicti

SUNDAY, MARCH 22

The medical examiner, Constance Verdi, greeted Kane and Gurson in the bland reception area of the morgue. Thankfully, Verdi, a highly respected and longtime veteran, had enough warmth to compensate for the contrasting chill of the job. Not to say that she was overtly compassionate or sympathetic. She'd seen too much. Floaters, eviscerations, defiled children. But somehow, through the worst of it, she refrained from blatant indifference, which was the way most in the business of homicide dealt with the unfathomable in order to survive.

"I like your hair," Kane told Verdi. "Very *Vogue.*"

It was short, jet black. "Easy," Verdi smiled. Verdi looked a good five years younger than she was despite the long hours. She was hardly what one could call vain, but at fifty-two she was certainly a woman well maintained. Hardly a wrinkle on her, save the subtle creases at each corner of her mouth and hazel eyes. She liked to joke that being around the dead could make anybody look younger. The nasty rumor going around was that she was extracting fatty tissue from her deceased boarders, injecting her own secret supply of human collagen to plump up gaunt facial features. A rumor started, according to Verdi herself, by an odious female coworker who'd tired of Verdi's brutal work ethic.

Kane inhaled before entering the stark, white room and prepared to hold her breath. Stainless steel tables were lined up like boxcars. One in the middle, occupied. A fingerless hand of the charred corpse hung limply off the table. The rest of the body covered.

Gurson read the preliminary report aloud. "'Female. Hispanic. Twenty-five to thirty. Approximate height: five six. Approximate weight: 120 pounds.'"

"Female." Kane cleared her throat.

"Never would have guessed that." Verdi crossed her long, slender arms in front of her and stared critically into the dead woman's burned-out eye sockets.

Gurson continued reading the report. "'*Time of death: two days to two weeks.*' Two days to two weeks? Which side of the scale you weighing in on, Verdi?"

"Temps have been below zero out there for over a week." Verdi lifted the white sheet and looked at the curled limbs of the corpse. "I'd say she's been under snow for at least that long, judging by the condition she's in. But then, when it's as cold as it's been, it's hard to tell for sure."

Gurson looked over at Verdi. "Cause of death?"

"Here's the strange thing. No CO in the blood, and no burn marks or soot in her throat." Verdi put a pair of rubber gloves on and handed a pair to Gurson.

"So she was dead before the fire started." Gurson put the gloves on.

"Correct."

"What do I need these for?" Gurson asked.

"The fire might have been an afterthought," said Verdi. "We need to turn her over. There's something I want you to see. Give me a hand." Verdi wheeled another table alongside the one the corpse was on. "We're going to lift her gently to the left and let her tip slowly."

Carefully, Gurson and Verdi maneuvered the leathery corpse, Verdi at the shoulders, Gurson at the feet. Kane stayed back, taking small, metered breaths. When the dead woman had been turned over, Gurson looked at his gloved hands, covered with a brown residue. "You got a clean pair of gloves?"

Verdi rolled her eyes and acquiesced. "Squeamish?"

"I'm going for Chinese tonight. No spicy sauce from column B to go, thanks." Gurson removed his dirty gloves, disposed of them, washed, and then put another pair of clean gloves on. He stood beside Verdi now.

"Have a look at this." Verdi pointed to the back. "You see the sym-metry in these lines on each side of her back, just below the shoulder blades?"

At first glance Gurson didn't see what Verdi was talking about.

Verdi ran a scalpel above the back, outlining the markings. "Of course, the gashes here could simply be disfigurement from the fire, the skin splitting under pressure. I'm not one hundred percent sure."

"You think these markings have been inflicted with a knife or some-thing?" asked Gurson.

"It's hard to tell," said Verdi. "The fire has damaged so much."

Gurson was now able to make out the two markings, one more evi-dent than the other. Symmetrical gashes about seven to eight inches long.

"Of course, fire doesn't usually have this kind of symmetry," said Verdi. "I'm thinking it may have been inflicted before she died. Possibly months before."

"Months?" asked Gurson.

"She may have had it done herself," said Verdi.

"Like some tattoo or something?" asked Kane.

"Could be. If she was part of some cult, maybe. I'd guess this was some kind of cult killing," said Verdi.

"Some ritual that ended with fire," Gurson added. "Could be more than one killer in that case."

"Used gasoline as the accelerant," said Verdi. "Sulfuric acid to dissolve the face and hands."

"You don't carry that kind of arsenal unless you're planning to torch *something*," said Gurson. "Whoever did this had a plan. Knew he needed time. Made sure he left nothing behind."

"Could be beginner's luck," offered Kane.

"I remember saying that about the last one, too," said Verdi.

"The last one used gasoline?" asked Gurson.

"Same high octane. Sulfuric acid on the face," said Verdi

"Any other bruises on this one?" asked Gurson.

"On her feet," said Verdi.

"Suggests she was dragged," said Gurson. "Might have killed her somewhere else, then brought her to the park. Sexual assault?"

"Body might have been played with post mortem," said Verdi.

"How's that?" asked Gurson.

"I found no semen in any orifice," said Verdi. "Nothing on any part of the body. But the wounds outside the vaginal vault suggest she was forcibly penetrated."

"Could be a drug overdose. Some psycho comes along, she's already dead. He does his business, makes it look like homicide," said Gurson.

"Find any fibers?" asked Kane.

"I've sent whatever was left of her clothes to Forensics. Full pathology work-up will take time but it may tell us more," said Verdi.

"Who are you?" Gurson looked at the ghoulish corpse.

"Whoever she was, she had nine lives." Verdi stood up and walked over to the counter to retrieve a bagged bullet. "Found this lodged near the spine. I'd say it's a few years old. Bet they couldn't remove it without cutting her cord." Verdi looked over at Kane. "You're turning a lovely shade of green."

Gurson looked over at Kane, who was slowly breathing into her hands.

"Not my best color," Kane said, looking ready to puke.

"Wish there were some way to reconstruct that face." Verdi lifted one of the incinerated hands.

"Or one of her fingers. You ever tag the last one?" Gurson asked.

"Nothing much to tag," huffed Verdi.

"What was the cause of death on that one?" asked Gurson.

Verdi groaned. "That one? Asphyxiation finished her off. Smoke residue in her lungs. Smoke inhalation." She shook her head. "But who knows what was done to her before that. I never found anything substantial. I suspected she'd been strangled. But there wasn't the usual damage to the trachea. Her eyes were cooked out, couldn't document broken blood vessels."

"Could argue that there was no way to really prove that one was homicide, either," said Gurson.

"I suppose," said Verdi.

"Maybe we got a necrophiliac troll living under the bridge. Waits for hookers and homeless to break down," said Gurson.

"There wasn't a tooth in that last girl's head. God knows what happened to her teeth. At least this girl has her molars," said Verdi.

"Gave the last one a name and buried her in Potter's. They figured she was a pross." Kane propped herself up against the wall. "Rounded up a group of suspects but no one confessed, never matched DNA."

"Race and age on that one?" asked Gurson.

"Hispanic. Twenty-five to thirty." Verdi sat down on a metal stool.

Gurson looked over at Kane. "You okay?"

"Little queasy," Kane said without looking up.

"We're finished here," Verdi told Kane. "Go out and get some air."

Relieved, Kane walked out the door.

Gurson gave the remains another look and then Verdi covered her up. "You say she's been dead about a week?"

Verdi took off her gloves, went to the sink and washed up. "Give or take."

"And nobody's reported her missing." Gurson rubbed his hands together. "How the hell do I find out who she is?"

"Piece of cake, Gurson. Just follow the psycho-path."

[7]

Dead Poets

Gurson and Kane canvassed the park but came up empty. All leads leading nowhere. Back at the precinct, Monday morning, Gurson watched the faces of the missing flash across a computer screen. He checked vitals. Nothing matched the dead girl or the suicide in the park. He glanced at the printout on the car. Registered to Orrin Gaylord Gretz, M.D., 211 Central Park West. Was it just a coincidence that the guy's car was brought to the wrong place Saturday night or was it something worth checking out? When in doubt, make a house call.

Kane settled into the passenger seat of Gurson's Jeep and turned up the heat. A burst of ice-cold air shot out.

"I see they fixed your heat." Kane zipped up her parka.

Gurson fiddled with the controls. Instead of heat, the radio came on. "Yeah, but the radio works."

"Try the radio, maybe you'll get the heat." Kane rubbed her hands in front of her face. "Bianchi doesn't think we need heat. If it's broke, why fix it?"

"Speaking of Bianchi, he wanted me to tell you he's counting your personal days." Gurson kept his eyes on the road.

"Really? Counting. Didn't think the man knew how."

"Doesn't look good, he says." Gurson pulled out of the precinct, taking a special exit that looped through the park. The area was empty.

"Neither does his face." Kane looked at her hands, then out the window. "I was cramming for exams."

"Hey, you don't have to make excuses for me."

"You trying to get on my good side?" Kane engaged Gurson in a moment of eye contact.

"You have one?"

His eyes caught the subtle curve of her frown. She was in there somewhere, a whole other story.

"Found the car in there." Gurson eased the car off the side of the road, deciding to make a pit stop. He parked in the thick of the Rambles amid a large grouping of shrubs and tall trees.

"Black tupelos."

"Huh?"

"The trees. Over there. *Nyssa sylvatica.* Listen hard. Might hear them tell you what happened to the good doctor."

"Bianchi tells me you're going to school."

She looked amused. "Working towards my master's. You know, to wipe my literary ass. What was your major?"

Gurson tugged on his right ear. "Psychology."

"I'll be careful what I say," said Kane.

"Or don't." Gurson smirked and sat back, setting his head on the headrest. "Your last partner was a woman. Charlene Leone. Must have made things easier for you," Gurson said in a fairly innocuous voice.

"Why?"

"No reason." Gurson tapped the steering wheel.

There was a long moment of silence. Then Gurson said, "So, what's Charlene Leone up to these days?"

"I don't keep tabs on her."

"Bianchi tells me they suspect she was on the take, says she's hooked on coke pretty bad. Nasty habit. How long she have that problem?" asked Gurson.

"You're the psych major, Gurson. Give her a call if you're so curious, see if she wants her head examined."

"Touchy, touchy." Gurson gazed out over the snowy vista.

"Let's just say I got my guard up, and I'm keeping it there. I'm sick of pricks pushing me around."

"Your guard's a feminist, huh?" Gurson smiled.

Kane scratched the back of her neck. "Sorry. I keep thinking you're one of them."

"I am." Gurson smiled. "Anatomically."

"But you love women, don't you? Respect them as your full equals."

"In fact, yes, I do. Seriously. Loved my mother too." He curbed a grin.

Kane shook her head. "'Green as eunuchs, your wishes hiss at my sins.'"

"What's that?"

"Dead poet."

"Which one?"

"Sylvia Plath."

"You into poetry too?"

"No, just dead poets." She laughed.

"What do you think of that line from the guy's car . . . 'I have become accessible to consolation'? You think it's poetry?"

She wrinkled her brow. "Not a clue."

"I think it is," said Gurson.

"Could mean anything."

Gurson shifted into drive and headed out of the park to get to where they were originally going. When he got to the corner of seventy-ninth and Central Park West, he turned right and parked. He looked at the sign on the building across the street. The Beresford.

"Swank address," said Kane.

"They call it Analyst's Row." Gurson opened his door and got out of the car. "I hear shrinks are getting one hundred fifty a pop these days."

"Sitting on their asses all day. You know, I've never met a shrink who didn't need a good shrink." Kane followed Gurson to the front of the building.

"You meet many shrinks?"

"All these guys defending lunatics. I figure they have to be crazy to do that." Kane gave a comic sigh. "So, what's our position here? Invite one of the doctor's kin to the morgue and then hit the woods again to look for the abominable snowman?"

Gurson squinted at the sun. "Sounds about right."

"You doing the talking?" asked Kane, walking up beside him.

"Feel free to cut in anytime," Gurson said as he pressed the buzzer. A gold plaque hung on the brick wall to the left of the entrance. ORRIN GAYLORD GRETZ, followed by a couple of dollar signs: M.D.

"Nobody home."

Gurson buzzed again. "Let's try the front entrance. Talk to a doorman."

Doorman was none too happy to let them in. Was Dr. Gretz here? Had he been here yesterday? Was there a Mrs. Gretz? *Una bonita muchacha? Poco* English? *No problemo.* Kane flashed her gold shield and *habla'*d *español.* One moment *por favor.* The doorman's perfect English was coming back to him. He called management. Management called the super. The super called the president of the board. Soon, the super arrived on the scene and opened the door. Introduced himself. Manny Benitez. Super for almost eighteen years. Never forgot names, faces yeah, but he was good with names. Told them Dr. Gretz had an unusual first name. "Orrin." Manny rolled the r's with flourish. Gretz was a quiet guy, according to Manny, had been a resident of the building before he bought the ground floor office. Never complained. Good tip at Christmas.

Gretz's back office was dark and quiet. The waiting room was the size of a newsstand. Glass table cluttered with magazines. Leather chairs against the wall. Reminded Gurson of purgatory. There was a musty smell in the air he identified as the residue of cigarettes. A ficus tree stood in a corner, forlorn. Gurson felt the soil, dry. There were two offices. One looked like it was being used for storage. Boxes parked in corners. The other looked like the main office, where he saw patients. Neater, brighter. Books lined the walls. Theology. Psychiatry. Philosophy. Nobody home but the cat. While Kane kept Manny busy talking about the weather, Gurson scanned the office and soon realized he had no quick job on his hands.

A series of about a dozen framed photographs caught Gurson's attention. Eleven-by-fourteens, matted, nice wood frames hung salon style on the north wall. Black and whites, all signed "Gretz." Studies of Central Park at different times of the year. Landscape shots. Winter, spring, summer, fall.

Gurson stood over the doctor's desk, flipped through his Rolodex and looked for an appointment book. A slim black leather ledger, the size of a lean paperback, its pages affixed inside by three small silver spirals, sat open on a corner of the desk. He scanned the opened pages, a week-at-a-glance, which recorded the days before Gretz's death. He noted the empty roster, a black slash running through the expired week. A couple of days marked "R & D." He flipped the page. Another blank week with the word "Cornell" scrawled and crossed out, suggesting a canceled engagement. Gurson deftly stashed the ledger in the pocket of his bulky parka and then joined Kane and the super in the other room.

Manny led them to the lobby, where they took the elevator to the doctor's residence, on the tenth floor. One bed, one bath. Small eat-in kitchen. He looked at the date on the milk in the fridge. Still good. Nothing out of line at first glance that suggested the guy hadn't intended to return.

Gurson looked in a desk drawer in the living room and found the guy's checkbook. Looked like the bills for the month of March had been paid on time. Why pay your bills on time if you're planning to exit out? He thought of the appointment book. R & D. He took a look at the bookshelves lined with books. "R and D," he said out loud.

Kane turned toward him. "Artie who?"

He took her aside, out of hearing range of Manny. "R and D. In his appointment book, week before he died. Research and development? Had Cornell crossed off the following week. Maybe the guy was writing a paper or something." Gurson ran his eyes along the shelf. Seemingly endless volumes by Freud, Jung, and Brill along with what looked to be first editions of literary works by authors such as Rousseau and Dostoyevsky, as well as lesser known heads and their disciples. "Rousseau and Dostoyevsky."

"Rocky and Bullwinkle," laughed Kane.

"Bullwinkle starts with a B," said Gurson.

"No shit," responded Kane.

They moved into the bedroom. Northern exposure, dark. Tidy. More books. Camera on the desk. Ten pictures taken. He advanced the roll, opened the camera, and popped the roll into his pocket.

Bathroom closet full of dirty laundry. No sign of anything bloodstained or burned. No apparent signs of foul play. He opened a couple of drawers, neatly arrayed with shirts, socks, underwear. Half-eaten candy bar on the night table. Snickers. Pair of reading glasses. He sat down on the bed, made up like a hotel bed with lots of pillows. A black-and-white photograph, this one large, hanging on the far wall, snagged Gurson's attention. Gurson tugged on Kane's arm and spoke softly. "Look at that."

"I'm looking."

It was a grotesque and yet alluring image. Back of a shapely nude. The bald, androgynous head deeply scarred. Waist cinched with what appeared to be a chastity belt. Gaping vertical slashes on each shoulder blade. Gurson went over for a closer look and tried to find a signature but found nothing on the photo. Then he took it off the wall and had Kane look on the back.

Kane read aloud. "Says 'Witkin. Nine-slash-fifteen'."

The photograph reminded Gurson of the bird he'd found in Gretz's car. The way the wings were cut off. He rehung the photograph. Made him think of the burned girl they'd found, the markings on her back.

Gurson turned his attention to a nearby shelf and took hold of a framed snapshot. He recognized the guy in the second row. A younger version of the guy in the Mercedes. He slipped the photo out of its frame and flipped the picture over. Yale conference. Spring 1975. Slipped the photograph into his jacket pocket. Then he hooked up with Manny. "You know if there's a Mrs. Gretz?" asked Gurson.

"No, no Mrs. Gretz."

"Anyone share the office?" asked Kane.

"Once. Few years ago. Another doctor. Always complaining. Too hot in winter, too cold in summer," Manny went on, seemingly oblivious.

"Got a name?" asked Gurson.

Manny smiled. He was good with names. "Like a dog. Collie. No, that's not it." Manny tugged his ear, impatient with himself. He passed a hand over his face, concentrating. "Collier. Yeah, that's it," he said, snapping his fingers. "Dr. Isaac Collier."

IF DR. ISAAC COLLIER'S WAITING ROOM WAS DESIGNED TO INTI-midate, it was indeed a great success. The walls were lined with signed heads, Freud, Jung, Rank, Brill, et al. A group shot of the Weimar Conference, dated September 1911. He had never met any of the men posed there, but as surely as they stood forever frozen in time, Isaac Collier counted himself among them.

Three days a week, Isaac Collier put in time at his Upper East Side office. 1120 Fifth. On Thursdays, he helped oversee a clinic downtown, supervising residents and their drug-addicted caseloads, a course in miracles: how to manage the unmanageable. Drugging drug addicts to help them kick was nothing new. Methadone was the old den mother of detox. And the newfangled drugs certainly had their place. But Collier insisted that without counseling, no drug in the world could ever stop an addict from wanting more. He viewed the contribution of his time at the clinic as a way to keep his sixty-four-year-old hands in the stew, a way to keep the great talking tradition of Freud alive in a world that consistently tried with pharmaceutical weaponry to prove the great godfather of all analysis wrong.

At the moment, he was sitting in his office with a full-blown hysteric, her mind set on vividly re-creating the sex she'd had with her sister's husband. A sordid tale, which vaguely piqued Collier's interest. He sat behind his patient, as was Freud's custom, and listened to the tearstained monologue. It was all he could do to help her. Listen. As no one else had for the better part of her life.

He vacillated between apathy and empathy. On the one hand, the patient was clearly acting out, reliving a painful childhood, the victim of a wicked older sister. On the other, of course, she was merely using that as her crutch, a feeble excuse for defective morality. Collier found most women to be duplicitous. In his opinion, the trick was possessing the wisdom to know the difference between pure emotions and feigned sorrows. With women, as far as he was concerned, this was a lifelong challenge.

The buzzer cut through his patient's sobs just moments before the session was over. He took the opportunity to sum up, offering a reminder of their next appointment, and said good-bye.

He closed the door behind her and then answered the persistent buzzer. Detectives? He checked his watch. In an hour he was due on the racquetball court. He looked at his coat and hat hanging on the wooden rack as he answered the door.

"Detectives Gurson and Kane, sir. Sorry to bother you, we're looking for Dr. Gretz." Gurson leaned into the door and wedged a foot forward. "Only take a moment."

"What makes you think he'd be here?" Collier asked wryly.

"Your name was on the doctor's lease," said Gurson.

"Why are you looking for him?" Collier ran a hand through his balding pate.

Gurson briefly explained the situation. Found a guy in the park, thought it might be connected to the doctor. Wanted to ask a few questions.

"Well, he isn't here." Collier looked behind him, then back at the police standing before him.

"Know where we might find him, then?" Kane slipped through the door and, to Collier's obvious dismay, stepped into the office, her tone easy and open.

Collier looked over at Kane and was suddenly struck by how beautiful she was. He held back his intended protest and allowed Gurson to enter the office as well. "I'm extremely busy," he began, his hand still clinging to the doorknob. "I've no idea where Dr. Gretz is. . . . I'm afraid I can't help you."

"We're trying to identify a man." Gurson looked around the waiting room.

"What man?" asked Collier, not comprehending the meaning of the statement.

"At the morgue," Gurson said plainly. "Would you happen to know what kind of car the doctor drives?"

The word "morgue" set a new tone. Collier closed the front door. "Old Mercedes, I think."

"Any chance you could point the doctor out in this photograph?" Gurson pulled out the photo of suits that he'd taken from Gretz's apartment.

Collier looked at the photo and took a bit of time before answering. "Quite dated. But that's him, right there." He put a finger on the man in the middle of the second row.

"So you say that's him, huh?" Gurson took Collier in now, recorded his physical attributes and deficits. About sixty-five, distinguished, five foot nine, 160, brown eyes, big ears, prominent nose, thin scar over his left brow. His breakfast sat half eaten on a plate on his desk, *New York Times* folded to the Op Ed. Roll with sausage and eggs. Omnivore, physically well maintained, New York intellectual, snob.

"Add a little gray and a few wrinkles," Collier ran a hand through his own balding pate.

"He have any immediate family?" asked Kane.

Collier was becoming impatient with all the questioning. It occurred to him he didn't have to answer any questions, that in fact he should be asking the questions. "Tell me, is Gretz dead?"

Gurson looked over at Kane.

Kane said, "If you could come with us to the morgue, it might help us get a positive ID."

"So you're saying Orrin Gretz is dead?" Collier rubbed the back of his neck.

"Like we said, we're not sure it's him," said Kane.

Collier became more rigid. "I'll have to make a few calls, cancel an appointment."

"Much appreciated," Gurson said, turning Collier's complaint into an acceptance of the task at hand. "Sooner the better."

Realizing it was futile to refuse, Collier left them seated in the waiting room and disappeared into his office, mumbling something.

Gurson browsed around, noting the view of the park. He clicked his internal shutter. He took the photograph from Gretz's apartment out of his pocket and looked at it again. But it wasn't a youthful Gretz, dead center smiling beside Collier, that gave him pause this time. It was the young woman seated below him on the bottom row. A bit heavyset, but the kind of face a guy could fall hard for fast. And the way those eyes looked back at you, he guessed she damn well knew it, too.

Gurson thought to ask Collier who she was. But thinking better of it, decided he'd wait awhile. Psychiatrists didn't like answering too many questions. He'd have to find out who she was on his own, then come and tell Collier how he *felt* about it.

[8]

Angel of the Waters

Ren blew a fifty on two vials of regret. Four rocks, a quarter carat each. Stuff on the street, aptly dubbed Body Bag, was risky, but her private dealer had been busted. She was feeling too desperate to discriminate. She'd been smoking garbage for almost two days running, long into the wee hours of Monday morning. One hit after the other, in search of oblivion. The acrid aftertaste of petroleum and chemical additives washed down with cheap wine had her on edge.

And then, at dawn, there was no more.

No more.

More. She wanted more. Her heart pumped an irregular beat, loud and fast. She tried to slow it all down with NyQuil, but her manic thoughts kept winding in smaller circles, tighter and tighter around her neck. She smoked her last pack of Marlboros down to the filters, her fingernails singed at the tips. The back of her throat raw. Needed more cigarettes. Needed more blow. Needed something to bring her down.

She fumbled in her bag and looked for the bottle of Xanax but couldn't find it. Shit. She unfolded a card with a downtown address. *Painless and free.* She had an appointment. Ten A.M. It was almost eight o'clock now. They'd bring her down for sure. All she had to do was get there. Let a bunch of white coats observe her. Rehearsed the part most of her life. Strung out druggie, no problem.

She locked herself in the bathroom and sat on the floor with the cordless phone. Head resting on the toilet, she thought of alternatives. There were no good ones. At 9 A.M., shaking, she put on her darkest shades and hit the street. Used all the cash she had to cab it to the clinic. Shivering in the waiting room, her leather boots wet, her feet cold.

They were expecting her, had her sign a form, asked the usual medical questions. Told her a bunch a shit she had no use for. They'd be throwing in some free psychotherapy. Like she'd ever show up for that. They'd want to see her back the following week, track her progress. Home phone? None. Home address? Under the Third Avenue Bridge. They'd be in touch with her doctor. Yeah, yeah. She had as many aliases as there were days in the year. She promised them whatever they wanted, never intending to ever see them again. All that mattered now was that they brought her down. After that, they'd have to be private eyes if they wanted to track her down. Nobody came that close, not unless she wanted them to.

After a while, a nurse finally came along. Took her blood, her urine, blood pressure, then ushered her into a changing room and gave her a locker. When would they take her, she just wanted something to bring her down. Soon, the nurse said, soon.

Others like her came and went. She undressed and put her things inside. Not much. Downtown thrift chic. Leather biker jacket, bell-bottom jeans, faded to a perfect patina, a vintage pair of black cowboy boots, and a moth-eaten gray cashmere sweater that she'd lifted from an old john. She thought of a god she'd forsaken long ago and played with the mandala around her neck. Thought of the wife, then. She rubbed the pendant as if it might bring her luck, then put it and all her other jewelry—bangles, hoops, and chains—into one of her wet socks, then into one of her boots. They gave her a paper robe and slippers and took her down a long, antiseptic hall to a small hospital-like room with two beds separated by a long white drape. Another release form to fill out.

At last, a doctor materialized. How long had she been getting high? he wanted to know. What drugs did she do? Did she shoot up? How often, how much? Just talking about it had her nose running and her bowels contracting. When were they going to knock her out? Talk, talk, talk. All these crazy shrinks. Didn't these guys know that the mouth was the most dangerous part of the body?

When the doctor finished taking his notes, he explained the procedure. Simple. They'd shoot her full of Demerol with a side of methadone, pack her off to dreamland. She sat on the edge of the bed and pushed back her cuticles.

The nurse reappeared and wheeled her out on a hard stretcher. The walls were painted pale green. The nurse wore pale green. The whole place made her feel pale green, like a frog, dying. Once in the treatment room, Ren reconsidered. What the hell was she doing there? But then her eyes caught sight of the metallic stand beside her and she breathed easy. There lay what she was waiting for. A full IV of space nectar.

"Okay," said the doctor, taking Ren's hand in his. "Are you ready?"

Ren looked up at the face of an angel. Sweet dreams were made of this. She stretched out her arm and pumped her fist, watching her poor excuse for a vein slowly surface.

Let it snow, let it snow, let it snow.

WHILE REN MADE ANGELS IN A FIELD OF IMAGINARY SNOW, Theodora and her dog Siggy loped across the real thing. Theodora maintained an even pace, jogging alongside the dog. She tossed a stick in the air. Catch. They rounded the reservoir. The water was nearly frozen. A loop around Angel of the Waters. One of her favorite places to meet Ren for a long walk. She glanced around now, as if by some wished-for coincidence the young woman might be there. She looked up into a gathering of dry trees, creaking with each gust of the wind, and felt a sudden chill. A quick stop at the playground before heading home.

Despite Siggy's protests, Theodora tied the leash to the iron bars. Reassuring the dog, she stroked the top of his head and spoke in a soft even tone, *Mommy will be back soon.* . . .

In this enclosed quarter-acre wood she found peace. Rays of light filtered between tire swings, tall oaks, and monkey bars. She took a seat, tilting her head up to the sun, the warmth comforting her, reshaping the taut frown into a half smile. She closed her eyes and began to meditate. Felt the weight of her body on the bench, the cool air on her face. Her discursive mind attempted to tug her back, back to unpleasant reminders of imperfection, back to the past. She paid these thoughts no attention. She was taking off now, a quarterback with the ball, two-hundred-pound linebackers in pursuit, grabbing for some part of her, just seconds too slow to tackle or knock her down. When she opened her eyes, she observed the scene before her with raw clarity.

A handful of children out to play. A young mother cooing to her tiny infant. The child, wrapped in a rainbow quilt, ceased its mournful cry as the mother placed the tip of a finger into the tiny mouth. Unconsciously, Theodora sucked on her bottom lip. The wanting had overcome her again, as it had so many times before. A child. A center of gravity that though demanding, would demand what she wanted to give.

"Ready or not, here I come. . . ." The words washed over her, an unexpected wave. She could see the child hiding there, beneath the slide, crouched in a kind of terrified excitement. Wanting and not wanting to be found. The mother crept slowly, hunched over, as if to make herself invisible, or at least as small as the five-year-old she was seeking. The child looked up, caught sight of Theodora watching, and smiled. The child put a finger to her mouth and whispered, "Shhh."

Ready or not . . . here I come. . . .

When mother and daughter were reunited in an embrace, Theodora turned away, envious. She thought of Ren, of an autumn afternoon they'd spent in the park. Ren had called saying she was in some trouble. They'd met at the conservatory garden. Walked the maze of landscaped paths, arms linked. Didn't speak much, didn't have to. Theodora held on to the feeling of that day. Of Ren looking to her for guidance and support. In this way, Ren became her center of gravity. A child needing what she so wanted to give . . .

Like a baby's cry, at once recognizable to its mother from another room, Siggy's bark called her back. She stood up, a sleepwalker, following the dog's call. The dog, catching sight of her, leapt about wildly. As soon as she untied him he lurched forward, pulling her back toward the playground. As if knowing he wasn't allowed any further, Siggy stopped short of the gates.

Together they stood, frozen in place. Access denied. Their faces pressed to the cold metallic bars.

From deep within the wooded green, her stalker watched it all. Well concealed in black woolen hood, he circled her orb and marveled at the sight of her. How the brisk air raised the blood to her cheeks. He inhaled, as if from this distance he might catch the wave of her misty breath on the breeze. Too far to inhale her exhale. And yet, not too far to capture the beauty of her, and the longing in her eyes. Her dance with her dog. A child at play . . . on this bright holiday of spring.

It was here he gained his insight. Here that he confirmed her vulnerability. He kept his distance and his feelings for her neatly in place. Dreams of her, of the two of them, together, were the covers that kept him warm. Here, at his imagined edge of the earth, they were alone. When the time was right, he'd take her there.

[9]

Somebody to Blame

Isaac Collier stood before the door of the Chief Medical Examiner's Office building, the wind blowing strands of gray hair across his face. The sun ducked behind a cloud, shading the block. Collier appeared nervous. "I hope this is all just a waste of my time." He rubbed his palms together and said, "Well then, let's get to it." Collier stepped in front of Gurson and Kane and led the way to the elevator.

They rode down to the basement level. The doors opened and Gurson walked up to the reception desk. "Verdi still around?"

The medical examiner soon appeared and produced a Polaroid. The bright red face in the photo looked sunburned. Collier looked at the photograph.

Gurson looked at Collier. "Is it Gretz?"

"Dear God." He held the photograph in his hands. "I was hoping not . . . but I believe it is."

"We'll need you to take a look at the body," said Verdi.

The room was cold. Lighting too high. Smell of formaldehyde, rot, and ammonia. Worse than milk gone sour. Verdi put gloves on and then pulled out the drawer. Before Collier came forward, Gurson positioned himself on the other side of the body, Collier's face in his view. Verdi lifted the white sheet. Collier looked down and swallowed hard. His lips trembled. "Orrin." He paused for a long moment. "He's so red—looks like carbon monoxide poisoning—"

"That's precisely right, Doctor. Classic lividity," explained Verdi. "The result of carboxyhemoglobin. Compound produced by the exposure of the hemoglobin to carbon monoxide. Whole body stays red for days."

The room went silent for a few moments and then Collier spoke in a whisper. "Suicide?"

Kane, Gurson, and Verdi led Collier to a waiting room outside. Kane sat down next to Collier, placing a hand on his shoulder. "When was the last time you spoke to him?"

"Spoke to him . . . not that long ago. . . . A month, maybe two. We were hoping to get together but we were both so busy."

"Did he seem upset, mention any problems?" asked Gurson.

Collier shook his head. "When did you say this happened?"

"Found him Saturday," said Gurson.

"Saturday," Collier echoed.

"You ever see this big print he has at his place . . . black and white of a woman's back with slashes?"

Collier cocked his head in a show of confusion. "No."

"When was the last time you were at his apartment?" asked Kane.

Collier scratched his jaw. "Five, maybe six months ago."

"And you say you didn't see this print there?" asked Gurson.

Collier shook his head no.

"You two, were you close?"

"We were colleagues. He trained with me at Yale."

Gurson zoned in on the wrinkle between Collier's brow, a deep indentation that seemed to grow deeper every time Collier spoke. "So, any idea why he might do this?"

Collier shook his head, sadly. "Not really, though his mother comes to mind. Took her own life. An overdose of pills, I believe."

"When?" asked Kane.

"Long time ago. She had Huntington's disease," said Collier.

"What's that?" asked Gurson.

"Progressive movement disorder. Causes seizures, dementia. No cure," said Verdi. "Fifty-fifty chance it can be passed from parent to child through a mutation in the normal gene."

"You know if your friend here had it?" Gurson asked Collier.

"Might have been his genetic inheritance," said Collier. "Of course, the same might be said for suicide. Greater incidence in such families."

Gurson had heard that line before. He brushed it off. Life was all about fifty-fifty chances. "Anyone else close to the doctor you think we should talk to?"

"No immediate family. Some friends, of course, colleagues," said Collier. "I'll give it some thought . . . put a list together."

"We found a note in the car, something about finding consolation. Found a dead bird in the car with him too. You know if the doctor had a pet bird?" asked Kane.

"Bird? What kind of bird?" asked Collier.

"Sparrow," said Gurson.

"I doubt he'd keep a wild bird for a pet." Collier looked at Gurson quizzically. "You say the bird was dead?"

"Wings cut off," said Gurson.

"None of this makes any sense to me." Collier shook his head.

Gurson offered Collier one of his cards. "Give me a call if anything comes to mind."

"Yes, of course." Collier took the card.

Kane turned to Gurson, then to Collier. "Will you be making the arrangements, then?" asked Kane.

"The arrangements?" asked Collier.

"We need someone to claim the body," Gurson filled in.

Collier nodded. "Yes, of course. I suppose I could attend to that."

"Good, we'll just need you to sign some papers," said Gurson.

After business was handled, Gurson asked Collier if he needed a lift.

"No, no. Just need some air and then I'll get a cab." Collier offered Gurson a firm handshake and let Kane escort him outside.

Gurson followed Verdi into her back office. A small cubicle with shadow boxes on the wall. X rays illuminated. A desk meticulously arrayed with medical books and well-marked folders. "Find any buried treasure in that head of hair?" The detective waited for Verdi to sit down at her desk, then took a seat.

"Nothing unusual. Looks like classic CO poisoning. What are you looking for?"

"Foul play. Found him parked in the Rambles Saturday morning. Next day, Jane Doe turns up barbecued in the Brambles. This guy has this photograph of a woman hanging on his bedroom wall. Nude with slashes on her back. Reminds me of the marks you found on the dead girl's back."

"I told you those markings could be from the fire," said Verdi. "Or a ritualistic or masochistic branding—"

"Yeah, okay. But then he has this amputated bird in his car. I'm starting to think there's more to this story."

"You comb the car?"

Gurson shook his head. "Bit of a fiasco. We're working on that."

"So what do you want me to do with him? He's taking up valuable drawer space." Verdi absently moved a book from one side of her desk to the other.

"If he killed the girl, you ought to be able to find some trace of her on him, right?"

"Under ideal circumstances, yeah."

"I want a full workup on this guy. Can you run some test for this Huntington's?"

"You want additional tests, I'll need paperwork," said Verdi.

"Paper takes time," said Gurson, tracing the outline of his bottom lip with his finger.

"Lack of it makes trouble," Verdi countered.

Verdi was overworked and Gurson knew it, but she was a professional, better than average at a job she'd been showing up for with pride for over two decades. She rarely missed a thing, her attention to detail and her commitment to veracity her industry trademark. On the other hand, her scrupulous rep gave her power. Power to call it quits when she felt a detective was being unjustly persistent.

"You want to know why he killed himself . . . or why he killed the girl?" Verdi raised her brow.

"Maybe one will answer the other."

"This one looks like an open-and-shut suicide, Gurson. No struggle, nothing. You said he was found with his fly open?"

"Yeah. That's how I found him."

"There was no semen, no saliva, no vaginal fluid. I say the guy was jerking off to the night sky, inhaling fumes. Lullaby and good night."

"But—" he began.

"Maybe he took a leak, forgot to zip his pants," Verdi cut him off. "That's what it appears to be."

"Since when are things what they appear to be? Aren't you the one who taught me that?"

"Get clearance."

Gurson nodded, then thought out loud: "What did they do with the dead bird in the car—"

"Ornithology's out of my league." Verdi closed her ledger. "They'd send that one to Fish and Fowl."

"You any good at suicide notes?"

"Try me."

"Said he became accessible to consolation."

"Consolation? Like the prize you get when you lose?"

"I was thinking more like remorse," said Gurson. "You know, maybe, for killing the girl."

"Sounds like he was just feeling sorry for himself, Gurson," said Verdi. "If the guy had this Huntington's disease, he knew he was a goner."

"Nothing to live for, nothing to lose. In my book that spells dangerous. Maybe this consolation bit has to do with something he was sorry he did." Gurson tapped his boot on the edge of Verdi's desk. "I mean, what's a respectable doctor doing parked in the Rambles? Unless he's not respectable . . ."

Verdi swiveled in her chair. "Park's a big place. World within a world. Maybe it's like they say, maybe nature's just more powerful than education. Maybe the guy liked the park, maybe he was in love with his car. Like some kind of shrine. You know, really *autoerotic*. Rest of it, sounds like coincidence."

"Maybe. But I don't generally subscribe to that."

"You look at any other suspects . . . any of the guys they lined up for the last arson killing?"

"Sure. Screening all the reruns." Gurson stood up and stretched. "Basic investigative procedure."

"If all else fails, use logic."

"Logic." Gurson put on his shades. "Now why didn't I think of that?"

Gurson took Gretz's agenda out of his pocket and flipped to the week before his death. Like a flat line on an EKG. Nothing. He flipped along. Didn't look like the guy had any long-term plans. He flipped backwards. Full roster of patients, months on end, and then suddenly nothing. He'd have to get a hold of the guy's medical records, get Verdi the clearance she needed. Pick up the pictures he'd had developed from that roll of film he'd found at Gretz's place. No suicide was simply open, shut. At least, not the way most cops wanted it to be. Suicide took cops off the hook. Death of choice. No one to blame. Kind of death that carried immunity. Cover it up with dirt, clear the land, next. Just like his old man. Quick wrap. But suicide *was* murder. Self-murder. And as far as Gurson was concerned, there ought to be somebody to blame.

[10]

Hot

First things first. Cleanliness. Theodora stepped into the bathroom. The steam fogging the mirror. He had drawn the bath for her and she knew the rules—he had tested the water, she need only get in, immerse.

She took a deep breath and sat down quickly.

The water, hot enough to poach an egg, scalded her legs, her vagina, the soft flesh of each breast. The impulse to leap out flashed.

"Sit."

But it wasn't pain she felt. Not precisely. Something about hurting herself, something so familiar, gave this scene its most primitive sensation—something close to comfort.

After a few moments, at his command, she stood slowly, her skin scalded crimson. He turned on the shower above her head. Ice. Opposites attracting.

"Come."

She stepped out of the tub and he swaddled her, from her neck to her thighs, in a large white cotton towel and led her into the bedroom.

There, he instructed her to lie down on the bed, ass up. She said nothing, simply followed orders.

He took off the towel and then, with the softest of silk scarves, tied her tightly to each post. He surveyed his possession.

She could feel the cool air on her bare ass now. She arched her back.

"You've made me wait too long."

Everything was going according to plan. Consenting adults. Top and bottom. Act One.

She felt . . . ashamed, and yet relieved. This was her theater, her place to conquer childhood fears. A shortcut back to the cause of all despair.

"I hate you." She sent the words cutting through the air.

"That's good."

She pulled against her restraints and bit the inside of her lip until the taste of blood filled her mouth. He pulled a rope around her waist, a double slipknot resting at her hips. He spread her legs wider for a good view of all points of entry. He began pulling tightly on the rope, laughing as she fought against him, the hemp burning a reminder of who dominated the game.

He played with himself, a futile gesture. His cock laid flaccid in his hand as worthless as a used condom. Channeling frustration into rage, he parted her cheeks and began a different journey. A finger, then a fist. The arrow through her heart.

Jerking off, he managed to conjure a slight hard-on and whimpered with elation. But this pale rush of endorphins was only briefly satisfying. Unable to maintain his erection long enough to climax, he untied her and rolled away to his side of the bed, pouting.

Theodora did not attempt to console or comfort him. She lay still, quieting her own resentment. The only indication of the roughness of their play a tumble of silk and hemp. Tucker sat up and lit a cigar. With the same match, he lit her cigarette.

"Why didn't you answer your page this afternoon?" Theodora asked, a burst of smoke billowed toward the ceiling. "I really hate being put off that way."

"Reversing roles so soon. I was just beginning to relax."

"This has nothing to do with fun and games."

"Reality? Please. Not yet."

A transparent floater sailed into her optic view, rimmed in black. She tried to follow it, to see where it could be going, but in an instant it was gone. She closed her eyes.

He looked at his watch. "Shit." He disappeared into his clothing so quickly, his nakedness just moments before seemed imagined.

She gingerly draped a towel around her, her skin, still raw to the touch, stinging.

He gently ran a finger across her back. "Too hot?"

"Never."

"So. You paged me. What was so important?"

She was thinking of telling him about going to the playground with Siggy. Something about seeing the children. She looked into his steel gray eyes. A handsome man. Strong jaw, full lips. She ran her hand through his still thick graying hair and enjoyed the way it felt between her fingers. He was her protector, in a most ironic way. Inflicting pain to give pleasure. Partners in a game where trust was all. On a stage where vulnerability played with extremes. Each knew the other's insecurities. Intimately. Until Tucker had firmly refused to pursue the issue of their fertility, neither one of them had paraded this knowledge unfairly. They'd had a mutual understanding. She filled her lungs with nicotine and oxygen.

The phone rang. They both looked at it.

"Don't answer it," said Tucker.

Theodora leaned over and picked up the receiver and began a stilted conversation. "My God," she murmured. "When . . . yes, of course."

Tucker, annoyed that she'd answered the phone, got out of bed. He was busy at the mirror now, refining the part in his hair.

Theodora said again, "Yes, of course," and then hung the phone up.

Tucker pretended not to give a shit, but asked anyway. "Who was that?"

"Isaac Collier."

"Collier?" He looked over toward the dresser with irritation; his beeper was going off, again. "Screw you." He cursed the little black box, the number of his caller flashing across its digital face.

"Tucker, dammit. Did you hear me?"

"Yeah. Collier. So what?"

Theodora pulled the bed covers up around her, a small gesture that gave her some comfort. "Orrin Gretz is dead."

[11]

Fragments

Gurson and Kane worked back-to-back shifts, buoyed by caffeine. They were mourning the loss of their window of opportunity. Over forty-eight hours in and they still had nothing. No ID on the girl. No trace evidence. Gretz's roll of film just a bunch of shots of trees and a frozen fountain in the park.

Knee-deep in snow and the usual suspects. Actually found a lunatic by the zoo who offered to take credit for the murder. Had the facts all wrong though. Said he'd thrown her off a bridge. Had a hell of a time convincing him that this murder wasn't his for the asking.

Tuesday morning brought gusty winds and freezing rain. Kane went home to hit a soft pillow for a few hours. Gurson flipped through the file on the first park bonfire. Plenty of similarities. First murder, the one last year, took place in the dead of winter. Same accelerant. No viable suspects, no evidence left behind. A lineup of mugs, all long shots. They would haul them all in again, sure, waste a week of snowy afternoons.

Gurson took five in the back room. A dimly lit mess hall for cops on downtime. Soda and candy machines. An old pool table, VCR and TV. Slopped together in a haphazard way, like some pop-art museum or a funky arcade, adorned with relics from the park. Old street signs, ancient traffic lights, remnants of old movie sets. Signed posters from the park's free concerts—Pavarotti, Paul Simon, an autographed photo of Hoffman in *Marathon Man*.

Gurson flopped down on one of the sofas. *Twister* was playing on the TV to an audience of one. Florio. Stale loaf of Italian bread. His once thick head of inky waves now thinning and his one-two street punch turning to paunch. He'd been at the Central Park precinct for almost ten years. A run-of-the-mill beat cop promoted to sleepy-eyed detective. In the park that meant he spent most days chasing squirrels.

"I can tell you straight off, the twister is going to win," said Gurson.

"Thanks for ruining it for me." Florio was doing serious damage to a bag of jalapeño Doritos. "You find that jerk's car yet?"

"Still at the pound. I was thinking of taking a ride there before heading home."

"You want company?"

"No thanks."

Florio made a sour puss. "You think the guy had something to do with the park killing?"

"Don't know yet."

"Any play on that gun they found?" asked Florio.

Gurson got up and walked over to the soda machine. He dropped his coins in, his back to Florio. "Shaved numbers. Running it down at the lab."

Florio lowered the volume on the TV. "Errand for fools."

Gurson popped open his soda and took a drink. "Reserve judgments until all the facts are in, Florio, didn't they teach you anything at the academy?"

"Oh, wait, I get it. Some fancy doctor, right? Family wants an inquiry, won't accept the fact the guy booked his own flight," Florio offered.

"Looking at all the angles," said Gurson.

"Why bother. No one gives two shits about the chick in the Brambles," said Florio. "You weren't here last year. I was. We chased our tails for six months on that one."

"That's because I wasn't here," Gurson said, smirking.

"Yeah, right." Florio cleared his throat and went on in a more cautious tone. "You know, I heard the boss saying you're taking this personal, probably paying this suicide too much attention. Something about your old man . . ."

Gurson felt the blood rise to his face. "Careful, Florio. You're sitting too close to the set." Gurson tapped his forehead. "Causes brain damage."

GURSON HANDED OVER HIS COPY OF THE AUTO VOUCHER. "I'm from the Central Park precinct. Campbell sent me." He was holding a shovel in his hand, figuring the car was dumped outside.

The cop took the voucher and laughed. "You planning to dig her out?"

The nameplate on the cop's desk said John Smith. Perfect name for the guy, thought Gurson. Middle-aged, middle of the road. "If I have to."

"Have a seat." Smith moved lethargically toward the files. "Relax . . . read the thoughts of the boys of summer." Smith nudged the newspaper in Gurson's direction. It was an old Dodgers saying. March hailed the coming of summer, a new baseball season.

Gurson watched Smith shuffle out of the room. A stooge, plopped at the dullest desk in town. Junkyard heap. The lot where stray vehicles were parked until somebody came to claim them. Gurson took the *Daily News* in his hands, folded to the sports section. Headline stories about baseball, the new spring season. Talk about all the big trades that he predicted would turn out to be a bust. His old man had been a big Mets fan. Hated the Yankees, something about a World Series game all the way back in '41 against the Brooklyn Dodgers. How the Yankees took the pennant on default, some wild pitch that should have ended the inning. Gurson still remembered the Dodgers' catcher's name, it was a name his father said he'd never forget because when the guy lost hold of the ball it changed baseball history. Mickey Owens, that was it. His father was only nine at the time, but that moment burned itself into his memory. The unfairness of it, his father had told him, had a real impact on him. From that moment on, his father wrote the Yankees off. In his mind, that instance signified something major, something he would ultimately teach his son about character. It was one of his first lessons about injustice. How winning without deserving the win meant less than zero.

When the Dodgers moved to L.A., his father continued to root for them anyway. Boys without a home team, until '61 when the Mets came along. From that day forward, father and son became devoted Mets fans. TV was always on when the old man was home, right through dinner in baseball season. Gurson was daydreaming about the '69 World Series now, how he really believed the Mets had won because he and his father were watching the game. How much he had wanted them to win! Needed them to, something he believed he willed by wishing, to give to his father, like a gift. His father celebrated the win with him, like it was their win. Bought him a mitt and all the trimmings, but never had much time to go to a real game, or toss the ball around.

Gurson turned the pages, away from baseball, away from the past, and landed on a short piece about the police asking for help in identifying the torched girl they'd found in the park. He put the paper aside when Smith returned.

"Car came in here Saturday morning . . . never should have come here," Smith was saying now. "Tow said Eighty-fifth Street was blocked with snow. Couldn't get it to the precinct so they brought it here."

"How convenient. Where is it?"

"Field 5. Row F, number 14."

"Outside, right?" Gurson laughed out loud. "Just what I figured. Car's a freakin' crime scene and they let it sit out in the open." Truth be told, they'd dusted for prints at the scene and come up empty. Still, the car ending up out here wouldn't help prosecuting arguments any. Made them all look like fools.

"Flatbed laid it down in field 5."

Gurson followed the cop out into the lot.

"First left, 'bout half a city block, row F, number 14." The cop pointed west.

"I'm going to need that flatbed. Have to tow this car over to the Central Park precinct's garage."

The cop shrugged. "We're talking twelve inches. Your car is snowed in."

"You got two hours," said Gurson.

"Pal, your guys dumped it here."

"Now you got till yesterday morning," Gurson said, letting him know he wasn't screwing around. "Catch my drift, wiseass?"

The cop looked at Gurson more closely. The rough-hewn good looks made him look more like a cowboy than a cop, too young to be bossing anybody around. Stood about five ten, rock hard. But it wasn't the size of him that made the guy pause. Not the big hands or the threatening stance. It was something in his eyes. Cocksure, unwavering. Not the look of a rookie. Compelled him to reconsider. "Let's see what I can do."

Gurson hiked out in the snow and walked toward field 5. Walking along, he started thinking about his old man again. For some kids it was the smell of cookies in the oven that took them back to their childhood home. For Gurson it was the choke of car exhaust.

He remembered the smallest of details. The hair on his father's hands; the saliva at each corner of his mouth; the Adam's apple perfectly still; the crease in his regulation blues. Memories that belonged to some other world. Not long after it all happened, his mother sent him to a shrink, tried to get him to talk about it.

What do you remember, James?

. . . old rusty garbage pails lining the walls, his long worktable, some tools . . . The car . . . black . . . a beauty, bought it at a police auction. Old Eldorado.

He's hanging over the steering wheel like he's looking for something . . . like he's praying maybe. Motor's running. Sound of the engine. Like some animal, loud. Then it's quiet . . . when I turn it off. I'm by myself. With him. It's cold. His face . . . is all red.

He's too heavy . . . I can't get him out.

Until her dying day, seven years ago this May, his mother had tried, unsuccessfully, to convince her son that it wasn't his fault. But to this day he held on to his own belief and his own anger.

If I'd come home sooner . . . could have stopped him, could have gotten him to change his mind. It wasn't fair what the old man did to them . . . leaving them feeling so damn guilty. . . .

Gurson stopped walking and let the sun's white light blind him. Row F, 12, 13, 14 . . . There it was, covered to the top of its steel wheel wells. It would take all day to get the freaking car out. He cleared a small section of snow away from the driver's side, enough to clear the winged door, and then popped it open. The inside of the car stank. He looked on the passenger seat and saw the dead bird. With gloved hands, he bagged it. Then he looked under the seats. The silver cigar cutter. Bagged that too, then opened the glove. Same as the first time. Maps, flashlight.

He cracked the trunk and had another look. The leather duffel. He hadn't thought much of it before. Just some dirty rags. He took a sniff. Grease and grime, and a touch of something else. Acetone? Typical accessories of your everyday car enthusiast . . . or the props of a park arson?

*　　*　　*

Ren fell through clouds of anesthesia. Thick, white cumulus clouds. A force pulled her through a long, dark tunnel without end. Comatose for over twenty-four hours straight. While her brain was on disconnect, her physical body convulsed through the trauma of detox. After a day out cold, she awoke feeling hollow. Like a carved pumpkin, her guts scooped out and the top of her head neatly replaced.

Back home, heavy limbed and exhausted, she wondered if she was really clean. Was the desire gone for good? Or would she soon crave a fix? In this moment, she simply felt empty, as if she'd left her drugged-out self in another world. A world of sleep and forgotten dreams. The sensation was odd, like losing your shadow.

But all that said and done, she was still Ren. No fairy godmother waiting to turn her rags to silk, no prince in the wings to pay overdue rent. Hell, she wasn't looking for any forever after. Just wanted to come down, get off the street, avoid the wrench of the cold kick. Her fingers were swollen, eyes red and drawn. She looked old, worn out. Her full lips cracked and dry. She'd lost the edge, but still felt restless. The red light flashed on her message machine. Four messages. Reluctantly, she listened in.

"Hey, girl, where you been?" Tommy. As expected, looking for her. She fast-forwarded the tape.

White noise. Like someone calling from inside a closet. And then nothing. Ren played it back, tried to make out the background static. Again, nothing.

Number three was short and to the point. "Call me." The wife. A request or an order? Either way, Ren wasn't ready to return that call, or the one right after it for that matter. Caller number 4 was her landlord looking for rent.

She needed money. Counted spare change. Thirteen dollars and twenty-six cents. Not enough to fill the bowl of a base pipe. She emptied pockets. Another two fifty. Her stash, not that she wanted any, was a refuge of empty plastic bags and bottles, their residue long ago licked clean. Her apartment, a cramped two-by-four, was cold and a far cry from cozy. Recent acquisitions that might have offered comfort—a pashmina throw, a crystal decanter, a sterling flask—all compliments of satisfied customers—had been hocked on receipt. A dreary view of the street revealed the weather. Cold and nasty. The movers and shakers of the city were most certainly under cover. Somewhere out there, somebody needed to get laid.

She needed to get back to work. Needed her lifeline. Time to dial for dollars.

"Superman?"

"That you, girl? Where the hell you been?" Tommy shouted into the phone.

Rule 1: Never tell your pimp you've been to detox. They think if you get a little healthy you might change your fabulous lifestyle. "Flu thing."

"You don't call. Makes me think you're cutting out."

Ren fished in a pocket for a tissue. Her nose was running. "I thought you were leaving last week."

"Something came up. But I ain't talking on the phone, you know what I'm saying. I see you, we talk," Tommy sang. "I got some friends, baby. Owe me favors. All you need's enough for a pair of shades. You understand what I'm saying? First class. You be my girl. Palm trees, sunshine, can you dig it?"

She knew exactly what he was saying. He was cutting out. A deal was going down and he'd need to get out of New York. She'd earned a warm place in his cold heart for all the times she'd covered for him with the cops. Besides, he liked her company.

Twisted Tommy was all right. He'd scraped her off the sidewalk. She owed him and she hated it, but without him she was just another doped-up whore scrounging for three-dollar blow jobs. "Let me think about it."

"Don't take too long, sweetheart. So, you working or what?"

Ren took a deep breath, then coughed. "Working. What you got?"

"Switchboard's hot, baby. Your regulars have been calling. They be asking for their sweet young thang." He fumbled with the phone. "Let me see what I got. . . . Guy downtown. Keeps calling."

Ren felt a surge of sudden energy. Money. She looked over toward her open closet. On a shelf there were boxes. In the boxes she had hair, all colors. "I'm in the mood to be blonde, long blonde."

"Knock yourself out, sugar."

"Who is he?"

"Calls hisself Rocco."

"Rocco. Don't know any Rocco. This guy clean?"

"Mr. Clean with the green."

"Set it up for tomorrow. And tell him I get my money up front."

"Listen to this, Joey, she wants it up front."

"Who's there with you?"

"My parakeet. Joey, say hello to Ren, hel . . . lo . . . hel . . . lo . . ."

"You talking to a parakeet? Sounds like it's time *you* got laid, Tommy."

"I'm flying on a full tank, baby. Come help me burn some fuel."

Ren let the line sit silent about a minute, then said, "You get those two tickets to paradise, then we'll take a slow ride on your full tank."

"Consider it booked, baby, but listen up. Don't make me come looking. And stay out of the park. I hear some 'droid's burning tricks."

[12]

Kiss and Tell

TUESDAY, MARCH 24

Driving up the FDR in his Jeep, Gurson turned up the radio and cruised to vintage Cream. He was thinking about the Mercedes he'd just left sitting at the pound. Kept wondering why the guy would take a car like that out in the snow. He was following this thought into the woods when his cellular rang.

Kane's voice came across the line, static and remote. ". . . girl in the park . . ."

The line went silent so long, Gurson thought he'd lost her. "You're breaking up. Where are you?"

"Brambles . . . crime scene . . ." Silence. "Got ID . . ." Sounded like Kane was crying. "The girl . . . gun—"

"Don't move. Can you hear me? I'm there." He pushed his foot toward the floor.

Gurson could see Kane sitting on a boulder, drumming the snow with a stick. He walked up, his hands tucked deep into his pockets. She looked up. Gurson shrugged his shoulders. Kane's eyes were red and wet. She'd been crying, all right. Nothing she'd ever admit to. He sat down next to her. "So . . . who's the girl?"

Kane stammered, "Leone."

"Charlene Leone?" Gurson did a double take. "For real? No shit. Who made the ID?"

Kane leaned her head back, letting the rich sound of the wind fill the silence between them. Kane looked at him, square. "You trust me?"

"What are my options?"

Kane contemplated. "The gun. I've seen the piece before." She paused again. "Drop gun."

Drop guns were illegal. Name for the piece some cops carried in case of trouble. In case something went down and you didn't want the gun coming back to you. All guns owned by cops were supposed to be registered.

"What are you saying?" asked Gurson.

"At first I wasn't sure," Kane said.

"At first? Sure about what, Kane?"

"Forensics raised the last two numbers. Three seven." She paused and looked at the sky. "Leone took a piece off a dealer. Chrome plated .25 auto. Shaved numbers. Except the last two. Three seven." She looked at the ground. "I thought she vouched for it. We were doing a shakedown, scooping up junkies, moving them out of the park. Charlene took this guy's gun, let him walk. A favor, you know, something he'd remember when she needed something."

"You saying Charlene took this piece off some dirtbag and then never turned it in?" Gurson didn't give her time to answer. "When she needed something? Like what? A suspension? When was the last time you saw it."

"Before she got suspended. About nine months ago."

"Why didn't *you* vouch for it?"

"She told me she'd take care of it."

"So you didn't report it?" asked Gurson.

"Like I said, I figured she took care of it."

"You figured she took care of it," Gurson repeated. "So you think it's her because you're saying the gun they found is that piece?"

"That's part of it."

"There's another part?" asked Gurson.

"That bullet Verdi pulled at the autopsy. The one lodged in that girl's back." Kane shook her head. "I had a feeling then, at the morgue . . . it was Charlene."

Gurson made a fist and gently tapped his thigh. "How's that?"

"Leone was hit during a raid, three years ago. Couldn't take the slug out." Kane breathed in deep and went on, "Too close to the spinal cord. Hoped maybe it was just a coincidence." She looked away. "I went looking for her. Everywhere. No one had seen her for a week or more. At first, I figured she was on a bender."

"Why didn't you say anything?"

"Couldn't take the chance until I was sure. Had to be sure."

"Couldn't take what chance? Jesus, Kane, why haven't you told any of this to Bianchi?"

"Thought I'd tell you first."

Gurson shook his head. "You *think* it's her gun, or you *know* it's her gun?"

Kane looked at Gurson. "It's the gun, Gurson."

"Okay, but maybe she gave it back to the dirtbag." Gurson kicked up some snow. "I mean, what's Charlene going to be doing out here? Hooking or copping?"

Kane mulled over the question awhile, then put it straight. "What's it matter what she was doing? She's dead."

"It matters plenty."

"I don't imagine you know what it's like to be a black cop, Gurson. A black *female* cop. Having to line up everything you say, everything you do, before you do it. Playing to a white captain who, by my estimation, isn't exactly color-blind. You just try to blend in. You don't make too much noise. Anybody fucks with you, you better make sure you got all your aces lined up before you make your call. And then, sometimes you don't bother to make the call. You just let it slide. Unless it's one of those rare times when it's convenient to be darker than NYPD blue."

"When is it convenient?"

Kane looked Gurson squarely in the eyes. "When they're filling quotas."

Gurson exhaled loudly. "When was the last time you saw Charlene?"

Kane put her hands on her hips. "Been a while. Month maybe. Said she was straightening out. Said she was working on an old case, something that might get her back her shield. I was worried about her."

Gurson pulled a low branch down from a pine tree he was leaning on and plucked the needles. "Suspension report says she was pretty messed up."

"When did you see the suspension report? I would have thought that was confidential." Kane laughed. "But then, when you're a white cop rubbing elbows in the good old boys' club, nothing's really confidential now, is it?" Kane's eyes reflected her anger. "She got too close to the shit doing busts." Her eyes were watering. "You ever try busting some of these seasoned guys? Try before you buy, you know what I'm saying?"

"Sure, taste testing. I understand, Kane. Your partner is like blood. You want to clear her, I know you do. But we're talking about your ass now."

Kane continued pacing. "Are we?"

"I'd say so."

Kane went on as if Gurson weren't there. "I didn't stand by her." She paused. "Could have done that. Me and Charlene, shit, we were more than partners, Gurson."

"What's that supposed to mean?"

"I should have known better than to try talking to you." Kane looked straight ahead of her, at the acres of snow.

"Listen, all I'm saying is, soon as Bianchi finds out about the gun, he's going to blow your house down. Then the D.A.'s gonna come around. Your name just made their list. Not vouching evidence. And I'm the one covering your ass. If you're keeping any secrets, now's the time to kiss and tell."

"Tell you what? What half the force already knows?" She stared at him. "That me and Charlene were lovers. There, I told you." Kane paced. "And believe me, I wouldn't be sharing any of this with you if not for this mess. I know what you're thinking."

"What am I thinking?"

"You're thinking I fit the profile. I got the temper . . . maybe I killed her."

"I heard all about how you got dumped in this precinct, if that's what you mean. How you attacked your sergeant—"

"Bet you missed the part where the bastard was attempting to rape me in the basement."

Gurson nodded. "Hadn't heard that part."

"No, didn't think so. He expected me to smile and take it. Black chick with attitude, just a girl from the gutter. Well, sorry to disappoint y'all."

"Your business is your business, Kane."

"My business is your business, Gurson. What's mine is yours. Like it or not, we're partners."

"I don't think I need to know who you're sleeping with."

"If she shows up dead you do."

"Alibi?"

"None."

Gurson leaned back on a tree. "So. When was the last time you saw her alive?"

"Like I said, we split up before the suspension. Occasionally she'd call, crying, you know, telling me she was having a hard time. But when I saw her about a month ago, she was straight."

"So you think she lost it and started using again."

Kane walked over to a tree and doubled over. "I should have stood by her."

Gurson came up behind her and rested his hand lightly on her back.

Kane stomped the cold ground. "When I close my eyes, all I see is that disfigured corpse, melted and mangled. When I think how it went down, how she died . . ." Kane swallowed hard, "I can't breathe."

"Probably wouldn't do any good to say I know how you feel."

"Probably not, but say it anyhow." She turned and faced him.

"I know how you feel." He handed her a handkerchief.

"You think you got me all figured out? In just three months, huh? How do you qualify that?" She stepped away from him.

"You're not going to listen."

"I'm listening."

Gurson was about to spill his guts, though he didn't know it. He just figured he was pulling his partner back from the edge, a thing he'd done before but without all the talking. "You know what went down with my father?"

Kane looked at Gurson. "I don't believe much of what I hear secondhand."

"Too bad you weren't on board when they tarred and feathered him." Gurson paused, then went on. "He checked out when I was thirteen. I was the one who found him in the freaking garage. Hunched over, you know, motor running. I turned the car off. I remember doing that first. Then I tried getting him up, you know. I remember that the weight of him surprised me. He was so heavy. I had his door open and I was tugging on him, talking to him, pleading with him to get up. Eventually, some register went off. Bing. Suddenly, I got it. He was dead, and there I was, alone in that freaking dark, cold garage holding on to him. I don't think I've ever been so scared in my life." Gurson cleared his throat.

"Why did he do it?" Kane looked at him.

"He'd popped some kid. On a raid. Swore he pulled a piece. But all they found on the kid was a black wad of plastic. Dime-store pistol. Family was connected. Waged a full-blown campaign, put a smear together. Came to the house . . . looked into an internal report of domestic trouble . . . some fights he'd had with my mother . . . souped it up into a 'tendency toward violence.' I'm upstairs, listening in . . . these two rookie schmucks are bringing her to tears in the kitchen while my old man's sitting in a cage downtown. It was total bullshit. Twenty years on the beat and they all turned their backs on him. Threatened to run his ass through the mud if he didn't plea bargain."

"But you became a cop anyway. . . ."

"Didn't really have a choice. His only son. Needed someone to clear the family name. You know, raise instead of fold."

"I'm sorry."

"No sorrier than I am that you came upon Leone the way you did." Gurson walked up to her. "Looks like we're both stuck clearing people who can't clear themselves."

Kane attempted a smile, but instead her lips began to tremble. "I want this guy."

"So do I." He looked at the snowy scene around them. "He's our ticket out of this igloo."

They walked to the car together. Kane slid into the passenger seat. Gurson behind the wheel. He focused his eyes on the road ahead of them.

Fifteen minutes later, Gurson and Kane were sitting in Bianchi's office. Bianchi sat calmly, taking in the details without any immediate reaction. When Kane finished her monologue, Bianchi rubbed his jaw. "You're off the case."

"Off the case?" Kane shouted. "But she was my partner. I need to work this case."

"She was sleeping in your bed," Bianchi barked.

"And the book says ninety-nine times out of ten, fags kill each other," Kane said through clenched teeth. "Isn't that what you're saying?"

"It's for your own good, Kane," said Bianchi, "you're too close to this."

"My own good? And what am I supposed to do now?" She settled into her chair.

"Restricted duty. Until you're cleared." The sergeant looked at her firmly.

"Cleared? Of what?"

"Not vouching evidence, for starters."

"That's bullshit, Sarge."

"Standard procedure."

Kane hung her head and exhaled loudly. She stood up.

"IAB will want to have a talk with you. In the meantime, turn in your shield . . . and your guns, Kane. All of them," said Bianchi.

"Internal Affairs?" Kane's voice intensified. "Thanks for the vote of confidence." She stood up and looked at Gurson. Then she stormed out of the room, slamming the door behind her.

Gurson sat in Bianchi's office waiting for the other black shoe to drop.

"While the M.E.'s comparing dentures, go live the last few days of Leone's life," said Bianchi. "By the time we talk to the D.A., I want to know what brand of toilet paper she used to wipe her ass. You'll be working with Florio."

"Florio's an asshole."

"So park him on Leone's toilet." Bianchi tapped a pencil on the desk.

"I was hoping you'd give me a warrant for the shrink's office."

"The shrink? You still sniffing around that? M.E. says it's open, shut. Forget about the shrink."

"I put in for a full workup. We get the final autopsy report yet?" asked Gurson.

Bianchi played with a rubber band.

"Gretz's mother had some disease, chance he had it too."

"We're not here to make sense of suicide, Gurson."

Gurson tried a different tack. "Photographs in his apartment—scenes of the park, some chick cut up."

"Sounds like you're fishing in a dry riverbed." Bianchi chortled. "Next thing you're gonna tell me, the guy's suicide note was written in blood."

"I sent the bird to Forensics. You hear anything?" Gurson began.

"In process."

Gurson remained undiscouraged. "Give me a warrant, what's the big deal?"

Bianchi looked over at the map of the park. "If the girl turns out to be Leone, every step we take will be on the front page. I can't have you wasting time snooping around this suicide when I need you on this arson case."

"And what if it turns out this doctor killed her? You saying we should just dismiss it?" Gurson shot Bianchi a stern glance.

Bianchi took a deep breath. "You think he killed her . . . go ahead, get your warrant . . . just don't trip over yourself doing it." Bianchi looked over at his wall calendar, again. The days marked off. "If a guy isn't careful, he could get life in this dump."

[13]

Smoke Signals

Cheerios and necrophilia.

Gurson set the table for one. He sat down and spooned up mouthfuls of sugarcoated cereal while intermittently reading up on the subtle nuances of sexual deviance. Not your run-of-the-mill voyeurs here. These authentic studies of aberrant behavior were highly classified. Documented pathologic variations on just about every gruesome theme. Deadly assaults performed on nonconsenting targets.

Gurson contemplated the time it took for Cheerios to soften in cold milk. Inspired by his reading about the decomposition of flesh. His appetite, remarkably, remained undaunted. The smell of sausage and eggs frying in a skillet kept his stomach pleasantly distracted. He turned the page of the hefty volume and unexpectedly came across the offbeat tune of a different drummer. "'Necrophagia,'" he read aloud to the empty room, "'eating of dead bodies.' Mmmm, lovely." A full-color picture of an eviscerated male accompanied the definition. He tossed his spoon into the half-full bowl and watched the mushy o's float. He got up and turned off the stove, taking a small, unenthusiastic bite of carcinogenic pork.

Despite his sudden loss of appetite, Gurson couldn't help but note that man preferred meat cooked, not raw. Might that explain the deviant use of fire? He'd have to pay close attention to what the autopsy found in Gretz's stomach. If the doctor's last supper had been human remains, for example, he might have the link Bianchi was looking for.

His hunger and his breakfast break effectively ruined, Gurson headed uptown to East Harlem to have a look in Leone's fourth-floor walk-up.

He was greeted at the door by Florio. The forensic squad was buzzing around behind him like a swarm of mosquitoes.

"We canvassed the hood. Nobody's seen her for a couple of weeks." Florio kicked a bin filled with laundry.

"Find anything out of the ordinary?" asked Gurson.

"Just these." Florio produced a set of handcuffs and a black lace G-string. "Kinky."

"She was a cop, for crissakes," Gurson said. "I'm sure you got a pair of those at home too." He looked first at the cuffs, then the black G-string.

Florio giggled like a kid. "Got that right."

"So you got nothing yet. If she's so dirty, where's all the dirt?" Gurson looked around the apartment. A basic one-bedroom lacking many of the comforts of home. Not much furniture, nothing hanging on the walls. No decorative ornaments suggesting the personality of the tenant, which in and of itself seemed suggestive. Looked like she'd just moved in. Boxes in corners. Hardly any dishware in the cupboards. Nothing but soda and an old loaf of bread in the fridge.

"Where's Kane?" asked Florio.

If Gurson had Kane pegged right, he figured she was still working. Off the record, of course, out of range. Staking the underground, the park's bowels, where street scum did its true creep and crawl. "Restricted duty. Sarge gave her a few days off."

"I hear she was banging Leone." Florio made some foolish gesture with his hips. "Bang, bang, she's dead."

Gurson ignored Florio's comments. Stepped around the forensic squad. They weren't wasting any time. The place was being treated like a freaking crime scene. Gurson walked into the bathroom. He picked up a hairbrush and looked at the long strands of jet black hair wound around the bristles. He carried the brush into the bedroom. "Bag this," he told the forensic squad. "M.E.'s holding follicles from the girl we found."

"What's the verdict?" Florio asked Gurson.

"Dead until found breathing." Gurson looked around at the boxes filled with books, papers, clothing.

"This place was a flophouse, if you ask me." Florio tapped a cardboard box with his foot.

Flophouse? Hardly. Gurson knew they were all hoping for a small scandal. Like a small fire, they would contain it, put it out. Dirty cop, dirty end. But Gurson knew firsthand it wasn't always that cut and dry. "You finished with these?" asked Gurson, pointing to a couple of boxes.

"We finished with these?" the investigator called out. He got an affirmative response and turned to Gurson. "Yeah."

Gurson examined the contents of a few of the boxes and stopped when he came upon a stack of clippings from the arson killing that went down in the park a year ago. Some xeroxed crime photos that eerily mirrored the case at hand. "Leone work the last park case?" Gurson yelled out to Florio.

"Sure. We all worked it," answered Florio.

"Any reason you can think of she might have been mixed up in it?" asked Gurson.

Florio shrugged. "Leone was a bleeding heart. Fed the pigeons, gave half her danish to the bum under the bridge. Paid her informant's phone bills, that kind of thing. Felt sorry for all of them."

"Looked out for the underdogs, then."

"Yeah, the girl they found last year, all burned up, really got to her."

"Identified with the victims and became one of them," Gurson said to himself. "Sounds like a good egg."

"Kane was always teasing her. You know, telling her one of these days she was going to give her address to the wrong informant. Said she'd find one of them sleeping in her bed."

"You friendly with Kane?" Gurson asked while flipping through a stack of business cards held together by an old rubber band.

"Kane? She's got no friends. Trusts nobody." Florio leaned against a wall.

"I was checking the files on the killing last year. Looks like Leone was working hard. Must have interrogated every bum and hooker in the park." Gurson held up a card embossed with an illustration of a sports car, the two doors extended like the wings of a bird. Like Gretz's old Mercedes gullwing. Vintage Motorworks. Boyd Cleary. He turned to Florio. "Boyd Cleary. I know that name."

Florio ran his tongue over his teeth. "Cleary?"

"Boyd Cleary," Gurson repeated out loud. "One of the suspects last year."

"Could have been."

Gurson did some simple arithmetic. Gretz had a gullwing. Pretty rare bird, not like any old Honda. Boyd Cleary restored gullwings. Cleary was a con. Gurson ran his hand over the little gullwing embossed in the corner of the card. It called out to him like an invitation to dance.

[14]

911

What to wear. Ren rummaged in her closet. Black was always a safe choice, but she wasn't in the mood for black. Red, too much, blue, too blue. She pulled out a burgundy dress. Precisely right. She laid her selections on the bed. Sheer stockings, black corset and garter, skimpy lace panties, come-fuck-me shoes. She wanted to put it all together, then she'd make it look impulsive, last minute, lived in. Best part was getting ready. Pretend it was a blind date. The anticipation of the unknown, and the thought of cash flow, got her going.

She turned on her radio, found a good tune and started dancing around. She sang loud, on key, moving like a schoolgirl in front of the full-length mirror on her door. She had enough makeup to start her own company. Lipsticks of every hue, mascaras for thickness and curl, liquid concealers, powders, potions, psychedelic eyeliners, smoky shadows.

Why not put on a happy face?

When she was finished, she had to admit: She looked great. Some guy ought to fall in love with her, like in the movies, carry her off in his limo to his big pie in the sky. She opened her medicine cabinet and perused the bottles. She took a swig of cough syrup and loaded her gun. An unlicensed .25, given to her by a cop she'd been doing. She tossed it in her bag. She kept her mind on the money, could already taste it.

She called Tommy to let him know she was leaving. The way they worked it, if he didn't hear from her in a couple of hours, he came looking.

Avenue A and Eighth. Building was a dump. Nameless buzzers. Take-out menus littered the entry steps. She pressed the bell for 6W and the front door promptly clicked open. Alone in the old elevator, she opened her bag, reapplied some lipstick and changed her shoes. She repositioned the gun. As the lights lit up, floor to floor, she stretched her neck and back, took a few deep breaths. She hoped the guy was a premature ejac-ulator, something short and sweet.

The elevator opened on the sixth floor. South, North, East . . . West. Front door was open. She ran a hand through her hair, tugged the hem of her dress and entered. Anybody home? She didn't notice the guy hanging back in the shadows. No lights on.

"Like the view?" he crooned.

The apartment offered a dismal view of rusted water towers and concrete rooftops. A maze of aging architecture, poorly planned. The sun was setting behind a building, casting its orange light over a snow-capped spire. "Hey, can't see you over there," said Ren.

The guy said nothing. She couldn't see his face but now she could make out the rest of him. Well built. He walked in closer, his head cov-ered by a black leather hood. Slits for his eyes, nostrils, mouth.

"Trick or treat?" Ren smiled.

"That's not your hair." He stood closer now, close enough to touch a strand of the wig.

"You like it?" She put out her hand, blocking his touch. "I get my money up front."

He walked up to her with the truest look of tenderness in his hooded eyes and passed her a handful of bills. She counted and smiled, stuffing the stash in the zipper pocket of her coat.

"Get undressed."

"I'm not into rough stuff. You don't want me, I'll leave. He'll send another girl."

"Like I told him, I wanted you."

"You and me, we know each other?" The voice seemed familiar, but it was muffled and distorted by the mask.

"We have mutual friends."

She set her bag down, took off her coat, began to relax. "Got a little music to cut the edge?" She turned to look around.

He went over to the stereo on a black metal stand and flicked a switch. A woman began chanting in a beautiful yet haunting way. She knew the music, but couldn't quite place it.

He lit a few candles. She began to relax. Then he moved toward her.

"Why not take off the mask, honey?"

She could feel the wind before the slap brought her down. Then he ripped off the wig. He held the synthetic hair over the burning candles and let it light up. She backed away, watching the long hair crackle and burn. He followed her, the fiery wig extended like a torch.

She tripped and fell, tucked into herself, curling up like a fist. If he planned to burn her or start kicking, she wanted her face to stay whole. But he had something else in mind.

"Get up."

She tried to establish distance and prepare herself for whatever was coming. He tossed the burning wig into a metal wastebasket. Flames turned into smelly plumes of black smoke.

She looked left. Her bag, too far away. If she could lance him with something, she might be able to get to her bag, get the gun, or better yet go for the door and get the hell out. But he was ahead of her there. He grabbed a book off the table and whacked the side of her head. Hard enough to stun her.

She was thinking of Tommy. By the time he came looking, she'd be dead. Where was her bag? He had her down on the floor and now he was dragging her into another room. She started to talk to him, slow and easy. They were in this together. He didn't have to hurt her.

She figured she was a goner. Whatever end he had planned was probably in the bedroom. One scream, that was all she'd get, and then he'd bash her head in. Besides, the music was too loud. No one would hear her. The music. And suddenly, she knew. She knew who he was. And she knew she had better go with it, give in. Dominance was his trip. If she succumbed, he'd finish his little scene maybe let her go.

But then, maybe not. Maybe she had this bastard all wrong. Mock fantasy wouldn't fly. For the price of admission maybe he wanted to smell real fear. He took off his shirt. His upper body a ripple of well-worked muscles. He caught her staring and slapped her face hard. Then he handcuffed her to the bed. She heard seams split. He was ripping her dress, clawing her panties, saying something about heat. She looked away. Nothing mattered now, the bastard was going to take his time. She tensed, but then laid back and detached, what else could she do? And then he kicked her so hard she nearly blacked out, stomped on her over and over, like he was putting out cigarettes.

Just when she thought she couldn't stand any more, her prayers were answered. He came on her face and promptly unlocked the cuffs. Like nothing, he scooped her up and put her outside the door like the evening's trash. The contents of her bag spilled onto the ground. Noticing the gun, he smiled, lifted the piece and aimed. She held her breath and closed her eyes, but instead of a shot she heard him empty the barrel and then dump the gun in her lap. Hadn't wanted to kill her, just wanted control.

She stood herself up, the pain between her legs enough to bring her back to her knees. She wasn't bleeding, and she couldn't imagine why not. How could it hurt so bad with no blood to show? "I'll—"

"Keep your fucking mouth shut," he hissed. He unzipped the back of the mask and pulled it over his head. "And stay the hell away from my wife."

"But I—"

"You weren't supposed to become her secret lover, you were just supposed to fuck her when I was around. I wasn't paying you to become her sweetheart."

"I'm—"

"Dead," he finished her sentence, then his own, "if you see her again."

She wondered if the wife knew about hubbie's little hideaway. How come all of a sudden he wanted her to fade so fast? Keep away from the wife? Play by his rules? For now. If there was justice, it would come up from the street. There were no swans living in this sewer. No one was dialing 911.

Back at the precinct, Gurson was randomly calling the numbers on Gretz's Rolodex. Past patients, present patients. Cross section of city life. Scanning names. Taking notes. Nothing hair-raising, except one overtly flirtatious Victoria that turned out to be a Victor. Over the phone, Vic sheepishly confessed that he enjoyed dressing up as a cop. When asked if he had obtained a uniform dubiously, Victor/Victoria swore he would never do anything illegal. Gurson sent a car to be sure. Found one totally harmless middle-aged male, living alone with his shih tzu, Ralph. Fully done up for the Easter parade, Victor/Victoria was found to be missing a few screws, his bonnet, and a left leg. Not a homicidal bone in his cross-gendered body. He joyfully commended the NYPD, Dr. Orrin Gretz, and anybody else who happened by.

Coming up empty, Gurson began surfing the Internet. Mercedes gullwings. Only fourteen hundred of them were made. Originally sold for about eight grand back in the fifties. Couldn't touch one now for under a hundred thou, and then you'd need to sink another hundred to hundred fifty more if you were talking *concours*. Gurson printed out a picture of a '57 coupe and tacked it to his bulletin board. Then he punched in Huntington's disease. Wasn't sure what he was looking for. For now, he was just looking. He downloaded a page of information posted by a foundation that fund-raised for the disorder. Kicked his feet back and read. The disease was invariably fatal. No cure. Pathogenesis still unknown. Some controversial research was being done, involved the implantation of fetal tissue in rodents. Government opposition, red tape hoopla. Genetic test was available for diagnosis. If Gretz knew he had the disease, how long had he been in the know? Had he started experiencing some early symptoms? Could that have triggered his rage? He read on. Large percentage of the children of these patients chose not to test. Positive result was a virtual death sentence. Ten to fifteen years max, guarantee of losing control of your mind and body. Anybody's worst nightmare.

Gurson wondered if he'd want to know. Proverbial question—how you're going to die. Know the deal or take the luck of the draw? Wouldn't want to unknowingly pass something like that on to your kids. But then, Gretz had no kids. He was a confirmed bachelor, according to Collier, a man who avoided entanglements. A man without a family was a man without a transferable future.

[15]

Headline Maker

By Thursday morning, the Central Park precinct was humming. The burned corpse found on Sunday was Charlene Leone. Same back molars, and the hair in her brush matched the DNA. NYPD had a publicity problem. Leone had been kicked off the force nine months back. Cop killing? Not precisely. According to the NYPD, Charlene Leone was an ex-cop, questionable citizen turned statistic. Unfortunately, the front page of the morning papers told a different story. The press touted Officer Leone as the first female cop killed in the city. A headline maker.

Gurson turned his attention to another matter. Boyd Cleary. Gurson ran Cleary's name on the BCI. Piece of shit with a long list of priors. Aggravated assault, attempted rape. Presently fresh out on parole after a six-month stay on Wards Island. Manhattan Psychiatric Center's state-of-the-art forensic hospital. Part of a plea bargain. Not enough evidence to prosecute. A deal, no doubt, arranged to relieve a clogged court system. Reduce the population in the state's prisons and jails. Going to trial was a roll of the dice. Most settlements were made outside the judge's chambers. Guilty bastards walked in exchange for time in psycho bins. Okay for prostitutes and first-time thieves. But some future killers in the bunch managed to sneak through. Cops could only hope half of them would leave a better trail next time around, or kill themselves trying. All those questions asked about repeat offenders, tossed off with a shrug. Blame it on the system. Police preferred letting the politicians explain, since it was usually the D.A.'s office that had agreed to sign off on the rotten deals, after the cops had risked their fool asses trying to nab the perps in the first place.

Bianchi sat in his office and twisted a paper clip with his fingers. He had been hoping, by some small miracle, that the girl wasn't Leone He looked over at the calendar, forlorn. This was one of those cases that would certainly revive his ulcer. No end in sight.

When Gurson came in, Bianchi looked up, his tired face a map of discontent. "What's with the shit-eating grin, Gurson?"

Gurson sat down. "I just got off the phone with one of Gretz's patients. Lady I'll call Olivia who prefers to remain anonymous." He rolled his eyes. "She thought it was a prank call, so I told her she could call me back, you know, told her to look up the number for the park precinct and ask for me. So she does it, you know, and you can tell she's nervous as hell. Starts sobbing, says Gretz was such a good doctor, all that shit, says she's recently divorced, in AA, that he was helping her through. By the time she hangs up, I know her whole freaking life story. She wants to know if I'm married."

"What did you tell her?" Bianchi smiled.

"I gave her your number, boss. She's about sixty-five."

"Sounds like a real reliable source, Gurson."

"They're all turning out to be like that, I'm afraid. Looks like Gretz was ruling the Prozac nation." He passed Bianchi a folder. "And then, there's this wild card."

Bianchi picked it up and read the name on the side. "Cleary."

"On a leash with a parole officer named Brady. D.A. let him cop a deal for an attempted rape. Defense called in a shrink. Shrink convinced the D.A. that Cleary was crazy as a bedbug. Middle of everything, victim decides she doesn't want to squeal in court. So they cut a deal. Cleary does six months on Wards Island, then he's released on probation. Was out and about at the time of the first arson killing a year ago. Pulled him in but had nothing solid to hold him. He walked."

"Who was the A.D.A.?"

"Alister."

"Don't know him." Bianchi sat back. "What led you back to Cleary?"

"I found his business card at Leone's along with some park memorabilia. Started thinking maybe Leone was onto him for something. Who knows, he could have offed Leone because she was getting too close." Gurson paused. "Parole agreement says he had to get counseling. Name of the shrink is in there."

Bianchi rummaged through some papers. "Here it is. Jeez. Theodora Weil."

"You know her?"

"Tucker Norville's wife." He shook his head.

"Norville's wife. No shit."

Bianchi gave Gurson an apprehensive look. "You know the D.A.'s office is placing bets that Kane killed Leone. Commissioner's not happy. One of the city's finest might have mud on her shoes, you know the deal. Wants us to handle the case with kid gloves. Doesn't want any fuckups, nothing embarrassing."

"NYPD's his ticket to a box seat at the Senate. Why put the heat on Kane? Needs the cops on his side."

"Kane's made herself one too many enemies."

"So we cut her loose, is that it, let her take all the heat?" Gurson looked at Bianchi warily. "We write the doctor off as suicide and let suspects like Cleary roll?"

"Before we go any further with this, Gurson, I got to ask you a personal question." Bianchi unfurled a paper clip he was holding in his hand and tapped the desk with it. "You fishing for answers on this case or your own?"

"Beg your pardon?"

"With all due respect, we both know your old man died in a similar fashion as this doctor here." Bianchi spoke without looking at him. "I mean, this Cleary connection has possibilities. But how does Gretz play into all this?"

Something inside Gurson howled with impatience and rage. "You want me to do my job or you want me to feed the pigeons?"

There was a long silence. The two men stared each other down.

Bianchi flipped a coin, checked the outcome, then spoke. "Question this Cleary's ass all you like . . . but try to keep Norville's wife out of this."

"Why's that?"

"Hassling the A.D.A.'s wife shows no respect for the law."

Gurson stood to leave, his response an inaudible murmur. "Guess that depends which side of the law we're talking about."

Cleary's shop was down a side street off the West Side Highway and the river. The cobblestone road was too narrow for his Jeep, so Gurson parked and walked the hundred yards. A garage door sporting a hand-painted sign—same as the one on the card: sports car, wings up. This one with a buxom blonde throwing her cares and her long, wild tresses to the wind. Gurson let himself in through a side entrance and browsed around the vast interior of the garage. The place was remarkably immaculate. Broken-down classics, dented and bruised, neatly stalled like retired thoroughbreds. Car doors, two dozen at least, shelved high on a metal rack, like dishes drying. A wall lined with tools and the requisite pinup calendar.

A pair of long legs were sticking out from under the belly of a jacked-up Porsche. Stripped to bare metal, hood off and guts displayed for its turn for redemption. The guy underneath was banging a pipe, cursing about the lack of light, about insects atomizing on paintwork. A radio played a country western tune about a train wreck. Another guy appeared from a room off to the left. When he saw Gurson standing there, he didn't stop, just carried on with his business.

"I'm looking for the boss." Gurson eased in, familiar, like he belonged right where he was. He'd decided to put Cleary and Gretz together. They had nothing but the car in common as far as he knew, but it was something more than anything else he had. If the math didn't add up, he figured he had nothing to lose but time. Time he'd otherwise spend sitting on his ass in the park. He was merely turning the engine over, cold, seeing what the rumble might tell him.

The guy put down his gadgets and gave a holler. "Yo, Boyd, company."

"Dammit, Coot, bring me that light." The guy under the car continued to work underneath.

The guy passed the torch under the car and repeated that they had company.

The air was dank and musty. A mix of stale heat, rusted metal, and high-gloss paint. Gurson waited. Eventually, Boyd rolled out from under the car holding a filthy toothbrush. He was wearing headphones. Tall, built like a linebacker, his large hands covered with axle grease. His hair in a ponytail, a long thick mane of black. Cleary had the gaunt look of a speed freak. Glassy eyed and strung out.

Cleary rested his headphones on his neck and took Gurson in. His eyes, the drab brown of old pennies, gave his face a dull feel. Gurson figured that worked for the guy. Hid the gray matter. Rebuilding one of these old Mercedes from the ground up had to take some focus. Patience. Guy had to have the kind of head that could take small things apart, fit them back together, make them work. Gurson looked at Cleary's hands. Huge, strong. Tinkering with high-end cars was more than just a hobby for this grease monkey. It was a cash business. Gurson pegged him just shy of thirty.

"Get kind of deaf from all this metal bashing. What can I do you for?" Boyd stretched out of his slouch to his full six-foot frame. Briefly, the two men stood eye to eye. He walked over to a table and began straightening a long line of tools with methodic care.

"I'm interested in a car." Sportscars had always intrigued Gurson, more for their effect on men than for their aerodynamics. Kind of the way he felt about guns.

"A car." Boyd's mouth widened into a full, toothy grin. "We got a few here."

Gurson felt confident. He'd done his homework. Internet provided a crash course. Rounded out the rough edges with a call to one of his old informants, a high-rolling Colombian coke dealer who collected expensive toys. He filled in the missing blanks. Gave him the slang, versed him in gullwing shop talk. More than enough to make this conversation. "I'm thinking of buying a '57 Mercedes, 300 SL."

"Coot, turn the volume down on the radio." Boyd now seemed interested. But Coot wasn't paying them much attention. Cleary asked again. Coot sauntered over to the radio, lowered the sound. Cleary's gopher. Boss's handy wipe. Not much going on upstairs. Coot played with a box of shiny screws and remained distracted. He soon disappeared from the room with the box of screws. A kid with a new toy. Didn't look like he was more than eighteen. Hell, none of them were born when most of these classic cars rolled off the production line.

With Coot gone, Gurson resumed his conversation with Cleary. It was time to bring Gretz and his gullwing out for air. "Yeah, this guy I know, he's got a beauty." Go with the flow. No, he didn't exactly look the part of a guy with a few hundred grand to burn, but then, he didn't look like a cop either. Could pass for some poor little rich boy. Soft features, brains that showed up in the tone of his voice, overconfident stride. "Guy named Gretz. You know him?"

Boyd answered with a question. "Who'd you say sent you?"

"Gretz." Gurson awaited some response but got none.

Boyd put some goop on his hands and started slowly cleaning each finger. "Gretz," Boyd said casually. "If it's who I think it is, the lucky bastard picked that gull up for squat. Talked about restoring her some time ago, but didn't sound like he had that kind of change."

Gurson rubbed his broad chin. "Well, I'm thinking of picking up the pieces. Thought you might be interested in finishing the job. Bit of a joint venture, you know. Wouldn't mind getting my hands dirty."

"Don't usually work that way. Strictly cash for art. I get the commission, you get visitation rights. Can't have people hobnobbing here, you know."

Gurson let a laugh go. "I get it."

"So, you say this dude's selling?" Boyd leaned back against the wall. His jeans hung low on his hips. His tight white T-shirt, stained with grease, ended just shy of his belt loops, exposing a patch of his pelvic hair and naked skin.

"Yep. Looks like he had some work done on it." Gurson popped a stick of Juicy Fruit gum in his mouth. "Stripped to metal. Primed. Ought to be able to bring it pretty damn close to original. Aluminum hood, trunk lid, rockers, door skins. Rest of the body is steel. Knock-off wheels."

Boyd stretched his jaw. He had a large mouth, set of pearly whites to match. Chipped front tooth. "Better make sure the guy has all the papers." He grinned. "Make sure all the numbers match."

"This one's the real deal," Gurson smiled. "Rudge knock-offs."

"Dunlop racing tires?"

"Shit yeah. Beautiful rear end assembly, standard ratio. Hear she stings at 160."

Boyd nodded, cracked the beginnings of a smile.

"Gretz must have garaged her somewhere and forgot about her. Rebuilt engine. Probably fixing her up little by little, you know."

"How much is he asking?" Boyd asked.

"Between me and him," Gurson hedged.

Boyd raised his thick brows and laughed. "No problem." He turned his back on Gurson. "So how much more work you think she needs?"

Gurson talked to Boyd's back, all the while studying his gestures. The guy was cool. Too cool. "Mechanical's done. Could use new rockers, paint job, odds and ends."

"Original color?" Boyd asked.

Gurson had no idea what the original color was. He stalled.

Boyd turned to face Gurson again. "Paint it anything but the original color, you're an asshole."

"I was thinking maybe you could have a look at it."

Boyd laughed. "You mean, tell you if she's worth it . . . you won't even tell me what he's asking." Boyd poked around in a wooden box of old screws. "Time's money, man. Where is she?"

Car was being hauled out of the police pound and brought over to the CP precinct to dry as they spoke. Gurson figured he could have it moved, with a little trouble, to a garage uptown somewhere. "Garage, uptown."

Boyd looked at his wrist but there was no watch there. "Not this month, man. Plate's full till summer."

"Car could be gone by then."

"Sorry I can't help you out."

Gurson thought a moment. "I suppose I could get it down here."

Boyd glanced at the wall clock, then looked around at the floor space. "Not really taking on anything new right now."

"So don't waste your time?" Gurson locked eyes with Boyd.

Coot returned holding a cold beer.

Cleary walked up to Coot, took the beer out of his hands, and slugged back a mouthful. He swallowed hard. "Give the man a card, Coot."

Coot took a card off the table, same as the one Gurson had found in Leone's place.

"Give me a call when she's yours," Cleary continued the game of hard to get. "Can't make any promises."

Gurson pocketed the card. "Mind if I have a look around? Looks like you have some real honeys in here." Gurson looked around him.

"Actually I was just heading out, man. Maybe next time."

"No problem." Gurson put his hands in his pockets. "Next time."

"Hey, I didn't catch your name."

"Baxter."

"Baxter." He nodded. "Let me know if you end up behind the wheel, Baxter." He smiled. "Coot, see Mr. Baxter finds his way out. Open the door."

Gurson watched Coot lift the heavy garage door. Boyd climbed into a banged-up MGBGT. He revved the engine a couple times, put her in drive, and squealed out of the garage. Coot closed the opened door, the cold air rushing in. Gurson stopped in front of an old Jaguar. "Three point eight liter Jag," Gurson was fast becoming a teenage boy. He wasn't ready to leave. Figured he could stall Coot's juvenile engine with a little high-octane bullshit. He waltzed around the silver bullet.

Coot nibbled at the bait. "In for some rewiring. A beauty but wicked hyper."

"Temperamental. Can't corner dick in the rain," Gurson fudged. "I'm more into the 300 SL's."

"Strat above." Coot was the big shot now. Liked playing the part when the boss man was gone. He closed the garage door then pointed to a car off to the left, covered in blue tarp, and walked up to the hood. "Fifty-six roadster." He peeled the tarp back a foot.

Gurson stepped up. The headlights peeked out, the eyes of something dangerous. Sexy, like a beautiful broad under wraps. Gurson whistled. "These cars you got here are worth a fortune."

"Finished? Shit yeah. But like this"—Coot shrugged—"just metal. It isn't easy to get to the finish line, if you know what I'm saying. Takes too much time to make it profitable." Coot lifted the tarp another foot.

"You're a lucky guy. Cleary's teaching you everything, I bet." Gurson tried putting wind in Coot's sail.

"Yeah, but you know, he likes working solo."

"Takes your breath away, don't it? Look at her lines, man," said Gurson.

"Rotted through, but she rocks on."

"Lacks convenience," said Gurson.

"But sure makes up for it with killer design. What a body, huh?" Coot stroked the hood of the car.

"Not a lot of storage space." Gurson looked in the driver's-side window.

"Nope. Not meant for robbing banks, dude, meant for hauling ass." Coot laughed, a boyish guffaw.

Gurson was hoping he could start talking about Gretz's car, maybe get the kid to spill something, anything. "I love how the custom luggage sits on the parcel shelf in back. Car I'm buying doesn't have any. I figure the guy's holding back. Keeping it for himself, you know."

"Bummer." Coot looked around like he was about to tell Gurson a secret. He walked over to a steel cabinet and pulled out a leather valise. "Check this out. Pigskin." Coot let out a lovesick sigh.

Gurson took a look at the case. In the back of the cabinet he saw another black case. "Mind if I have a look?"

Coot looked around him, hesitated.

"I won't touch anything."

Coot shrugged. He pulled the black case out.

"Can you open it?"

"If it ain't locked." He popped the case open.

Lined up like the instruments of a surgeon sat a set of shiny tools. Gurson took a look at the tools. "What's this?" Gurson pointed to one of the tools.

"Wrench combination. Adjusts the valves."

Gurson wanted to hold the tool in his hands, hold it up to the light. He nonchalantly reached for the wrench. Coot wasn't quick enough, or smart enough, to stop him. Gurson held the tool to the light. Three small letters. OGG. "What's with this?"

"Most people engrave their tools."

"No shit."

"These? Hell, yeah. Good as gold. Can't use any other tools on your car. Custom fitted."

Gurson twirled the wrench in his hands and wondered. If Gretz's car was never here, then what the hell were his custom tools doing in this garage?

Coot put out his hand and waited for Gurson to return the wrench.

Instead of the wrench, Gurson showed the kid his shield. Good as gold. Just the ticket to haul Cleary's ass in for questioning. It was time for Gurson to properly introduce himself.

Cleary sat in the interrogation room, high on more than his own bad attitude. They'd made him take a leak in a paper cup, threatened to call his p.o. because he failed the drug test. Gurson walked in and laid a folder on the table. A shot of Cleary's mug clipped to the cover. Cleary stared uneasily at his image. Then Gurson put a plastic bag filled with the dirty rags that he'd pulled out of Gretz's exhaust pipe next to the folder. Thick cheesecloth saturated with grime.

"Guess you're not really buying that car," Boyd said sarcastically. "What they got you in, a Pinto?"

"Be nice. Wouldn't want me to talk to your parole officer. Tell him your piss is full of methamphetamine. He'll have you modeling a new straitjacket."

"All the rage," Boyd said, smirking.

Gurson looked at the rap sheet on Cleary. "You're just the guy I'm looking for."

Boyd remained unphased.

"Hard to believe you've never seen Gretz's car when you got his tools in your closet," Gurson began again.

"Who says they're his tools?" Boyd said. "And even if they are, who says I had to ever see his car to have them?"

Gurson ignored him. "You dip and strip with acid, don't you?"

"It works."

"I bet it does," Gurson shot back. "I got a cadaver that underwent a particular type of acid work."

Boyd looked away again. "What's this got to do with me?"

"Good question, Boyd. Why are you pretending you didn't know Charlene Leone or Orrin Gretz?" demanded Gurson.

The heater in the interrogation room hissed. "You're the detective, you tell me."

"I got plenty of time."

"Good for you." Boyd snorted.

Gurson looked into Boyd's file again. "Says here you have a tattoo. Mind rolling up your sleeves? Of course, I can get your parole officer to strip-search you at Central Booking—"

"Roll away." Boyd rolled up his right shirtsleeve. On his bicep, there was an evil eye.

"Superstitious?"

"Keeping the bats at bay."

"Working out?" Gurson flexed his own biceps.

"Working." Boyd looked at the floor and rolled up his left sleeve.

"Nice brand. Crow with a carnation."

"Raven and a rose, man."

"You into birds, Cleary?" Gurson looked at the tattoo more closely.

"I like ravens. What's it to you?"

"Ravens still flying around the mountain?"

"Huh?"

"Old German legend. If you're into ravens, you should know it. One of Grimm's fairy tales. Story about this chick who's been turned into a raven because her mother's sick and tired of her whining."

Boyd yawned.

Gurson went on. "This hunter's in the woods, right? Hears this raven talking, asking him to set her free, turn her back into a maiden. She tells him to lay low until she flies back. Can't sleep or eat for days or else he might miss her when she comes back. Hunter tries to hold out, but he can't. Nods off, just as she's flying back around. There's a giant in the story who's supposed to eat him up, but the guy's a hero, right, so he works it all out. Comes upon some bad guys, pinches their magic—a stick that opens locked doors, a cloak that makes him invisible, a fast horse. Rides to the top of this glass mountain, and poof, finds the raven and sets her free. They live happily ever after."

"You're putting me to sleep." Boyd closed his eyes.

"Wake up, 'cause here's the good part. I figure the gullwing is your magic horse. Gretz is the giant. Leone and us cops—we're all the bad guys."

"It's your fairy tale," said Boyd. "I don't talk to birds."

"You like cutting their wings off, maybe."

"You're sick, man."

"What happened to your hand, Boyd?" Gurson stared at the gauze wrapped around Boyd's left palm.

"Sanding rockers."

"You sure?"

"What the hell's the difference? You guys are making up fairy tales no matter what I say." Cleary put his fists on the table.

"Difference between tossing your ugly ass in or out of Rikers." Gurson paused. "How about this line—'I have become accessible to consolation.'"

Nothing.

Boyd shuffled his feet. "I'm no street dog. I know my rights."

"I'm sure you do. You know exactly how to pass Go and stay out of jail. Just start acting a little loony. Get a good shrink to work a plea bargain."

"Fuck off."

Gurson smiled. "Be nice."

"Man, I got places to be."

"Like where?"

"None of your goddamn business," Boyd snarled.

Gurson got up and sat in a chair next to Boyd. He tossed a newspaper in front of him. Front-page headline. Pyro Kills Cop. "You read the papers, Boyd?"

"I can read."

Gurson smiled. "Got to rough them up every now and then, show them who's boss." Gurson paused, then threw the crime scene photo in front of him. "Make what's beautiful ugly."

"Man, what—"

"Last year, we had one burned up so bad we couldn't tag her. Remember her? We hauled your ass in here a year ago. But this one still had a few teeth in her head. Though of course, you'd never know it from looking at her here."

"Man, I don't have to look at this shit." Boyd looked away. "You're messing with my civil rights."

"Come off it, Boyd. This is good stuff. Kind of thing a guy like you would be proud to take credit for." Gurson pointed to the photo. "Tell me something, is it true what they say about the taste of flesh?"

Boyd sat back. He closed his eyes. Like he was putting himself in a trance.

Gurson gave Boyd's shoulder a firm tap. "I got two killings . . . almost identical . . . except for the teeth. One with, one without. You making a necklace?"

Boyd said nothing.

Gurson let a good minute pass, then said, "Let's talk about Gretz. How'd you meet him?"

"Don't you got it all right there?"

"I say maybe he was whispering in some cop's ear. Telling her how he thought you killed a girl in the park. This is your payback." He showed Cleary a picture of Gretz in his Mercedes in the park. "Nice touch, making it look like he killed himself."

"Payback, shit."

"You pretty familiar with Central Park?"

"I love the park." Boyd smirked.

"You like the ladies of the night that hang in the Brambles?"

Boyd looked at his hands. "I want a lawyer."

"You call a lawyer, I call Brady. Or better yet, maybe we should call your shrink."

Boyd blew out a gust of hot air.

Gurson continued. "Restoring cars is hard work, Boyd. You're good with your hands, mechanical. Like you said, no street dog." Gurson thought aloud. "Still, the fumes must get to your head. Dangerous too. Flammable shit. Listen, I can probably get you another deal. Claim you were out of your mind, you know the ticket. Blame the system. Or maybe, this time, we send you to Rikers."

"I've had enough."

"Enough? Of what?"

"I didn't kill nobody."

Gurson looked up at Boyd. "Who said you did?" Gurson gave Boyd a smirk.

"You're fucking with me."

"Am I? You know, I'm confused. You're telling me you hardly remember the guy, but his custom tools are in your shop."

"You guys planted those tools."

Gurson didn't answer him right away. "Sounds like you're getting paranoid." Gurson flipped a file open.

Boyd glared at him.

Gurson closed the file. Boyd was getting tired. Gurson forged on. "I'm thinking Gretz had to be crazy to take such a beautiful car out in that snow."

"Maybe he wanted to see the stars." Boyd looked Gurson over, up and down, as if he were a car in need of a paint job.

"In New York City? Nah. I figure a guy takes a car like that out in the snow for a damn good reason. Either he's getting laid or he's up to no good. Of course, I bet that's one and the same in your book."

Cleary laughed. "The car killed him, man."

"Real funny. Too bad this isn't a tryout for a comedy club. We're thinking of locking your ass in a four-by-four and you're cutting jokes. Don't be stupid."

For a moment Boyd was silent. His face remained impassive. Then he looked at Gurson with a strange watchfulness. "Maybe Gretz went to the park to kill this girl you're talking about. That gull handles like a wet dream. Set of new Pirellis, she could take the snow like a tank."

Gurson gave Boyd a sidelong glance.

"Anything's possible, man."

"Anything always is." Cleary had a point, however moot. Leone was working the park undercover. She could have been copping drugs, playing the part of a pross when her path and Gretz's converged.

Gurson looked through the file on Cleary to help him focus. "It interests the powers that be that your card turned up in Detective Leone's files."

Boyd tapped his fingers on the table. He shifted in his chair uneasily. Gurson stayed quiet.

"All you cops want to ride in fancy cars. Makes you feel like big dicks. With or without a dick, Leone could never afford one of those cars," said Boyd. "But then, she was a dirty cop, according to the papers, maybe she had money."

Gurson got up and parked himself behind Boyd. "Is that why you killed her? Because she was dirty? Or maybe she owed you something. Some drug money?" He paused. "Or maybe you just forgot to take your meds that day."

"Back off."

Boyd rocked in place. "I got rights, man. When I call my lawyer, you're toast."

"Burnt toast?"

Boyd cleared his throat. "You got no reason to arrest me."

To Cleary's surprise, Gurson unlocked his cuffs. "Okay. I'm unarresting you."

Cleary rubbed his wrists, rolled his shoulders back. "Smart move."

Gurson knew it worked better to let him go. Evidence against him so far was at best circumstantial. Better to put a few cops on his ass. Keep an eye on him. Feed his paranoia. "You're free as a bird."

Boyd stretched out his arms.

". . . trapped on a glass mountain," Gurson added, smiling. "And last I heard, Cleary, nobody's giving out any more magic cloaks or daggers in this fairy tale."

"Who needs magic cloaks and daggers," Boyd hissed, "when you cops can't even see the back of your own heads."

Gurson had something better than eyes behind his head. He had high-tech surveillance. As of now, the volume was up. Mr. Cleary wouldn't be able to fart without the NYPD knowing all about it.

[16]

Privileged Information

Tucker Norville tossed the *Daily News* onto Bianchi's desk. The headline read CORRUPT COP DEAD. "They're hanging Leone's soiled panties out to dry."

Norville rolled a fat cigar between his long fingers. He poked the brown tip inside a silver splicer and clipped the end. He slid his tongue over his lips and then stuck the cigar in the right corner of his mouth.

"No smoking." Bianchi pointed to a sign above his head.

Norville ignored the comment and the sign. He lit a match and took a deep drag, directing his smoky exhale at Bianchi's face. "Honduran Astral. Call them dogwalkers. Wife won't let me smoke 'em in the house."

Bianchi waved the stink away. The phone rang. He picked it up. "You're calling me from where? What the hell you doing in the Bronx?"

Norville looked around. A cockroach the size of a walnut cruised up a heat pipe. What a mess. Papers everywhere. Pix of the commissioner and the mayor thumbtacked to the bulletin board like Most Wanted mugs. A blueprint of the park hung over the sergeant's desk, each beat sectioned off and numbered. He zeroed in on Sector 7.

"Bet you can't wait to get out of here," Norville said to Bianchi, now off the phone.

Bianchi smiled. Finding out the ashes were Leone's had just added another six months to his run and Norville knew it. They'd keep Bianchi plugged in until the case was cleared. Could be years before they'd pack him off.

"I was in here Sunday, Bianchi. Why didn't you bother telling me your boys found that suicide?"

"Had no idea who he was on Sunday, Counselor. Didn't look like something to interest you."

Norville straightened his tie and continued smoking his cigar. "Suicide in the park, fancy doctor, in that kind of car? Really." He blew out a cloud of smoke. "Not interesting enough to mention to me?"

Bianchi rifled through some papers. The other phone rang, Bianchi picked it up. He spoke in cryptic sentences. "You sure? You got a name? Get me a goddamn name." He hung up and returned to Norville. "So you say you're interested in the suicide."

"I knew the guy. Peripherally. Expert witness for the D.A." He was cool, inscrutable. "I'm interested in the car actually."

"The car went to the pound." This was the kind of screwup to cover up. Might trickle down slowly, but it was sure to surface like a bloated floater eventually. Better to let Norville know about it up front, toss it off, not make a big deal about it.

"What did they hand you here, Bianchi? The extras from *Pocahontas?*"

Bianchi smiled. "Guy left a note." Bianchi slid a Xerox of the line in front of Norville.

"'I have become accessible to consolation,'" Norville read it aloud in a disinterested voice. He fingered the edge of the paper. "That's all you've got?"

"That and a dead bird without wings."

Norville cocked his head. "Dead bird?"

"Sitting next to him on the passenger seat."

"So you think the guy killed himself."

"I'm looking for a filthy cop killer, not the meaning of some poor schmuck's life. But you know how it is, Norville. You got to cast your net."

"Mind if I make a copy of this?" Norville waved the copy of the suicide note.

"Not at all," said Bianchi. "I'll have one of the guys do it for you now." He buzzed for a cop and barked an order. "Before you go, Norville, I wanted you to have a look at something." He took the mug shot of Boyd Cleary out of the file. "Boyd Cleary. On parole for attempted rape. Turns out he may have been Gretz's mechanic. Found some of Gretz's belongings in his shop."

Norville looked at the photo. "Looks like your typical sleazebag."

Bianchi took a pack of Rolaids out of his top drawer. He peeled the wrapper back and popped two tabs in his mouth. Then he slipped the next line in fast. "I understand he may be a patient of your wife's."

Norville picked up the photograph, then put it down. "We don't bring our work home."

"Good philosophy," said Bianchi. "But maybe you could make an exception on this one." It was a statement, but it came out sounding like a question. "We think he may have had something to do with Leone."

"You think he killed her?" Norville put out his cigar, retaining the butt in a silver case for later use.

"Maybe." The cop returned with the Xerox and left.

Norville pocketed the paper, stood up and walked to the door. "As I see it, you've got it all wrapped up, Bianchi. The doctor offed himself. Sitting around all day listening to cranky melodrama got too goddamn depressing. You pin some lunatic with Leone's murder, let the mayor's p.r. guys sweep the dirt, restore the park to its former tranquility and pack your bags." He ran his tongue over his front teeth. "Call me if they auction off that car."

"That would be nice. But not likely to happen," Bianchi dropped the bomb. "Gurson's convinced Gretz had something to do with Leone's murder. Thinks maybe Gretz knew something, doesn't buy the suicide."

Norville laughed. "You guys are really something. I heard of guys trying to turn homicides into suicides, but you got a perfectly good suicide, Bianchi. What's with you? Depressed shrink commits suicide in the park and now you want to call it murder. Stop wasting your time. You ought to be looking at Leone's old partner. What's her name . . . Kane. That one's attitude problem followed her here. Forgetting to vouch for that drop gun for crissakes . . . you know what they say about gays . . . nine times out of ten they kill each other. You drug test Kane?"

"Clean."

"And as for this kid Gurson . . . his old man was a dirty cop too, come to think of it."

"You never proved that, though, did you?" Bianchi reminded him.

"Never got the chance. The fucking guy killed himself." Norville scratched his chin. "Just like this guy Gretz. In the family garage. Maybe your golden boy's stuck in a flashback, if you know what I'm saying."

Bianchi flicked a crumb across his desk. Bianchi thought of Gurson. How he'd left the scene with the wallet. Maybe Norville was right. Maybe Gurson had inherited his old man's lousy luck. Bianchi could feel the acid in his stomach churn. He ate another two Rolaids.

Norville looked at the picture of Cleary. "Who told you he's connected to my wife?"

"In his record."

"I'll talk to her, but if I were you, I'd be frisking your dynamic duo for answers." He looked around him. "This place is a dump. You know it and I know it. We both got more important things to do." He walked over to the bulletin board and straightened the picture of the mayor.

Bianchi tapped a pencil on his desk.

Tucker fiddled with his cufflinks, a pair of gold handcuffs. "Tell Kane she can plea for a lesser sentence if she wants to save herself some trouble . . . and some time."

Bianchi swallowed hard as he watched Norville leave.

Norville bumped into Gurson going through the door. Gurson backed up as if he'd just stepped in shit.

"Hey, where's the fire?" huffed Norville. "Watch my Tims." Norville bent to dust off his shoes.

"Norville, right?"

"Right," he said, straightening up. "And you are . . ."

"Gurson."

Dead quiet fell between them.

"I hear you guys are trying to pin Leone's murder on that suicide."

"We've got reason to believe he may have been involved, yeah," said Gurson.

"Towed his mechanic in for questioning too, I hear."

"Guy was questioned for the first arson. I got a hunch he got off too easy."

"Really." Norville grinned widely. "A grease monkey is the mastermind thwarting the investigation," Norville said in a patronizing tone. "This part of your third-eye intuition Bianchi talks about?"

Gurson was suddenly sorry he'd said anything.

"This mechanic confess to anything?"

Keep it simple. Black and white. Yes or no. "No."

"That's too bad." Norville clapped his hands together. "Frankly, I feel Leone's killer is keenly aware of Central Park police procedures," Norville said, alluding to Kane. He waved his copy of the suicide note at

Gurson. "I assume you're analyzing the original suicide note, checking for prints. On the car too." Norville laughed. "At the pound."

He'd taken the note home along with the wallet. Only fingerprints they'd find on it now were his.

Norville was in mid-sentence. ". . . sounds like the whole thing's been bungled from the gitgo."

Gurson narrowed his gaze. "You trying to antagonize me, Norville?"

"Careful. You're starting to sound just like your old man."

Gurson thought about popping Norville in the jaw, or at the very least, rattling off a worthy retort. But a knowing voice kept him quiet. He watched Norville leave and considered ways to even the score. Unfortunately for Norville, killing himself wasn't an option.

COLLIER SAT AT HIS DESK, PHONE CRADLED IN THE NOOK OF HIS neck. He was on hold, waiting for the director of the Riverside Chapel. While baroque music played on the line Collier did some accounting. Flipped through papers on his desk. By the time the director picked up, Collier had nearly forgotten who he'd been waiting for. Annoyed by this senior moment, Collier sat up and attempted to give the conversation his full attention.

"I see, so the cremation hasn't taken place," Collier droned in response to the condition of the remains. "The memorial service . . . yes . . ." He looked at his calendar. "I was calling to discuss arrangements . . . payment . . . it all seems quite high. . . ."

The director cut in, defending the cost of dying. A subject that displeased Collier. The money would come out of Collier's pockets, of course. The irony of this situation was not lost on him.

He and Orrin had parted ways over profound differences in principles as well as economics. The old guard versus the new age, as Orrin so indelicately put it to him. Freudian psychotherapy was a primitive tool, according to Orrin. Why chisel away at the architecture of the psyche with endless words when one could so easily transform the landscape with psychotropics? Zoloft, Prozac, Serazone. Give your patient a chemical lobotomy. Isn't that all they deserved with *managed care?* The idea of it all violated Collier's deepest psychoanalytic ethics. The new politics of health care. Forced reporting to insurance companies that breached a patient's coveted confidentiality.

Get with the program, Orrin advised him; analysis as he knew it was a thing of the past. Doctor and patient no longer had an hour to kill.

In his opinion, Orrin placed far too much emphasis on economics. Speed, efficiency. Instead of asking about a patient's well-being, Orrin Gretz, M.D., was more likely to ask about a patient's insurance coverage. A pittance when it came to psychiatrics, though Gretz most surely must have managed to finagle the system, no doubt.

But the straw that had really broken the couch's back was the office at the Beresford. Initially, Orrin had rented the space, letting the second office to Collier. This was bearable for over five years, until, as a residential insider, Orrin managed to nab the prime ground floor before it ever went on the market. When Collier attempted to buy in, Orrin kept the gate closed. Expected to play landlord, have Collier pay his monthly mortgage. When push came to shove, Orrin shoved Collier right out the door.

Absolute ingratitude toward the mentor who'd given him the goddamned keys to the analytic kingdom. Collier took a deep breath to steady his nerves.

Unavoidably, they continued to move within the same professional circles. For years, Orrin fueled Collier's anger with his published condemnations of what he termed Freudian demagogy. Orrin went so far as to become a spokesperson for the drug companies. In Collier's opinion, this was the ultimate sellout. Grandstanding like a prodigal son. Collier attempted to engage Orrin in correspondence, tried to remind him that without Freud they'd all still be sitting on their hands. His efforts were met with measured doses of avoidance and denial. In Collier's mind, Orrin had betrayed more than just Collier himself, he had betrayed the essential foundation of psychoanalysis.

Collier looked at the papers on his desk once again. Orrin's unfinished business. Turned out that neither the office nor the apartment was worth a dime. Should have known the properties would be remortgaged to the hilt. How else could Orrin have afforded his extravagant material world? Fancy cars, custom monogrammed wardrobe, artwork by the notably avant-garde, dinners at Lespinasse, to which, he ruefully noted, he'd never been invited.

The memorial service would take place Sunday. No sordid details would be mentioned. Old friends and colleagues would recall happy times. Proverbial casket closed.

Speaking of old friends and colleagues, Collier was expecting a visit from Theodora Weil at four-thirty. He checked his watch. Half past three. Collier turned to daily office affairs and began reviewing case-work. He was mildly annoyed when the buzzer rang.

"Theodora." Collier greeted her at the door and took her hand. "It's been too long."

"Years." Theodora tentatively stepped in. "I'm sorry it's taken such a tragedy to bring us together again, Dr. Collier."

"Such formality. Please, call me Isaac."

"I couldn't. To me, you'll always be Dr. Collier."

He enjoyed the adulation and led the way into his office. "Please sit down."

Theodora took a seat and looked around her. No light reading here. Latin, French, German . . . languages Collier could slip in and out of with ease. "I appreciate that you called . . . letting me know about Orrin last week."

"I hope I didn't forget to notify anyone. I ran an announcement in the *Times*."

"Yes, I saw that. Memorial service will be held Sunday morning at the Riverside Chapel."

"Yes. I've received a number of calls . . . people wanting to say a few words." Isaac unbuttoned his suit jacket, a brown Harris tweed, a touch too tight. He crossed his arms decisively. "The first time Orrin and I met, we spoke for hours into the night. Felt I'd known him all my life. I feel now as if I hardly knew him. Of course, that makes all of this no less upsetting."

Theodora reached for a glass paperweight and ran her fingers along the contour of the smooth egg-shaped veneer. "I'm flooded with memories."

Isaac offered a look of sympathy. "I believe you were his first patient."

"That was a long time ago," sighed Theodora.

An uncomfortable silence passed.

"So, will you be taking over his practice, then?" asked Theodora.

"I'll parcel out some of his casework, I suppose. Why, are you interested in taking some of it on?"

"At the moment, no. I'm so busy with my own practice." Theodora sat in closer to his desk. "Actually I was hoping to gain access to *my* old file."

Isaac removed his glasses and laid them on his desk. "If I come across it, I'll be happy to release it to you."

Theodora looked at Collier with as much sweetness as she could muster. "I'd hate for such privileged information to get into strange hands." She paused. "It would give me great comfort . . ."

"Of course." His eyebrows bent inward, intensifying the deep crease between his brows. His tone was patronizing. "I'll see what I can do, then."

His words, though agreeable, did nothing to reassure her. Theodora indulged him with another smile. She knew he was putting her off. He would not likely admit to finding her file, nor surrender it, without a court order.

Isaac returned the conversation to his more pressing details. "I've contacted most of his patients. Orrin requested cremation . . . police investigation holding that up. Disbursing his last effects. Turns out he carried no insurance. Suppose he felt there was no one to leave it all to. Not that there's anything to leave anyone." He exhaled. "As it turns out, I'll have to sell everything just to pay off outstanding debt." Collier put a stiff handkerchief to his nose and blew. He looked at Theodora, who seemed to be listening intently. "Well, no need to trouble you with senseless technicalities."

"Sometimes that's all we're left with," Theodora said, arching an eyebrow.

"How true." Collier nodded. "I've spoken to the police." He opened his top drawer and extracted a card. "A Detective James Gurson," he read aloud. "I wasn't much help to him, I'm afraid." He smiled at her. "Perhaps you should talk to him, too."

"If you think it would help." She hung her head sadly.

Isaac came around the desk and rested a gentle hand on her shoulder. "Are you all right, Theodora?"

Theodora dabbed the corners of her eyes. "Must be seeing you after all these years, Dr. Collier. I'm reminded how the time has passed." She smoothed her hair, collected herself.

He took a sterling bookmarker out of his desk drawer. "I thought you might want this." He handed it to her. "I found it among Orrin's things. The inscription suggests you gave it to him years ago." Collier passed her the trinket.

Theodora took the bookmarker. The sight of it embarrassed her. A schoolgirl gift for a teacher. A simple slim rectangle, the length of a paperback, with an indigo silk cord dangling from one end. The inscription read: *With fond appreciation, Dora. March, 1979.*

They stood a moment without speaking. Then Collier led Theodora to the door. "It's been so good to see you, Theodora." Collier shook his head. "Hard to believe . . . over twenty years."

"You know what they say . . . time flies."

"Yes," said Isaac, "like a little bird."

When she left, Collier unlocked the side drawer of his desk and extracted a folder, thick with yellowed paper. He laid the dossier inside his briefcase. Before deciding whether to pass the dated contents of the file to Theodora, Collier intended to read through Orrin's old notes himself.

From across the avenue, he strained to read her lips but could only imagine the content of the stilted conversation. As she left the office, clicking pavement in her high heels, she didn't see him take the corner behind her. But he saw her.

He lost her in a crowd, but then regained sight of her walking along the park on Fifth Avenue. She maintained a slow and steady pace, frequently dabbing her eyes with gloved hands. Was she crying? Or was the wind stinging her eyes? He licked his lips and imagined the taste of her. He walked in time with her now. Left, right, left. Stop, look. How many times had she looked right past him, right through him? Must not reveal himself too soon. All would be in vain. Must trace her steps. Piss on every place she'd been. Mark his territory.

[17]

Real People

Early Friday evening, Tucker lay in bed, remote in hand. He stared at the TV images with glazed interest. A deserted, snow-swept corner of the park, cops dodging questions. No further details on the cop killing, pending investigation. A few passersby being asked if they would continue using the park after dark.

The room was cool and lamplit. Shades drawn. The way he liked it. He sat up in bed, sipping an icy glass of Black Label, the newspaper spread out on the bed.

Theodora walked in, dressed in Tucker's favorite suit. The herringbone jacket and cream cable-knit sweater that made her look like an equestrian. "Where's the whip and stirrups?"

Theodora ignored the comment and picked up a section of the paper Tucker had been reading. "Prominent West Side psychiatrist commits suicide . . . Orrin Gaylord Gretz . . . it's all over the news." Theodora paused. "I saw Isaac Collier today. He's arranging the memorial. Sunday at Riverside Chapel. I'll have to go."

Tucker put the paper aside. "Of course."

"He said Orrin was broke. Said he has to sell everything to pay off his debts." Theodora took off her jacket and placed it neatly over a chair.

"That's what he's telling you. . . ." Tucker laughed while he reached for his drink. "Bastard's probably cashing in. Who do you think gets the car?"

"The car?"

"They found Gretz in his car. Mercedes gullwing. Where'd Gretz get the flow for a car like that?"

"I tend to believe Collier. He said Orrin was in debt to the hilt. Had bills spread all over his desk."

"Suddenly you believe Collier. That's a switch." He made this comment to rile her, which it did.

She felt inclined to laugh. "Now what am I to say to that?"

Tucker pretended to be her, his voice melodic. "You're attempting to antagonize me, Tucker. It won't work."

"That's good. That's precisely what I was thinking."

"You see. I can read your mind." Tucker smiled.

"Really. What am I thinking now?"

Tucker put his hands to his temples. "You're thinking of poor Orrin Gretz. . . ."

Theodora walked over to the window. A light rain was falling. She strained to see the moon, a sliver in a starless sky. "Collier said he spoke to the police . . . thought perhaps I ought to talk to them also."

This irked Tucker. She always wanted to meddle in his affairs. Nose around police stations, help the helpless. Surely, she'd expect him to dissuade her. "The Central Park police are a bunch of idiots."

"He thinks maybe I could give them some information that might help them," said Theodora.

"As you like." She'd do what she wanted anyway. He had no interest in playing that game. He had another, more interesting deck to shuffle.

Tucker downed his scotch. "They had one of your loons down there today. Boyd Cleary."

Theodora knelt beside Siegfried, kissing the top of his head, whispering in his ear.

"Your name was in the guy's probation file. Gretz's mechanic or some such thing. Young guy there named Gurson heading up the investigation. Stepping on his own feet. Maybe you ought to talk to him."

"You can't fool me, Tucker. It's not like you to court my interest in police work. What's the catch?"

"What do you call it?" He smirked. "Reverse psychology, isn't that it? I say black, you say white. You say you want to stick your nose in, I say don't. We go at this for how long before you do what you please anyway."

Theodora kissed her dog.

"Damn dog," hissed Tucker. "Better taken care of than anyone else around here."

Theodora continued to disregard him.

Tucker wiped his mouth with the back of his hand and walked up behind her. Dressed in nothing but his boxers, he took hold of her and rubbed his cock against her ass.

She could feel his chest against her back. "I thought we agreed not to bring our work home."

"Is this work?" Their reflection was captured in a beveled antique wall mirror, head to torso. Tucker looked at himself in the mirror, looked at her there too. She pulled away from him.

Thwarted, he retaliated. "I suppose your life ends now that Orrin's gone and you're left with me. As if the prick had any honorable intentions."

"What are you going on about?" Theodora asked.

He had her now and therefore began to ignore her. He brushed her off like a fly, walked to the bureau, poured himself another drink.

"Stop taunting me. Treating me like one of your inmates seeking an appeal."

"That is exactly what you are though, isn't it? Thought I could give you the child you wanted, but when that didn't pan out, you went back to him. Now he's dead. I figure soon you'll be coming to your senses, begging for my forgiveness."

"You're insane."

"Insane." Tucker laughed. "Now that's funny." He held his head in mock drama. He went to her, put a hand on her shoulder and turned her toward him, her face in his hands. "Isn't that what they called you?"

"You're drunk."

"You ought to join me. Let's drink to infidelity."

"That I share history with Orrin is hardly a secret between us, Tucker."

He moved closer to her, put his lips to her forehead as if to feel for a fever. A loving gesture that unsettled her.

"His story?" Tucker looked at her with obvious dissatisfaction. "Let's see. You mean the one where he blamed your inability to grasp reality on the rather inappropriate relationship you had with your father? Or the one where he insisted his vows of undying love were simply a figment of your emotionally immature and damaged imagination?"

Theodora took a slow, deep breath to regain her balance. She faced him. "I thought I could trust you, Tucker. It hurts when you fling the past at me this way."

"Trust." Tucker said the word with deliberate sarcasm.

"Yes, you know when two people actually count on one another, unconditionally."

Tucker picked up one of his cigars and placed it in the corner of his mouth. "I'm right behind you, Theo."

"That's what worries me." Theodora turned and left the room.

Tucker went for his half-empty glass of scotch and lifted it to his nose. The dense, heady aroma pleased him. He talked drunkenly to himself. "Trust." He took another swallow, the alcohol burning the back of his throat as it went down. He opened his bureau drawer and took out a baggie with a sample of the small white pills that he'd found in a bottle earlier in the week, stashed away in her closet. Visit to the lab confirmed the pills were a chemical compound of propranolol hydrochloride. Normally prescribed for high blood pressure. Something neither he nor Theodora had. On a hunch, he had a test run on his Black Label. Couldn't help thinking like a lawyer. Confirmed his suspicions. Sources down at Forensics said the whiskey contained high traces of the stuff.

Quickly figured out why was she putting the pills in his booze. The main side effect from taking these particular pills was guaranteed impotence. Since they'd discovered his sperm couldn't make it upstream, she'd no doubt lost interest in satisfying his frequent sexual demands. He thought back on it. Indeed, the timing went hand in hand. Tried to conceive for two years. Turned himself into a lab rat to determine the cause of their infertility. Doctors pointed their fingers at him. Made efforts to bolster his sperm count but their efforts failed. Along with a damaged ego came the gradual decline of his virility. Of course, he had thought Theodora was right— suggesting it was all in his head. He was getting older, she reminded him, said maybe he should cut back on his drinking. Cut back on his drinking. Just what she knew he couldn't do. His addiction was really quite a convenience for her. How frequently was she polluting his stash? He wasn't certain, but she had to have been going at it awhile. His research told him the effects were cumulative. Off the shit, it would take weeks to see any change in his boner. If all went well, his virility would be fully restored. Of course, ideally, for the best result, he should stay off the booze entirely. A concession he was neither willing nor able to make. Had to admire her ingenuity. She had learned something from him after all.

He carefully marked an untainted bottle of scotch and tucked it in a locked drawer. Then he removed a fresh bottle of scotch from his private cache and left it out on the top of the desk. It was a shame to waste good whiskey, but the ruse served him well. He would continue to make it easy for her. Not change a goddamned thing.

Not yet.

GURSON ENTERED THE INTERNATIONAL CENTER OF PHOTOGRA-phy on Forty-third Street and Sixth Avenue. An appointment with an old girlfriend of his. Mae Chin, expert on contemporary photography. He took the elevator to the fourth floor and found her in a small corner office, compulsively tidy. A tall window defined the space and saved it from feeling claustrophobic. A full-color poster of a Helmut Newton photograph took up one wall, two long-legged beauties scantily clad in black bikinis lounging poolside in compromising positions. A rather vicious looking Doberman, parked by the diving board standing guard.

Mae stood to take Gurson's hand in both of hers. He pulled her in close and kissed the nape of her neck and got a deep whiff of her trade-mark fragrance. Fleur de something. It was a smell he'd come to associate her with. A dream in green. He'd bought her some of it when they were hot and heavy last fall. Bottle the size of a small syringe had set him back a hundred and a quarter. As he recalled, their affair lasted halfway through that bottle. An accomplishment, as the majority of Gurson's postmarital trysts barely made it fragrantly through the night.

"Still running late for appointments." She looked at her watch.

"Nah. You're still setting your watch ten minutes fast." He smiled, taking her hand. A diamond on her ring finger told him what was new. He held up her hand, twisting the ring around and letting the gem reflect its brilliant facets in the light. "Guess a lot can happen in ten minutes," he quipped.

"Guess so." She looked at the ring, then up at him. "Still friends, though, right?"

He slid a finger down the bridge of her nose, over her lips, along the outline of her chin and neck. She stopped him short at the second button on her blouse. "Friends," she repeated.

"Sure." He let his hand drop. Friends. That would be a creative leap. He'd miss her bedroom acrobatics. Mae loved a good romp in the sheets but always said she wanted more. Felt she deserved a better exchange rate for her efforts—a lifestyle, a loft, a few million. He was just the blue collar in her closet.

She played with her long black braid. "You said you needed a favor. What's the emergency?"

"I need some information about a photographer. Witkin. Joel-Peter."

"Controversial." She walked over to a tightly stacked shelf of books, extracting one. She placed the book on the table before them.

Gurson looked at the spine. Witkin. He opened the book and began studying the startling images. Amputees, hermaphrodites, dwarves. Severed limbs, heads, torsos. Flipping along, he found the photograph of the nude he'd seen in Gretz's apartment. "What can you tell me about this one?"

She looked at the photograph thoughtfully a moment. "'Woman Once a Bird.'" She paused. "Remarkable, isn't it?"

"Seems contrived."

"Don't be so sure." She smiled.

"Looks like good makeup to me." He ran a finger over the photograph, gently touching the page where the scars on the woman's back were.

Mae raised her brow. "I think she's for real."

"No way." Gurson studied the photograph more intently. "Looks like she was hung up on meat hooks or something."

They both stared at the photograph: the back of a bald-headed woman, her shoulders deeply scarred with gaping wounds, her waist cinched unnaturally tight by what appeared to be a medieval metal belt.

"If she's real, then somebody ought to call the cops," said Gurson.

"And tell them what?" Mae looked at him blankly.

"Report her missing wings." Gurson wrinkled his nose. "This stuff hangs in public?"

"Museums, galleries, private collections. He's received numerous honors, international awards. He's considered something of a hero."

"To who?"

"Collectors all over the world pay tons for his work."

"We busted a ring of those collectors. Into child porn too." Gurson shrugged off her artsy dialogue. "Looks like he doesn't like women much." Gurson studied the black-and-white images of dismemberment and mutilation.

"Witkin's work usually provokes debate. Debate is good."

"I'm sure they provoke more than debate."

"You're just too used to filtered images from *Playboy* and *Vogue* to define female beauty for you, James."

Outside, a pigeon was perched on the sill. The guttural cooing gave Gurson a moment to consider. Mae's flippant comment was predictable, but so, he supposed, was his reaction to the photographs. He thought to refer to his attraction to her to prove his appreciation for something other than the candy-coated Americana she was referring to, but thought better of it. Women like Mae Chin loved to put *Playboy* and *Vogue* down while visiting their plastic surgeons to explore ways to look more like the women between those pages.

"Witkin's looking for a different way to define beauty," Mae added.

Gurson turned the book upside down. "Guess we're all in the same water, just not in the same boat."

What defined beauty? One of life's circular questions. At best, esoteric, a debate without end. Not the question he was asking or trying to answer. He looked up at the Helmut Newton photograph hanging on her wall.

She looked at the photograph on the wall, too. "You're wondering what makes a violent image like that erotic and images like Witkin's repulsive, aren't you?" She paused, her years of artistic training filtering into the conversation. "It's got something to do with instinctual drives. Intellectually, you expect something to repulse you but it gives you pleasure. The image overstimulates your brain; other parts of the body get in on the act. Hormones are innocent bystanders. They don't judge the image, not the way the mind does, they simply respond to it."

Gurson thought about this a moment. He recalled his own training, pouring over crime scene photographs. The odd sensation of wanting to look at the gruesome scenarios. He flipped a page. Eviscerated dog. "Sort of like rubbernecking, huh? You don't want to look, but you do."

"You're catching on."

Gurson wasn't sure he was catching on to anything. "You won't find this book on my coffee table."

"How about under your bed, then . . . along with those textbooks on homicide?" Mae retorted.

"What are you saying? That we ought to publish homicide books and sell them to the public? Distribute them to kids in school, maybe, show them how tough the world really is? There's a black market for that sort of thing too, you know."

"And you work hard to keep those worlds separate, don't you?"

"You could say that."

"So you believe in censorship," Mae said. "You'd like to deny the existence of this side of reality."

"There are times to defend the First Amendment, I'm just not sure this is one of them." He looked at another photograph.

"Line the streets with lemon drops, James? Come on. How about freedom of expression?"

Gurson had come to think of freedom of expression as an overrated privilege. Too many people felt they had something important to say. "Tell me the deeper meaning behind a photograph of a guy hammering a railroad tie into his nose." Gurson pointed to the image on the next page.

Mae put her hand to her chin, taking a moment to formulate a response. Gurson didn't wait for the artsy philosophic monologue. He cut off what he anticipated would be a long-winded defense of art for art's sake. If he had the time, he might engage her in a discussion of values: good versus evil, the fine lines blurring normal from pathological, the relative aesthetic merits of fauna and flora. He summed it up as best he could. "I guess I've just seen a few too many fresh kills to develop any appreciation for fantasy images like these here. These get into the wrong hands, they inspire already twisted behavior. To be honest, Mae, you're right, I can't wish it away but want to."

"Slow down. Try not to accept or reject it. No one here will blame you if you enjoy it." Mae turned to a photograph of three women, nude, blindfolded.

"Enjoy what?"

"Unrepressed sexual desire." She smiled.

Gurson sucked in his cheeks and turned a page. The image of a man lying naked, tied to a slab of wood, his penis rigged to a pulley, a heavy metal disk hanging precariously over his masked face. No, he would not enjoy this. "This one here makes me feel downright lonesome." Gurson arched his back. "People really hang these on their walls?"

"If they can afford them."

"Bet they claim these photographs have biblical significance. Suffer the little children to come unto me. . . ." Gurson turned the pages. A masked woman, holding a masked baby, the woman's mouth contorted and held open with what appeared to be wires. It seemed harmless compared to some of the other gothic images, but nonetheless eerie and disturbing. "Witkin's take on the Madonna?"

Mae suppressed a smile.

"I suppose severed heads ought to make me think of John the Baptist, too. But they don't." Gurson turned to a photograph of a naked woman without arms, two flabby stumps cut off above the elbow, the rest of her body blacked out so you could just see her from her large breasts up, kind of like a cartoon cutout. Her droopy mammaries were hanging like water-filled balloons, each nipple resting on what looked to Gurson like erect penile pedestals. Her eyes were masked by a hennalike tattoo, and she was adorned with a pair of large bird's wings. "Bird of Queveda." The image confused him the way bad dreams did. What did it really mean? Some punishment trip? He reached into his jacket pocket and took out a handful of photographs, four-by-six, black-and-white. "Tell me what you think of these." He showed her the one of Gretz that the detective squad had taken at the scene. Side view. Gretz in the driver's seat, head back, a tinge of crimson. "Taken by a guy named Crenshaw."

"Crenshaw?" Mae Chin puzzled over the photograph.

"Took this one too." He showed her an autopsy photo of Leone, the burnt flesh, gashes in her back.

"I'm not familiar with this photographer." She looked at the photograph carefully. "Interesting. Who represents him?"

"The New York City Police Department."

"Crime scene photographs . . . Jeez."

"You don't want to look at them but you can't help yourself, can you?"

"You know who did this?" asked Mae.

"Classic organized offender. Influenced by artistic metaphors." Gurson smiled boyishly. "Claims his work has biblical significance."

"In jail?"

"Not yet."

"That's reassuring."

Gurson closed the book of photographs, the blank black cover a refreshing backdrop for their eyes. But Gurson kept seeing the images in his mind's eye. Physically he was still in the room with Mae, but in his mind he was back in the park. Tracking a killer who knew exactly what he'd done and what little evidence he'd left behind. He hated knowing that he'd be smarter after the fact.

"Mind if I borrow this inspiring volume of photographs?" Gurson took hold of the Witkin book.

Mae played with the diamond ring on her finger. "Let me know when you catch the guy."

Catch the guy.

Gurson looked at the clock on the wall. Another minute ticked off. Somewhere out there somebody was committing another murder.

[18]

Conspiracy of Silence

Ren had gotten a couple of pages on her beeper from the wife. But still achy from her romp with the lunatic husband, she had no desire to go any-where near her. She flicked on the TV. A round of commercials and then a news update. The man who had been found in his car early in the morn-ing of that big snow, in Central Park. Apparent suicide, prominent West Side psychiatrist, Dr. Orrin Gretz. Cops were conducting an investigation.

She stared at the screen filled with the top story of the day. They'd identified the body of the burn victim found buried in the snow in the Brambles. A cop by the name of Charlene Leone. Detective with the NYPD.

Ren went to turn up the volume but unintentionally pressed mute. The screen filled with images but no sound. A snapshot of Leone in full uniform and a separate shot of assorted drugs. She fumbled to restore the volume, catching the last of the report.

. . . due to the sensitive nature of the case . . . pending a full investiga-tion . . . police refuse to comment at this time. . . .

Her throat swelled with fear. She'd been an informant for Leone for years. Cased the park for her. Passed her information on the local wildlife. Leone had looked out for her. They'd shared more than useful information. They'd shared illicit favors. Sex and drugs. And now Leone had been found dead in the park. And so had Gretz. How long before someone noticed she was a line that connected the dots . . .

She started looking in her closet. Tearing boxes down from shelves. Tossing wigs and shoes aside. Looking for a box of papers, an envelope with photographs. When she found it, she dumped the contents out on the floor. A collection of souvenirs that she'd kept over the years in case of something like this. High rollers, too drunk or stoned to have remembered the moment she took their souvenir photo. Where was the one she was looking for now? The banker, the baker, the candlestick maker. The husband.

She held the snapshot between the tips of her fingers. One wasted bigwig, dressed in drag, test tasting a pile of Peruvian snow . . .

It was risky to play this game of show and tell. It was risky not to. She looked out the window, at the snow slowly coming down. She'd go to the corner, buy a paper, see what the rags had to say. They'd be looking through Leone's things, looking for her informants. Asking questions.

Should she call the wife? Bid for sympathy. Get some money, get out of town.

Or take the husband's advice and keep quiet?

Quiet as snowfall on an early winter morning . . .

Quiet as the dead.

SUNDAY MORNING. TIME TO POUR A DRINK. TUCKER THREW BACK a shot of uncontaminated scotch too fast to appreciate the vintage. Drunkenly, he finished knotting his tie in the foyer mirror. He could hear Theodora down the hall cooing to the dog.

He put on his coat and joined her at the door. "Are you ready or you going to spend all morning making love to that dog?"

"You're drunk again." She sniffed the air around him.

He held the door open. Mock chivalry.

"I don't see why you have to come with me." She brushed past him.

Tucker laughed. "Like I need your permission."

They took a cab to Riverside Chapel, hardly speaking a word en route. Theodora dashed from the cab. When she entered the chapel, she distanced herself from Tucker, mingling with the crowd.

"The most terrifying challenge for humanity." Isaac Collier was addressing a small group of his colleagues, all former students. "Which explains our hopeless belief in the fiction of immortality. Speak not of death . . . it's a conspiracy of silence. Why, Theodora"—Isaac turned to take her in—"there you are."

Theodora adjusted her dark glasses.

Collier looped her arm in his and turned back to his audience. "An old friend, gentlemen. Ms. Theodora Weil. You know most of these people, don't you, my dear?"

Theodora looked over the small assembled group.

"Rumson, Hoffman, Cantor," he pointed them out, "older and wiser, the lot of them." He smiled.

The gathering acknowledged her.

One of the men picked up where Collier left off. "Are you suggesting suicide offers the best alternative, Isaac?"

Collier sighed. "I'd never prescribe it to my patients, of course, though one must admit, burdened by the past . . . fearful of the future . . . for some there's no more effective means to gain a feeling of control."

Theodora thought of responding, but Tucker came into view, bending toward her. He kissed her cheek. Mildly intoxicated. "Dr. Collier, this is my husband, Tucker." Theodora threw a quick glance Tucker's way.

"Tucker." Collier extended his hand. "Pleased to meet you."

Tucker clasped Collier's hand firmly. "Theodora has spoken so highly of you."

"Dr. Collier has been reassigning Orrin's practice," Theodora inserted. "Planned this service so quickly. Not to mention tying up all the loose ends."

"These things are never easy," Collier sighed.

"Really," said Tucker. "Sure provides a patient with the perfect solution to the question of termination though."

Isaac drew himself up, unsure how to take the comment. "Of course, when I die, I've instructed my secretary to burn all of my files. Wouldn't want years of confidentiality jeopardized. Wouldn't you agree, Theodora?"

Theodora only smiled.

Collier moved on. "Police seem to think Orrin's mixed up in some park shenanigans. Will probably subpoena his files . . . spoke to a Detective Gurson—"

Norville brushed the issue aside. "His old man killed himself the same way Gretz did. He's just dragging it out, pulling on threads."

Collier rubbed his chin. "Really, how interesting."

Tucker chewed on his unlit cigar. "Bet you curse the day you gave him his start, Collier . . . but hey, they can't hold you accountable for that."

At this, Theodora excused herself. Norville and Collier looked down the hall and watched Theodora enter the ladies' room.

The words that followed rolled off Collier's tongue with ease. "Reminds me of something Freud once said . . . 'The way these women manage to charm us with every conceivable psychic perfection . . . until they have attained their purpose . . . one of nature's greatest spectacles. . . . '"

Tucker heard every word, but pretended not to. Distracted, he walked off, leaving Collier in mid-sentence, alone in his Freudian reverie.

* * *

The group moved into the chapel and took their seats. Standing room only. People crowded in, many leaning close to one another. The doors were kept shut against the wind. Inside, the air seemed to evaporate; the warmth of body heat creating an unseasonable clemency.

A rabbi stood at the pulpit. He had come to know Orrin over the years, he said, through the doctor's fine charitable work at Columbia Presbyterian. He noted the size of the crowd, how the passing of one man, taken so abruptly in mid life, could bring so many people together. His voice reverberated off the arched walls with acoustic resonance:

"Some might say that Dr. Orrin Gretz was not a religious man, and yet, we see he did God's work. Let us pray:

"Lord, make us an instrument of Thy peace. Where there is hatred, let us sow love. Where there is injury, pardon. Where there is doubt, faith. Where there is despair, hope. Where there is darkness, light. Where there is sadness, joy . . .

"Amen. . . ."

Florio sat curbside in the Jeep, keeping an eye on the street. Gurson made his way out of the chapel, out onto the sidewalk, and stood on the sidelines. He looked left and caught sight of Norville making his way through the crowd straight toward him.

"Detective Gurson . . ." Norville smiled. "I see they let you out of the zoo."

When Gurson didn't react, Norville filled the silence. "I hear your investigation's in the toilet." Norville clamped his unlit cigar between his teeth.

Gurson produced the little silver guillotine that he'd found in Gretz's car. He held it up to the sunlight, in Norville's plain view, but didn't tell him where he'd found it.

Norville looked at the cutter quizzically, then looked around him at the thinning crowd. "Decent turnout."

Gurson repeated the rabbi's closing line about Gretz. "He did God's work. . . ."

Norville looked at Gurson. "Must bring back a rush of old memories, huh? Seeing how Gretz and your old man both met their maker sucking fumes. What's it been, about twenty years now?" Norville looked up at the sky, thinking. "How old were you when your old man died, Gurson?" Norville didn't wait for an answer. "Thirteen or fourteen, as I recall. What did they tell you back then? They say your old man was framed? That he exercised a *justifiable use of force?*" Norville shook his head. "Hate to burst your bubble, kid. But that wasn't the case. He killed an innocent kid. Used poor judgment."

Norville had been there. At his father's wake and funeral. An uninvited caller, there to further antagonize his family.

Norville was going on. "I remember it like it was yesterday. You were a real little man. Didn't cry. Not one tear."

"I remember you too, Norville." Gurson stepped in closer to Norville.

"Go on, Gurson, take a swing at me. Give me a reason to put your ass where your father's belonged."

Gurson took hold of Tucker's collar. Taken by surprise, Norville lost his balance, toppling over onto Gurson's shoulder. Norville looked like a man in need of consolation, a man in need of a good cry. Gurson pulled Norville into him and then, in an instant, steadied him back on his own two feet. Gurson spoke in a clear, loud tone. "Sober up, Counselor."

Norville dusted himself off and straightened his tie. "Before you clock an A.D.A.," he uttered in a forced whisper, "you ought to consider the consequences."

"Stop, Norville, you're scaring me." Gurson, still furious, spoke through clenched teeth now.

"Rotten apples fall from rotten trees," Norville deadpanned.

"You ought to know. Your old man was a drunk too."

"Far as I'm concerned, Gurson, your father saved us all a lot of trouble. You ought to try it. Sit your ass in the front seat of a car, park in a nice warm garage till the twelfth of never. Remember to shut all the windows and let the motor hum."

In the middle of this quarrel, they were joined by an attractive woman. For Gurson, the recognition was instant. She was the looker in the photograph on Gretz's bookshelf, the one seated in the bottom row. The extra pounds shed. Dowdy dress replaced by a classier package. The color of her lipstick matched the highlights in her shoulder-length auburn hair. Delicate white pearls adorned her ears and her long, white neck. He clocked her in just under forty, give or take a second hand.

The woman mentioned something to Norville about leaving.

"Where's your manners, Norville?" Gurson put a hand out to the woman and introduced himself.

Gurson's smile disarmed her. She extended her hand. "Theodora Weil."

"Pleased to meet you." Gurson firmly held her hand in his before letting go.

After a long moment of eye contact with Gurson, too long for Norville's taste, Theodora asked, "Central Park precinct?"

"That's correct."

Without turning to Tucker, she said, "Dr. Collier mentioned that he'd spoken to you . . . about Orrin. He suggested you might want to speak with me."

"How well did you know Dr. Gretz?" Gurson asked, interested.

Before Theodora had a chance to respond, Norville, who'd been tolerating this chitchat in silence, cut in. "She has nothing of value to say to you, Gurson." He turned to Theodora, his look severe.

Theodora said nothing.

Gurson looked at Theodora. "Mind if I call you?"

Theodora nodded her approval. "Not at all."

Norville took his wife's arm. "Now, if you'll excuse us—"

"No problem," said Gurson.

"Who's the good-looking broad?" asked Florio, now joining Gurson from his post in the car.

"Norville's better half." Gurson watched as Norville moved his wife into the crowd and disappeared into the daylight.

[19]

Blue Line

Kane sat at her kitchen table in Morningside Heights. The afternoon sun filled the room with natural light. She lifted the sharp scissors and cut the corners of each photograph carefully. The table was covered with a morbid display of crime scene photos, homicide news clippings, and miscellaneous quotations and trinkets. A pile of dried leaves, brush, botanical artifacts. She set a large sheet of poster board aside and selected another item to include in the grim collage.

Charlene's funeral had taken place that morning. A closed casket and a handful of family. A mother's tears. No hero's farewell. No cops folding flags. Dead and buried, a Saint Christopher's medal, the one she wore on the beat, buried with her. One short life died blue. Charlene Leone. History at thirty-two.

Kane glued down another strip. This one of Charlene on graduation day from the police academy; over it she would layer a headline denouncing her career, and over that an earlier commendation, and over that, a slice of a photo documenting her charred remains. Life was like that sometimes. Just a series of contradictions. She was interrupted by a knock at the door. She wasn't expecting anyone. She washed her hands at the sink, drying them on her jeans, and went to answer the call.

It was Gurson, downstairs, his voice coming through static, asking to be let in.

Reluctantly, she buzzed him up and waited for him to climb the four flights to her door, which she opened a few inches.

Gurson arrived on the landing and Kane let him stand there a moment in awkward silence. She wasn't in the mood for company.

"Can I come in?" Gurson asked.

"You have a warrant?" Kane blocked the entrance to her apartment.

"Do I need one?"

Kane took a closer look at him.

"Hey, you going to let me in or what, it's cold out here."

Kane freed the chain, waved him through, and led him into the living room.

Gurson waited for Kane to sit down. When she did, he took a seat on a worn brown sofa next to her. He looked at the high ceilings, walls painted white. Books stacked in piles beside an old pine desk. Tape cassettes lined up in cardboard boxes. A trio of white geraniums on the windowsill, their leaves plump and green. A large piece of artwork hung on a wall. Looked like it was made of wood, each geometric shape painted a different color. Magenta, yellow, blue, green. A series of collages on another wall. Photographs. One he could make out of Leone. "Nice place."

"Rent control. Been here for years." Kane looked him over. "You here for small talk?"

Gurson rubbed his hands together. "I want you to know I think it's all bullshit."

"Which part?" asked Kane, sitting back in her chair.

"Your deal, the whole thing."

"That makes one of you."

"I would have been at Charlene's funeral . . ."

She stopped him from apologizing. "But you had to go to that memorial service."

"How'd the funeral go?"

"As funerals go? Pretty depressing. You could be a stone-cold junkie, but you're still someone's child." Kane clenched and unclenched her fists. "I saw a couple of Bianchi's weasels on the sidelines. Grave digging. There to gauge my reaction, no doubt."

"Just there to see who showed up."

"Nobody worth mentioning, far as I could tell. But I'm sure you heard all about it." Kane stood up. "Off-duty?"

Gurson nodded yes.

"Want a beer?"

"Sure." Gurson followed her into the kitchen. He saw the papers laid out on the table. He picked up one of the photos. He recognized the scene. From the first arson killing in the park. The one they were comparing Leone's to.

Kane took two beers from the refrigerator and handed Gurson one.

"Where did you get these?" Gurson looked at the cropped crime scene photo of Leone's defiled face.

Kane gathered some of the papers on the table into a neat pile, turning the photos over. "Homework." Kane covered the pile with a newspaper.

Gurson looked at the covered pile. Like pulling the sheet over a dead body. Don't have to look at it, but it's still under there. "Took home a few mementos from the office, huh?"

"It's a hobby."

"You take these with that Instamatic of yours? Where do you get them developed?"

"I have a darkroom. No big deal."

"If you say so." Gurson shrugged.

"You got a hobby?"

Gurson thought a moment. "Horses."

"Racetrack?"

"No. Roping and riding."

"No shit. What kind of horses?"

"Quarter horses. Cowboy horses, you know. My mother was from California. Her family had a small ranch. Horses, cows. Spent summers there."

"Miss it?"

Gurson stared out the window. "Miss that sky sometimes."

"You should have been a park mountie." Kane smiled. "You still ride?"

"Not much."

Long, hot summer he and his mother spent at his grandparents' ranch, after his father's death. His mother losing herself in the place she'd grown up in, letting her mother care for her as if she were still a child, while he spent most of his time with his grandfather, mending fences, riding horses, learning to herd cattle. He was too young to really help her, too old to cry.

In the fall, they went back east, sold the house, and moved into a small two-bedroom apartment in another school district. Shut the garage door and started fresh. Or so it seemed to him at the time. He made some new friends. His mother got a decent job as an administrator at the local community college. Lived off her income and the generosity of her parents and in-laws. She lived long enough to see her son become a cop, much to her dismay. Long enough to meet Val and welcome her only grandson into the world. In the end, when the cancer overtook her, she held on to him and told him to be a good father. When he asked her how, she told him, "Live long enough."

Kane took an orange from a bowl on the table and began to peel it. "You're a million miles from here. Where'd you go?"

Gurson ran a finger along the lip of the beer bottle.

"Think I have something to bring you back." Kane picked up one of the books on the table, opening it where a marker rested midway through. "You read poetry?"

Gurson looked at the page.

"'Ptichka.' Written by Alexander Pushkin. It means 'little bird' in Russian. Go on. Read it."

"In a strange country I religiously observe / my own land's ancient custom: I set at liberty a little bird / on the bright holiday of Spring / I have become accessible to consolation. . . ." He stopped reading and looked at her. "Where did you find this?"

"Keep reading."

". . . why should I murmur against God if even to a single creature the gift of freedom I could grant."

"Ran the line by one of my professors at Columbia. Only took about fifty hours."

Gurson read it again. ". . . little bird on the bright holiday of Spring." He paused. "Were you planning to hold this out on me?"

"I don't know. I hadn't decided."

"Like with the drop gun, maybe, and Leone's ID?" Gurson put the book on the table. He leaned back and folded his arms on his chest.

Kane snapped, irritated. "I'm off this case, I don't owe you anything."

"No. You don't. And I don't owe you anything." He went to his bag and pulled the book of Witkin photographs out. "But maybe we owe Leone something." Gurson opened the book and Kane looked at the photo. "You remember the one on Gretz's wall? This is the same one. I don't think the markings were from the fire," said Gurson. "Leone into birds?"

Kane thought a moment and turned back to the Pushkin poem. "I set at liberty a little bird / on the bright holiday of Spring." She looked at the Witkin photo. "What did they do with the bird you found in the car?"

"Sent it to Forensics, nothing yet." Gurson paused. "Any reason you can think of why Leone might have been sticking her nose in the park case after she got tossed out . . . without telling anybody she was still working it?"

"She wasn't the type to give up."

"Like you, then." Gurson wanted to say something else. Wanted to say he was like that too, but he figured she knew that already.

Kane looked down and picked at the sleeve of her shirt. "Got that right."

"Some of the guys are saying Leone was on a mission, you know, felt sorry for junkyard dogs."

"She didn't treat whores and junkies like shit, if that's what you mean."

"So she understood them, then. Like she was one of them, you mean?"

"What are you getting at?"

Gurson looked over at the covered collage and thought of the cropped crime scene photograph of Leone. Kane looked at him looking at the collage. "She kept looking for that first girl's killer."

"She didn't stop working after she was suspended, if that's what you're getting at."

"And she kept using too, didn't she?"

"You're thinking that's why I killed her. Because she was a druggie whore? And that other girl last year. Mine too? Maybe Leone found out, huh, and I had no choice." Kane took a guzzle of beer.

Gurson took a sip of beer. "Crossed my mind."

Kane narrowed her gaze.

"And then it took a left turn out my ass and kept going."

Her mouth curled up at the edges.

"You don't fit the profile." Gurson reached for her collage; she didn't stop him. "That's what this is about, isn't it? Your collage here. You're thinking power assertive." He drew a circle with his fingers around one of the photos she had clipped of Charlene in the park. "Covered all his bases," Gurson acknowledged.

"Organized offender." Kane pointed to the photo. "Carefully arranged setting."

"Superior intelligence. Streetwise. Could fit well in society."

"Sexual sadist turned on by his victim's response to pain." Kane ran her hand over an excerpt from the autopsy report that she'd glued down and sprinkled with dirt. "But then I started thinking anger excitation."

"Seems more like anger retaliatory to me. As if the killer is getting even with women, to punish or degrade them. Retaliatory's the outdoors type. A hunter, maybe, or a fantasy of hunting women down. Possibly someone who has a significant woman in his life. Macho image."

"The few clues we have suggest a common pattern to the killing last year. This time the killer seems to have been more prepared," said Kane.

"Killing may have been an afterthought. Not the main satisfaction," said Gurson. "Have to consider the geographics too."

"I say he met his hookers in the same place every time. Lured them with money, then tortured them. Didn't have intercourse with them, but definite penetration with something. Knew the risk of apprehension would be low in the park."

"If he transported his victims in his car, we'd have found trace evidence. I say he killed them outside, where he planned to dump their bodies. Built a bonfire . . . created a kind of altar . . . a place he could return to from time to time to remember."

"Doctor by day, monster at night." Kane looked down at the collage as if disappointed. Gretz's obit was the center of her attention. "Motive?"

"Unconscious or conscious?"

"Either way a million explanations. You majored in psychology, right?" Kane ate a sliver of orange.

"Behavioral science, yeah."

"So you ought to have some idea."

"This kind of violence?" Gurson paused. "A way to resolve conflict. Brutalized as kids . . . or witness to the brutalization of someone close to them."

"Save the children."

"You got it."

"But instead, here we are, on the other side, prosecuting adults. A little too little a lot too late. You ever think of that?"

"Plenty."

"Ass backwards. We come in at the end of the story. Doesn't do anybody any damn good," said Kane.

"We're cops. We catch the bad guys. Let the shrinks and social workers worry about timely intervention."

"Social services," Kane said casually. "Ineffectual bullshit. We might as well be garbagemen if that's all there is to it."

"You got a point there." Gurson took a swig of beer. "All I know is somebody's dead and somebody's guilty." Gurson started looking in a shoe box that was lying on the table. Acorns, pine cones, horse chestnuts. He picked up something that looked like a dried snow pea. "What's this?"

"Seedpod." There were about two dozen in the box.

"From this amazing tree, an Evodia, grows over in the Brambles. Almost sixty feet tall."

"You say this tree is in the Brambles?"

"Only one I know of inside the park. There's a smaller one over by Columbus Circle, not the kind of tree you find everywhere."

"You wouldn't find it in the Rambles, then."

"In the Rambles? No. Mostly American elms over there. Some Chinese cherries, a lot of pine trees."

"Mind if I take a couple?"

"Maybe. Why?"

Gurson shrugged. "Could come in handy."

"For what?" she asked, suspiciously.

Gurson peeled the label off his beer. "Gretz liked taking pictures of trees in the park. Developed a roll of his film. I'll explain later if it works. It's no skin off your back, is it?"

Kane took two perfectly formed pods out of the box and laid them on the table, along with a baggie.

"Thanks." Gurson pocketed the pods. "Saw that old shrink Collier at the memorial."

"You think he knows something?" asked Kane.

"I figure he's not giving all he's got. Saw Norville there too," Gurson grimaced. "Got to meet his lovely wife."

"Pretty?" asked Kane.

"Skin deep."

"You going to talk to her?" asked Kane.

"Bianchi doesn't want me to hassle her."

"What are you planning to do?" asked Kane.

"Hassle her." He smiled.

The smell in the kitchen reminded Gurson of the early days of his marriage. Garlic and oil. A pot of tomatoes simmering. He looked over at the stove. "What's cooking?"

"Hungry?" Kane carefully cleared the table and set down a large bowl of something in front of him.

Gurson downed a forkful. "This is good."

"Vegetarian stew."

"Good."

"Who you got at home cooking for you?" She sat down and watched him eat.

"Miss Stouffer." He pulled out his wallet. "I ever show you my kid?" He flipped it open and flashed her a photo of his son.

"You . . . only better looking." She held the photo closer. "How old is he?"

"Almost eight. I was reading some of his schoolwork. Compositions, you know. Had a list of things in there about how to be a perfect person in just three days. He spells perfect p-e-r-f-e-t." Gurson thought of his son and smiled. "He's got this line in there, 'Treat everybody as a person, even if they're small.'" His smile went flat. "But the one that really hit home. When you make a promise, keep it. Got me thinking how I've let him down, you know. Haven't been there for him."

"Got a girlfriend?"

"Who? My kid or me?" Gurson laughed.

"You."

"A few easy pieces. Nobody special. Why, you know somebody?"

"Straight male cop seeks beautiful masochist," Kane wrote the ad in the air. "Nah. I don't know anybody like that."

Gurson took hold of the book of poetry. "Mind if I show this to Bianchi?"

Kane put her hand over his. "If Bianchi finds out you were here, he'll fry your balls."

"Who says I was here?"

"What are you going to tell him?"

"I was at the library reading. I'll tell him it's my *hobby*." He held up the book of poetry. "Don't worry about Bianchi. He's not looking for problems, he's looking for the quickest way out the precinct door."

"I'd like to retire now," said Kane. "I got my eye on a farm upstate. Moo-lah."

"A farm? Somehow I don't see you on a farm, Kane."

"Where do you see me, Gurson?"

"The one nine, Kane. Upper East Side. Sunny side of the street."

"No thanks. Too sunny. I appreciate the thought, but I'm not interested. To tell you the truth, I was ready to quit before all this happened."

"Yeah, and do what?" asked Gurson.

"Watch cop shows on TV." Kane looked out the window and watched a couple of pigeons fight over a scrap of bread. "I'm sick of all this bullshit. Some lunatic's dousing women out there and you know he's smarter than we are. Say we do find him—then what? You know they'll plead insanity. We'll have to hear how his mother chained him to the radiator. They'll stash him in some Motel 6 for maniacs but that won't change his ass one bit. Time off for good behavior. Few years later he's back out, some young kid's missing and we start all over again."

Gurson's pager vibrated against his hip. He looked at the number.

"You're not even listening to me." Kane smiled.

"Now you sound like my ex-wife."

He flipped open his cellular phone and dialed. Kane listened to one side of the conversation. When Gurson hung up, he looked at her.

"Well, that's interesting." Gurson wiped the corners of his mouth with a napkin. "That was Florio. Says Norville's wife called. She's looking for me." He deleted the call. In case his phone got into the wrong hands.

"I thought you were off-duty," said Kane.

"You know how it is." He smiled.

"What are you going to do?" asked Kane.

"Let her find me."

"Any news on that patient of hers?" asked Kane.

"Cleary? Yeah. We put a tail on him. He's been hanging out in Hoboken. Guys lost him for a few hours yesterday. Found him in New York having a chili dog. At the counter of Papaya King on Eighty-sixth and Third. Then he drove back to Jersey."

"What's in Hoboken?" asked Kane.

"Some broad he's banging. Looks like he's laying low."

"If you're going to see this wife of Norville's, you better get yourself a haircut and a shave." Kane tipped back in her chair.

Gurson rubbed his finely stubbled jaw. "Anything else?"

"Yeah, watch your back."

"Yes, ma'am." Gurson gave her a commanding salute. "But I'd feel a whole lot better knowing you were watching it for me."

Gurson stood up to leave. Kane walked him to the door.

"Hey, that book has a due date," Kane called out when he was halfway down the flight of stairs.

"So do I," Gurson called back.

[20]

Truthseekers

MONDAY, MARCH 30

Theodora looked out the window of her ground floor office and concluded that spring had arrived once again. The sun in the east was perched higher, and the young trees, planted in the courtyard behind the townhouse, were finally free of ice and frost, their thin branches showing the early buds of an almost April bloom.

Tucker had been drinking heavily since the memorial, making his life and hers even more miserable than usual. But they carried on. Mechanical. Getting dressed, going to work, assuming their respected roles in society. Distant and detached. Their own frustration with the world and their particular lot in it the single focus of their attention. Occasionally, they had no choice but to interact. Even the simplest dialogues resulted in fiery accusations. Their fights, malicious and ironic, only served to precipitate unwanted intimacy. Sexual pretense that neither pleased nor deceived either one of them. It was hard to imagine she had once been able to excite Tucker's sympathy. Perhaps he was no longer willing to suffer the humiliation of their one-sided love affair. It wasn't her fault that she didn't love him. Not the way he loved her.

After walking the dog and bidding a detached good-bye to an office-bound Tucker, she had come downstairs to her office, with coffee and the morning paper. An hour and a half later, and there she still sat, in the same leather armchair. She had been commandeering her mind around bends and curves, speeding by unpleasant reminders of the past. She lit a cigarette and focused on her day. She finished her coffee, opened her agenda, reviewed the lineup. Detective James Gurson leading the roster. When he'd taken her hand she had felt oddly at ease. She sat at her desk and pressed the four numbers on the lock that opened her file drawer. Even the drawer whined, sick, as she was, of the twisted life stories held within. She caught sight of the small black case instantly. A foreign object, out of place. When was the last time she'd opened the drawer? Last week. But when. Thursday? Friday? She eyed the case and wondered how it had gotten there. Had she forgotten to lock it?

Annoyed, she lifted the box out of the drawer and set it on her desk. A pretty velvet jewelry case, hinged at back, large enough to hold a bracelet or a watch. A light shake offered no clue. She set the case down again, reluctant to open it. Its appearance unnerved her.

She should not open it, she should discard it.

On first glance, it looked like a feathered hair comb, affixed to the black silk cushion backing. But the small arch of feathers was not a comb at all. It was the diminutive wing of a bird, the taupe and ebony feathers perfectly preserved. Horrified, Theodora closed the case and dropped it on her desk.

Theodora inspected the drawer again. Had she forgotten to lock it? The files inside contained highly sensitive information. Her inability to remember her own actions only complicated her next grim discovery. In the sun's light she could make out two prints on her window. Handprints. She wiped the inside of the window with her own hand, but the large ominous prints remained. Hands up. On the outside.

DEEP IN THE PARK, THE SNOW PROVIDED RECREATION. ON THE street, mountains of blackened ice melted into deep puddles of filthy slush. Gurson watched the people come and go, slipping and sloshing. A light breeze was blowing and the sun was high in a sky thick with clouds. He was parked in his Jeep across the street from Theodora Weil's office. Handsomely restored prewar townhouse off Seventy-fifth and Park. A wrought iron gate separated entry from the street. He assumed the set of stone steps led down to her office, while another set led up to their living domain. He counted. Three stories, all belonging to the Norvilles. Plenty of room for two.

Keep it friendly, Bianchi warned. No problem. Ms. Norville had extended the invitation. He'd be so friendly she'd invite him back. He looked over on the front seat. Gretz's cat in a travel case. Knowing the ASPCA would probably gas it, he'd taken the cat home with him. Figured if nobody wanted it, he'd keep it for his kid. He and the fur had become fast friends, found they shared a fondness for Cheerios and the Cartoon Network. A pet, a purr. Easy company.

He opened the gate with a flick of a metal bar and noted the slim camera, strategically placed above the left corner of the door. A slow mo detector. Easy to avoid, though, for a professional. He marveled at the apparent lack of security, and then, thinking better of it, realized that considering the occupants in question, it must be more sophisticated than it appeared. A buzzer on the exterior wall, marked Office, gave a low ring when he pressed it. A woman's voice asked, who is it?

Gurson checked his watch. He was ten minutes early. He turned up the collar on his black leather trench and smiled for the camera. "Detective James Gurson," he said, holding his shield in full view of the roving eye, and in a few moments she was opening the door.

Theodora looked at the shield, then up at him. The way she looked at him made him glad he'd followed Kane's advice about getting a shave and a haircut. He removed his black Ray-Bans and extended his hand to her. Strong handshake. Eye contact. He liked that.

"Come in," she said, leading the way with an outstretched arm. "Can I take your coat?"

"I'll hold on to it, thanks." He stepped inside and she led him down a short foyer through an airy waiting room that led to her office. All the walls were painted the color of tea-stained parchment, bordered in intricate antique molding. Tasteful hurricane lamps hung from the ceiling, their heavy glass etched with clover. A crystal vase sat on her desk, filled with purple and white orchids. Each item on her desk selected for its excellence and quality. Leather agenda-holder, glass paperweight, fancy silver cup to hold fancy pencils. The desk itself, a heavy mahogany number, carved along the edges in a wide scroll, the claw feet resting on an intricate Persian rug, the pattern dark and complex. Framed diplomas announcing her medical pedigree. M.D., Yale.

They engaged in small talk.

"Nice place," said Gurson, "been here long?"

"About ten years," she said. "It was a wreck when we bought it."

"I love old townhouses," said Gurson, "don't get to see the inside of too many." He looked up at the ceiling. "Great light."

"Thank you. A beast to rewire." She sat down behind her desk. "Please have a seat."

Gurson remained standing. He set the case with the cat on the floor.

Theodora looked down at the carry case, then back at him. "What have you got there?"

"This? I think it's Dr. Gretz's cat. Found him at the office last week. Poor thing was starving. Figured I better take him till we find a new owner."

"That's kind of you."

"Didn't have much choice. Cried like a baby when I tried to leave." He looked at the cat. "I was hoping that you might take him."

From behind smart gold-rimmed glasses, her eyes filled with amusement. "Oh, no, I couldn't. My dog would have a fit."

He shook his head. "That's too bad, ma'am."

"Ma'am." She took off her glasses. "Now that makes me feel old. Please, call me Theodora."

"Theodora, then." He finally took off his coat and folded it over his chair, then sat down.

"Mind if I ask you a few questions?"

"That's usually my line."

Theodora smiled. "Then you won't mind relinquishing it, this once."

"That all depends."

"Are you familiar with Chekhov?"

"Anton? Sure, old friend from college."

"Really. Then maybe you know a little piece he did called 'To His Excellency the Commissioner of Police of the Second Class.' It's just a paragraph long. A report of a suicide. In this case, a man found hanged on a tree. The policeman in charge suggests the man drank too much." She stopped talking as if waiting for a response.

"So, what's your question?"

"It's about Dr. Gretz. I was wondering who makes the official report."

"When all the facts are in? You're looking at him."

"I see. So all the facts aren't in?"

"Nope."

"And that's why you're here."

"You called me."

He smiled, she didn't.

"My husband told me that you were questioning the cause of Orrin Gretz's death."

"He's got that much right."

"He also told me that your father killed himself the same way Orrin Gretz did. No thanks to litigious pressure from him, no doubt. He was the prosecutor on the case. Young, full of himself. Determined to take your father down. He believes you're on a campaign to even the score."

Gurson watched her carefully, couldn't detect any false bravado. He returned the volley, a smooth swing. "And how does he think I'm going to do that?"

"By sleeping with me."

Gurson was surprised to find himself still sitting in his chair. Surely, she had just tossed him across the room. "Does he now." The stale questions he'd had in mind were growing mildew. Dull, routine questions about Orrin Gretz, his practice, his patients. In an instant, she had made sure the past and all its boring minutia didn't exist. It was just this moment and what they made of it. Between them and the four walls. He looked around for hidden cameras. Saw one.

Theodora brushed a hair from her eyes. "It's not on."

"Why not?"

Theodora looked at the camera. "It's broken."

Gurson saw a small red light on the side of the camera, lit. Looked like it was working to him. He smiled. "You usually tape your sessions?"

"It's a security measure."

"Your patients don't mind?"

"Nobody has complained yet."

Silent witness. Gurson looked at the camera, then at her. He wondered where the line fed to. Was he being watched by Norville right now?

Theodora reached across her desk for a slender silver case. Cigarettes. "Mind if I . . ."

"Nah, go ahead."

She offered him one, but he waved her off.

"Let me guess. You're an ex-smoker." She looked at his hands.

Next she'd be asking about his ex-wife. Gurson reached for the lighter and lit her cigarette. "I'm into secondhand smoke."

She exhaled with satisfaction. When the small billow of smoke cleared, Gurson could see she was smiling. He wanted to ask her for a glass of water. His throat felt dry. "That little Chekhov story, you suggesting Gretz was a drunk?"

"Perhaps." She set her cigarette down in a glass ashtray. The small stream of smoke rising was somewhat hypnotic. "But even if Orrin drank to excess, which I'm not aware he did, that would only be the result of some deeper torment."

"So what was he holding back? What made the dam give way?"

"Some threat, perhaps, real or imagined, could no longer be repressed," Theodora said coolly.

"Or maybe somebody was making his life miserable," suggested Gurson.

"Is that what happened to your father?"

She had balls. Refined, well-mannered balls. "I'm not here to talk about my father."

"No, of course you're not." Theodora held his gaze.

"You trying to turn this into a therapy session?" He remained calm, very still.

"Forgive me, Detective. It's a bad habit of mine." She crushed her cigarette out.

"If you're looking for my weak spot, it's not up here." He pointed to his head.

"One has the right to be curious."

"One has the right to remain silent."

"I'll remember that," she said.

She was either flirting with him or making him out to be a fool. Either way, it didn't much matter. Not in the long run. He redirected the conversation. "Dr. Collier mentioned something about Gretz's mother.

Some genetic disease. Said something about Gretz following her example, said his mother took some pills. You know anything about that?"

"I'm sure Dr. Collier painted the picture of a hysterical woman. Someone seeking attention," Theodora began.

"Collier seems like an old-fashioned guy. Bet that's his take on most women."

Theodora smiled widely. "That's remarkably insightful, Detective."

Gurson took a photograph out of his inside jacket pocket. "A guy into this kind of thing, for example, I figure he's got that kind of attitude too." He showed her a copy of the photograph hanging on Gretz's wall. The nude with the slash marks.

She cocked her head, wrinkled up her nose.

"Ever seen it before?" asked Gurson.

"No, thankfully."

He wondered if she was lying. "Hard to miss," he said, "Gretz hung it on his wall. Strange image to look at on your downtime, don't you think?"

"I suppose considering Orrin's specialty, it's not really that hard to understand."

"What's that?"

"Post-oedipal erotic transference."

He knew what the term meant, but he wanted her version. "What's it mean?"

"The nature of sexual desire. The unpredictable and sometimes shocking way it manifests itself in our lives."

The way it was manifesting itself right now, thought Gurson.

"Are you familiar with the terms 'repression' and 'sublimation'?" she arched her brow, still high on her horse.

It was his turn to surprise her. "You mean the way people deny all their fear and guilt? Common enough."

"So you understand that?"

He'd had enough of her patronizing air. Time to prick her balloon. "We all disassociate from reality to avoid pain, don't we, Doc. Incidents that cause us embarrassment, for example, or shame. Or disappointment. We pretend they never happened. Freud called it self-censorship." Psych 101.

She looked at him squarely, impressed. "A kind of emotional suicide."

"Right," he continued. "We ignore or cover up whatever upsets us. I think the word commonly used is 'denial.'"

She pointed to the photograph on the table. "Some seek creative outlets as a way to express rather than repress these powerful impulses."

"And when there's no creative outlet?" Gurson asked.

"The severely neurotic can lose touch with reality. One part of the personality battles the other for a while, confusing fact with fantasy." Theodora sat back.

"But the tension keeps building, needs release. Can blow up, create havoc, a desire to punish or be punished." Gurson was right with her now, on her level. He waited to see if she'd cut the shit.

She did, but with a dull knife. "I had no idea you were so knowledgeable."

"Never judge a man by his father's shoes." He looked down at his feet. Gurson shifted in his chair, thought a moment. "Gretz ever mention his mother to you?"

"I know she died when he was very young. I don't know the details."

"That's odd. I mean, seeing how she died of a genetic neurological disorder. Affects the mind, seems she could have passed it on to him. Kind of thing I'd think he might talk about with his friends. I assume you were friends?"

Theodora looked at him steadily. "Yes, of course."

"But he never shared any of that with you? Never invited you to any of those benefits he supported?" He watched her shake her head no.

"You know if he had any unusual sexual preferences? Any repressed sexual desires?"

Theodora tapped her cigarette case. "You think I have information about Orrin's sexual preferences," she said, laughing. "I'm afraid I can't help you there."

"But you're a good judge of character. Have to be. It's your area of expertise, right?" He tapped the photograph. "The woman we found in the park had similar markings on her back."

"And you think Orrin Gretz is connected to all that?" Theodora's eyes settled on him with determination. "Let me get this straight. You think Orrin Gretz killed this woman in the park and then killed himself?"

"Possibly." Gurson took out the picture of Cleary from his jacket pocket. "You know this guy?"

She eyed the photograph. "You know that I do."

"And you're going to say that you can't discuss anything about him, right?"

"What do you want to know?"

"Everything."

Theodora pushed her chair back and looked at her watch. A signal, Gurson predicted, that their meeting would soon be over.

"I don't know everything," she said.

"Tell me what you know, then."

Silence.

More silence.

"Who referred him to you?" Gurson asked.

"Orrin. But you know that too."

"Did Cleary tell you he killed somebody . . . that he wanted to kill again?"

"There are always patients who fantasize about death." Theodora sighed.

"Cops and psychiatrists have a lot in common." He smiled.

"You think so?"

"If we do our job right, we're both usually on the other end of a confession." Gurson crossed his legs, watched her eye the revolver strapped to his ankle. He'd put it there intentionally. Didn't hide it, wanted her to see it, see that he wanted her to see it, too. It was a conscious thing. A Freudian transgression of his infantile sexuality.

She looked away from the gun, into his eyes. "I suppose you could draw some remote similarities."

"Sometimes we even work together. The way Gretz helped the D.A.'s office. As an expert witness."

She nodded, but said nothing, so Gurson continued. "Boyd Cleary was being tried for rape. Gretz suggested to the D.A. that Cleary was sane. If that was true, Cleary would be found guilty. You were the psychiatrist assigned to Boyd's case. You felt differently. You wanted to give him a chance to change his evil ways. There wasn't really enough evidence to prove the charges, so you made a plea for rehabilitation."

"Why would I go to so much trouble?"

"Because you felt sorry for him, maybe. You're a Good Samaritan. You care about your patients, you're their only hope. It's either you or a jail cell."

"And I'm sure you'd sooner put the mentally ill in a jail cell, rather than have them counseled, Detective." She held her hands prayerlike to her face. "By the time they find their way into your hands, I'm sure you feel it's too late for empathy." She took the words right out of his mouth and kept talking. "We can't hold the criminal justice system accountable for a killer's crummy childhood, can we, Detective?" She crossed her hands under her chin.

He knew both sides of this argument. "How's the criminal justice system responsible if you go out and kill somebody?"

"How about if you kill yourself instead."

There was a long silence between them. Gurson knew damn well what she was referring to. His father, again. He was here for information. Not to defend or defy the criminal justice system. She knew his father hadn't gotten much in the way of justice or empathy. She was spinning the tables on him and he kept setting it up for her to do it. "Where do you draw the line between mental illness and depraved thinking, Doctor?"

"I don't," she said flatly.

He pulled out a crime scene photo. Leone burnt beyond recognition. "You know what was in the mind of this killer?"

She looked at the photograph, undaunted. "Are you asking for an analytic opinion or a judgment?"

"Judgment's guilty. The woman's dead. Give me your opinion."

"If guilt has already been proven, then what does it matter?"

"Which means what? Insanity? Take the killer off the hook?" Gurson thought about that for a moment, then said, "This killing was organized and premeditated. Which in my book means the killer was in their right mind. Which means that their evil self should be held responsible and their 'kinder gentler self' can go knocking on heaven's door in another life and try again."

"Perpetuate violence with more violence, then." Theodora lowered her gaze.

"There are about fifty serial killers on the loose in America right now. Before getting caught, each one of them will kill again. That's one hundred innocent victims, in most cases people they never knew, children for crissakes. Some of them will never get caught and go on killing for years. Do they need a good shrink? Shit yeah and a couple of volts of electricity."

Theodora tugged on the pearls around her neck. "When an officer makes a mistake, he's handled by Internal Affairs, isn't that right?"

"IAB. Internal Affairs Bureau. Yeah, I guess you could say that's our front line."

"Officers aren't immediately held up for public condemnation," she went on. "They're not thrown right in jail or put to death."

"No. Unless they mess up real bad."

"Well, the psychoanalytic community has a similar system."

"Which system's that?"

"The Medical Board of Professional Conduct, Detective. A regulatory board that sets professional standards."

"Guys who sort out the weeds, you mean?" Gurson looked at the soles of his boots.

Theodora reached for her cigarettes, but didn't take another out.

"You suggesting Gretz crossed some line?"

"I'm suggesting certain people receive professional immunity from the law. While others pay for their mistakes."

Gurson took a pack of cherry Lifesavers out of his pocket and popped one in his mouth. They stared at each other for a moment. Board of Professional Conduct. He drummed his knee. Was she trying to help him, or just giving him a lecture about ethics? He looked around the room, scanned her bookshelves. His eye caught a title. *The Dialogue of Dreams.* He decided to use it, to connect with her, change the tone of their heated debate. "I had this dream. In it, I'm falling. I want to know what it means. You do that, right? Tell people what their dreams mean?"

"Dreams about falling?" Theodora sat back in her chair. "Suggests a person whose ideas outweigh his capabilities. Could be a warning."

"Warning. Oh yeah, how's that?"

"Jung called dreams the forgotten language of the instincts. We're often attracted to danger even when our unconscious warns us to stay away." She stood up and reached for a book out of the bookcase. "Of course, the dream could simply mean that you're overworked. Or stressed." She handed him a slim volume. "You might find this of interest."

He took the book and watched her walk past him to the door. His invitation to leave. He stood up and took hold of the cat's carrying case. He made his way slowly to the door and shook her hand. "Thanks for your time."

"You don't mean that." Her smile was too much. One of those mouths that could give a guy vertigo. He had the uncomfortable feeling that she could read his mind. He looked about the room. He gave the case a tentative shake, causing the cat to whine. "By the way, you know anything about Fritz the cat?"

Theodora bent to look into the case. She placed a finger inside the wire mesh to offer the cat a tender pat on the nose. "His name is Sasha. Dr. Gretz was very fond of him."

"You know, I think no normal guy hangs that kind of picture on his wall. But then, what do I know?" Gurson moved toward her a step. "Maybe a guy with such a cute cat couldn't be all that bad, huh?"

She looked at the cat, then looked at him, the space between them charged. "I don't know, Detective. You're the guy with the cat now. You tell me."

[21]

Bedtime Stories

TUESDAY, MARCH 31

Icy cold morning at the precinct. Bianchi sat alone at his desk, six-pack of donuts parked on the corner. Hands free to roam over drawers, donuts, and paperwork, he cradled the phone between his right ear and shoulder, paying the caller on the other end as little attention as possible. "I understand what you're saying, Norville." He licked the powdered sugar off his thumb and forefinger. "But as I understand it, your wife called him. . . ." He now held the phone out at arm's length, Norville's voice reduced to a tinny annoyance. "No, he shouldn't hassle your wife . . . yes, Counselor. Yes, I'll talk to Gurson." He hung up, rubbed the kink in his neck. As he was lifting another donut, Gurson breezed in.

"Nothing missing but his gallbladder." Gurson was holding Gretz's final autopsy report. "And there's no Huntington's disease." He handed the report to Bianchi.

Bianchi looked the report over. "I was hoping he had a couple of Leone's fingers down there." He swallowed a mouthful of donut.

Gurson eyed a small cloud of powdered dust at the corners of Bianchi's mouth. Caused him to reflexively wipe his own. "Park's closed to traffic Friday at 7 P.M., right?"

"The road that circles the park. Transverses are open."

"Circle opens up to traffic again Monday morning 6 A.M."

"So?"

"So I found the guy Saturday morning. Which suggests he managed to find a way to sneak in."

"Pretty easy to do, people do it all the time."

"Or maybe that's what we're supposed to think." Gurson paced back and forth. "Maybe the car was there but he wasn't."

"Who?"

"Gretz, maybe he wasn't there. Not until later." Gurson examined his hands. "Maybe somebody else put the car there, hid it, late Friday night maybe . . . or before the park closed to traffic." Gurson paused. "Maybe Cleary had something on him, some dirt, blackmail or something."

"You check Cleary's alibi?"

"Of course his grease monkey covers for him. Real gumball. And the attendant at Gretz's garage says he thinks the car was there Friday. But there's no record. I ask him where the car is usually kept, you know, nice car like that has to have a special spot. He tells me on the second floor. We go there, have a look. He shows me an empty corner, clean. I get the feeling he's lying. I tell him there's an investigation going on, Gretz is dead. Now he looks nervous. Starts telling me sometimes the car is parked on the first floor. He starts saying maybe the car wasn't there Friday, he's not sure. Guy makes three bucks an hour, sends half of it home to Mexico. I figure he could be on the take."

"You check his record?"

"One misdemeanor, shoplifting."

"So you got nothing credible."

Gurson huffed, Bianchi was right. "I'm weeding through Gretz's phone records now, week leading to his death, the days after. Looking into local calls too. Rung up a handful of his patients. Your average neurotic New Yorkers. Uptight about the NYPD having their phone numbers. Swearing Gretz seemed like such a together guy. So far, I'm still hard pressed to find a motive for suicide." He paused. "I'm following a tip Norville's wife gave me though, that may prove otherwise."

Bianchi put his hand up. Stop sign. "Now I remember what I was supposed to do."

"What's that?"

"When you walked in here. Norville was chewing me out on the phone. Thought I told you to leave his wife alone."

"She likes me." Gurson reached for a donut.

"She likes you." Bianchi laughed in spite of himself. "Get too close to Weil, you got yourself a problem."

"What else is new. You mean Norville?" Gurson took a bite of the donut, tossed what was left in the trash.

Bianchi closed the box. "The broad's his wife, Gurson; he's a goddamned A.D.A."

"He's a prick."

"Don't underestimate Norville, Gurson. He's connected. Could make your life miserable."

"Already has," Gurson mumbled to himself.

"Norville thrives on conflict. He loves to come into a precinct and cause trouble," said Bianchi. "Personally, I don't like the guy. But messing with the A.D.A. is bad politics, Gurson."

"I'm a cop, not a politician."

Bianchi spoke before thinking. "That was your old man's problem too."

If he were younger, Gurson might have picked something breakable up and thrown it across the room. Now he just had to laugh. Bianchi's thoughtlessness ran deep. He knew enough not to take him personally.

The phone rang, sparing both men discomfort.

Bianchi had a brief conversation and hung up. "That was the lab. Faxing over some report you asked for."

"About time."

"You act like we're the only ones giving them stiffs in New York."

In a few moments, Bianchi's fax machine began to whir and beep.

"Don't get yourself all worked up, Gurson." Bianchi took out each sheet with a deliberately slow hand. "It's just the autopsy on the bird." But his tune changed as he read aloud. ". . . rapidly broken down in the body . . . succinic acid and choline . . . normal components of the tissues . . . could prevent swift detection. . . . '" Bianchi looked up at Gurson, then back down at the report and continued reading. "' . . . used to cause muscle relaxation . . . doctors use it in surgery. Too much can cause paralysis or death.' What the hell?"

Gurson shrugged. "What if Gretz had some of this shit in him, just not enough to trace?"

"Then where's the syringe?" asked Bianchi.

"Who the hell knows. Maybe a junkie stole it before I got there." Gurson took the report from Bianchi. "' . . . rapidly broken down in the body . . . could prevent swift detection . . . too much can cause paralysis or death.'" He thought a moment. "Say Gretz gets enough to paralyze him but not enough to trace. The bird gets too much."

Bianchi frowned. "Why shoot the bird up?"

"Who knows. Mercy killing."

Bianchi shook his head. "Mercy killing? More like a white-collar sicko, if you ask me, into torturing little animals. Goes for a nice drive in the woods to commune with nature. Maybe planning some sexual asphyxiation trip. Dies trying. Who knows what he had in mind for that poor little bird." Bianchi leaned back in his chair.

"You serious?"

"Nothing would surprise me, Gurson. Rambles is full of nut jobs at night. Maybe this guy was AC/DC, into pleasuring himself while sniffing a CO chaser." Bianchi shrugged. "You know, like those things the gays use in discos, nitrates . . . what do they call them? . . . Poppers."

Gurson's mood darkened. "Where the hell are the bird's wings?"

"Good question." Bianchi stretched his jaw. "Maybe he ate them. Says here his last meal included chicken. Sparrow, chicken, what's the difference?"

Gurson gave this some thought.

"It's obvious, Gurson. He shot the bird up and cut the wings off *before* he went to the park. Some sacrificial thing. Made an offering to the gods. Trashed the needle and the flappers."

"The photograph on Gretz's wall, the marks on the woman's back, the bird . . . it seems connected to the markings on Leone."

"Verdi said the marks on Leone could have been caused by the fire," Bianchi began. "Or she could have had it done at some tattoo parlor. Dykes are into that shit, you know. Piercing, tattoos, branding each other like—"

Gurson interrupted Bianchi's bigoted monologue, midstream. "Wings weren't just ripped off. They were surgically removed, boss. Whoever took the wings off knew how to slice and dice."

"You check that other shrink out, what's his name?"

"Collier? Yeah. He's holding some grudge against Gretz, some competitive thing. Collier's smart enough to have orchestrated Gretz's good-bye song. Could do it himself if he wanted to bad enough with the right planning, or he could have had someone else do it for him. You know, the maestro routine. But that doesn't explain Leone."

Bianchi sniffed around his desk, losing interest. "You'll have to do better than that."

"I got a couple of other theories."

"Shoot."

"Okay. Say Leone was onto Cleary for the first park killing. I found Cleary's card in her files and I say it's no coincidence it was there. She was digging and hit pay dirt. Maybe Leone tries talking to Weil, but Weil won't talk to her. Claims some kind of doctor-patient privilege. Leone stumbles onto Gretz, expert witnesses for the D.A., maybe Leone knew him from working the case. She asks for his help. Tells what she knows about Cleary, asks for a little cooperation." Gurson was grasping. "Gretz has nothing to lose helping Leone, he's on her side. Who knows, maybe he was scared of Cleary, maybe Cleary threatened him, said something about his wanting to kill him for trying to send him away. With a little help from Gretz, Leone starts putting heat on Cleary. In the middle of all this, Leone starts slipping, using again, you know. She gets sloppy. She gets suspended. But it's not like her to give up, from what I'm hearing about her, so she keeps on Cleary, figures if she clears the case, she clears herself in the process."

Bianchi held up his left hand and looked into his own palm. "Not bad. But how does Cleary know she's so close?"

"Maybe she gets sloppy on that end too. Cleary picks up her scent, decides to put her and Gretz permanently off duty."

"Let's go back to the original thinking. Gretz kills himself for no good reason."

"Okay," said Gurson. "We go looking for Leone's killer elsewhere. We scour the park for the usual suspects. Moonies, cult freaks, crazy kids. We still come up with Cleary."

"It's a stretch, Gurson. No trace evidence. Not one goddamn hair."

"Cleary's meticulous. Guy's into taking things apart, putting them together. Likes to take his time, likes to clean up after he's done." Gurson walked across the room, thinking on his feet. "We got nothing to imply Leone was up to anything dirty. There weren't any drugs at her place."

"Leone's past is sufficient to mark her, Gurson. I keep coming up with Kane . . . withholding information, not vouching evidence . . . makes her look capable of anything."

"You want to go that way, I say you'll be reading about the next park killing while you're teeing off on retirement somewhere." Gurson rubbed his hands together.

Bianchi gave Gurson a stern look. "You go sticking your neck out for Kane, you might get it chopped off, Gurson."

"Listen, cut me loose, boss. I need full clearance. Let me run Leone and Gretz's tissue samples again, have Verdi take a closer look. I don't know what I'll find, but it may be something to lift this fog. I want a warrant for Cleary's place. Who the hell knows what he's got in those twenty-gallon steel drums." Gurson remained persistent. "And I need access to Weil."

"You'll have your warrant for Cleary's place. I'm with you on that. You want to chase your tail with Gretz, go on. But hands off Weil."

Gurson drew a deep breath and was about to argue when Bianchi cut in.

"I won't say it again."

Eight p.m. and Gurson knew just where his kid was. Right there, on the couch beside him. He had picked him up after school for a visit to the Planetarium, where they left the city behind and became citizens of the cosmos for an hour and a half. Touching back down, they ate burgers and fries at the Dinersaurus cafe. Before heading home, they hit the museum gift shop to buy a big book on dinosaurs. Like old times, only after school tomorrow he'd be going back to his mother. "I have a surprise for you."

"What? What is it?" The boy's eyes were bright with anticipation. He watched his father's hands. "Gum?"

"Better than gum." Gurson walked to the bedroom and called to his son. "Come with me."

The boy came into the room and stood by him, taking in each corner. "I don't want to go to bed."

"Look."

"What is it?"

"On the bed."

Jack saw the cat lounging by a pillow and froze for a moment. "A cat, it's a cat."

"He's just visiting right now."

"Can we keep him, can we?" The boy approached the bed and the cat stretched out to greet him. "Why can't we keep him?"

"He belongs to somebody."

"What's his name?" The boy was on the bed now, petting the cat. The cat gave a few purrs, stood up, and made himself at home in the boy's lap. "Can we keep him, can we? Come on, Daddy." The boy looked at the cat, then at his father.

"You know how your mother feels about fur."

"He could stay here. With you. Okay?"

"If nobody else wants him, maybe."

"What should we call him? I know, we'll call him Lucky."

Gurson stroked the cat's back. "His name is Sasha."

"I don't like that name." The boy laid on the bed stroking the cat. "Can he sleep with me?"

"If you brush your teeth."

"I don't want to."

"Come on. You want your teeth to turn green?"

"Yeah," the boy said enthusiastically.

A few minutes later, Gurson cuddled up beside his son and ruffled his hair. "Let me see your teeth."

The boy smiled a toothless grin. "You still owe me for this one." He pointed to an empty space where a front tooth was missing.

Gurson looked at his son's face. Like looking in his father's blue eyes. Same strong chin, same thick, wavy brown hair. "You know, you look just like Grandpa Jack."

"Grandpa Jack." He said the name as if it were part of a school lesson, something he'd been asked to spell.

"We named you after him."

"He's in heaven, right?"

Gurson laid on his back looking up at the ceiling. "Heaven. Right."

The boy stroked the cat. "Was Grandpa Jack old?"

"Not too old."

"I don't want to get old."

"Why not?"

"I don't want to die."

Gurson swallowed hard.

"Are you old?"

"No way."

"Old people work. You work."

"Old people sleep. I have to work."

"Why?"

"So you can play."

The boy's face brightened. "Is that why you became a policeman, like Grandpa Jack?"

Like father, like son.

"Daddy, is that why?" The boy tugged on his shirtsleeve.

Gurson was trying to remember his father, any time at all spent like this, just hanging out together at home. But all he could conjure up were his father's hands, resting on that steering wheel.

"Why don't you come back home?" The boy had returned to the drama of his life now, his two lives. Here, there. His head full of questions and worry. The boy looked at him sadly. "I want you to come home."

"Hey, what's this? Come here." He pulled the boy to him, smelled the top of his head, and then began tickling him. "No matter where I live, I love you. If I lived on Jupiter, I'd still love you."

"Jupiter." This random image amused the boy. "Then you'd be really far away."

"You see, we're in good shape. All I have to do is take a bus and I'm right there to see you. Of course, if I were on Jupiter, I'd have to take a rocket."

Out of the blue, the boy asked, "How come you don't love Mommy?" He wiped his nose on his pajama sleeve.

"How old are you?" Gurson looked over at the boy.

"Seven. And a half."

"It must be that half. It's hard to answer all your questions."

"Why?"

Gurson pulled the boy to him. "I love you. I love you and that's why."

"Read me a story. . . ."

"One."

"Three."

"Two."

"Before I go to sleep, look under the bed."

"What are we looking for?"

"Monsters."

Gurson bent over, looked under the bed. "Nothing but dust balls."

The boy looked with him. "Monsters can make themselves look like dust balls."

"Nah." He wiped a hand under the bed, sprinkling the dust between his fingers. "These dust balls are just dust balls."

"Are you sure?"

"Hey, I'm a detective. Of course I'm sure."

Soon the boy was asleep, cat by his side. Gurson tucked him in and turned out the bedroom light. Technically, he was off-duty, but his meter was still running. He put up the coffee. Had some bedtime reading of his own. Back issues of psychoanalytic journals that he'd gathered, featuring a selection of articles. Each one written by one of a trio of head doctors. Collier, Weil, and Gretz. A wordy labyrinth that for the most part made him drowsy.

Earlier in the day, he'd returned a couple of calls. One from the Ricco/Maresca Gallery on West Twentieth and Tenth. Exclusive dealer in New York for Joel-Peter Witkin. Gurson had inquired about the unique and enigmatic "Woman Once a Bird." The enthusiastic young dealer commended his good taste and informed him that the hand-painted gelatin silver with encaustic was one of her favorites too. An astounding work that exemplified, in its singular way, the profound, universal struggle of all women. With such depth and complexity, she wanted to add, that a complete grasp of the piece could profoundly alter the viewer's idea of beauty and the sublime. No less sacred, in her opinion, than perhaps a vision of the Virgin Mary.

Gurson stopped listening for a moment and looked at the earpiece. Was he really having this conversation?

There was a limited edition of only fifteen, which had long ago been sold out? Gretz's print had said 9/15. Nine in a series of fifteen. The current value of the print? An estimated twenty grand. The current owners? Strictly confidential. Why? *Private* collectors prefer to remain *private.* Yes, Gurson acknowledged, of course, didn't want him trying to buy outside the gallery. But what if he were interested in making an offer, wouldn't she be able to help facilitate? Oh no, she exhaled in mild exasperation. The piece, as she mentioned before, was sold out. If he was interested in purchasing that particular print, she advised he watch for it at auction. We don't, she stressed emphatically, deal *secondhand.*

Perhaps she had something else he might find of interest?

She had limited Witkin inventory, but it was all equally impressive; would he like to make an appointment? A further inquiry as to the present owners of "Woman Once a Bird" was met with chilled laughter. A little encouragement from the police, Gurson noted privately, might help this devout young woman loosen up. He'd pay a visit to the gallery tomorrow.

A call to the office of the director of Yale University's medical school confirmed only that Gretz was a graduate. Gurson wasn't surprised that they wouldn't confirm any incidents of impropriety over the phone. No, that did not imply there were incidents. They'd have to subpoena records.

Click, dial tone.

Then a call to Cornell. Gretz was scheduled to give a talk the week before he died but had canceled at the last moment. The topic? Erotic post-oedipal transference. The nature of repressed sexual desire. Gretz's specialty.

Gurson's final call hooked him up to a well-placed friend at the Department of Health. Had him fax over some information on medical misconduct. The pages now before him defined nearly fifty punishable offenses within the medical profession. Negligence, incompetence, sexual misconduct. Gurson wondered. Assuming Gretz had committed suicide, which road led to the end of his life?

Gurson took hold of the journal Theodora Weil had given him. *Essays on Clinical Process.* He flipped to the table of contents in search of her article. He was expecting a short discourse on falling dreams, some road map to guide him through his own unconscious meandering. Instead, he found "Sexual Deviance: A Case Study."

Intrigued by the title, Gurson began reading. The four-page article skimmed the surface of V., a sexual psychopath who functioned mainstream. Above average IQ, well organized, socially adept. Textbook exception to most of the rules.

V.'s recurring fantasies involved brutal homicidal rape. Torture, disfigurement, random mutilation. The fantasies of a lust murderer. Sex wasn't the priority. The notion of control and postmortem play with the "subject" put the fizz in this phantom's cocktail.

Gurson thought of Leone. Had V.'s nightmarish fantasy merged with reality?

Gurson read on. V. enjoyed taunting authority. The kind who would never leave a trace of evidence behind.

On a good day.

When V. was really down and out, his twisted longings turned toward self-mutilation. Fantasized about performing his own castration with a straight-edged razor. Something he had actually tried, to free himself from his perverse desires.

For an instant, Gurson wondered if Theodora Weil had mistakenly given him the wrong volume to read. But after further deliberation, it seemed not. Gurson had met V. . . . Many times in the course of his law-enforcing career. V. lived on both sides of the barbed wire fence. Angry boys who grew up to be angry men. Hiding behind all different guises.

Who was V. this time around? Was Theodora Weil attempting to give him some analytic explanation for Boyd Cleary's adult neurosis? Or offering up some insight concerning the two-faced machinations of Orrin Gretz?

Or none of the above.

Gurson flipped to the cover. The article was three years old. He flipped back to the article and read Weil's synopsis. Filled with psychological jargon, it only confirmed what Gurson already knew.

"Considering how widespread severe mental illness really is, and how inept the legal and health systems remain, it's surprising how few like V. rage against us. . . ."

He decided to have another look through Witkin's scrapbook. To his surprise, he found himself drawn to the images this time. In the same curious way he was drawn to police work. The rush he got when entering a crime scene was a hard thing to explain, or comprehend. Not that he'd ever really tried making sense of it to anyone before. Who would understand? He'd never openly admitted to anyone, not even Val, the sense of power it gave him to be part of that world. Val had once suggested that it was the authority and all that came with it that had him so hooked. He'd denied it, turned into a fight. He thought now that maybe she'd been right, that he should have opened up, let go. Told her what it was really like, being in it, a part of it, firsthand. There was nothing else like it. The way adrenaline pumped high when you were closing in and tracking a killer. How it was hard to live in both worlds. How it was hard to come to terms with his own destructive imaginings. Of being fully in control, of getting even.

He closed the book, but he still saw the images. Inside the book, inside his head, inside the walls. The monsters he feared meeting face-to-face. In himself and in others. Childhood fairy tales with no happy outcomes, that still haunted his adult dreams. A fatherless boy's fears . . . of being devoured, torn limb from limb, burned beyond recognition.

Gurson walked down the hall and checked on his son. He listened to his boy's measured breathing. He sat on the edge of the bed and found comfort there. But he knew that even if he nabbed this particular monster under the bed, it was likely there'd be another one right behind him waiting to take his place.

[22]

Twelve Steps

Of course, Collier said, he would make time for Gurson. Still in shock about his dear friend and colleague.

Gurson arrived at the Yale Club in time to watch Collier chasing balls, up against an opponent some ten years younger. Showing some strain, but holding his own, Collier returned each volley with a loud groan.

While Collier showered and got dressed, Gurson waited in the members' lounge, a spacious, well-appointed parlor that reminded him of the rectory in Catholic school, days spent atoning for schoolboy pranks. High vaulted ceilings, walls lined with leather spines. The kind of acoustics and filtered light that Gurson was sure gave rise to lofty discourse—politics, philosophy, and most surely the whisper of the more than occasional scandal. When Isaac appeared he smiled as if he had all the time in the world. He motioned Gurson to a table located in a quiet corner of the room. Now dressed in a suit, his cheeks still ruddy from his workout, he walked with Gurson to the lounge and found a quiet, comfortable corner for conversation.

"Nice place." Gurson sank into a plush leather chair and Collier did the same.

"The benefits of being an alumnus," said Collier. "One of the few places I find time loses meaning."

"Central Park's like that too." Gurson tapped his fingers on the armrest. Gurson's eyes wandered across the room to where two men sat quietly talking. Gurson watched as they both enjoyed a stifled laugh, then returned his attention to Collier. "So you said that you and Gretz shared an office. Ten years. Long time."

Isaac put a hand in the air, summoning a waiter and waving off the question. A bottle of spring water and two glasses quickly arrived.

"How'd Gretz get started in New York?"

"After Yale he did his residency at Sinai. I helped get him the spot."

"How long was he there?"

"Two years."

"Then what?"

"He was offered a position at the Rockefeller Institute in New York. They were doing some groundbreaking research. He became part of a psychoanalytic team. Prolific writer, published numerous articles. His work on psychogenic illness was highly praised."

"Psychogenic illness? I thought his specialty had to do with . . . what did Dr. Weil call it? Real mouthful. Something post-oedipal . . . repressed sexual desire." Gurson smirked. "But then everything you guys deal with has to do with sex, doesn't it? The old undertow of the unconscious."

"Indeed."

"So then what?"

"He felt he was spending too much time with his nose in the books. He set up a private practice. I stopped teaching at Yale around that time, wanted to move back to New York. He offered to share the space."

"Why'd you go your separate ways?" asked Gurson.

"An opportunity came up for me on the East Side. I bought my own office. It was never meant to be a permanent situation."

"Gretz mention any problems to you, recently, any patients giving him a hard time?"

"On the contrary. He loved to boast. The plate was always full on Orrin's table."

"You sound sarcastic."

"Not at all." Collier folded his hands in his lap. "But it was a game of charades, apparently."

Gurson kept his eyes on Collier but he was thinking about Theodora Weil. How she told him that the medical profession, like the police force, could protect the reputation of one of their own, until maybe it wasn't convenient anymore. He kept feeling there was something about Gretz he should know, something no one was saying. If Gretz had skeletons in his closet, there had to be some record somewhere. "I hear the psychoanalytic community functions kind of like our police force does. You guys have an incident review committee, right? The Medical Board of Professional Conduct."

Isaac unbuttoned his navy wool blazer. He shifted in his chair, crossing his legs and then his arms.

"Come on, Doc, it's not your reputation we're talking about." Gurson paused. "Or is it?"

Collier tugged on the cuff of his blazer, as if the answer were hidden up his sleeve. "Are you suggesting that the problem here is about my credibility?" Collier eyed Gurson up and down.

"Your credibility and your cooperation, Dr. Collier."

For a moment, Collier closed his eyes, dismissing Gurson.

Gurson went on talking. "You know I'll go digging myself. But I figured you could help me put things together in a more timely fashion. Since there's nothing to hide, of course, you could save me some trouble. Give me some personal insight." Gurson took a shot of Leone out of his pocket—one from before she'd been lit up. "You know her?"

Collier studied the photograph, then looked blankly up at Gurson.

"Ever see this?" Gurson showed him a small copy of the print on Gretz's wall.

Collier's face became stern. "No. I've never seen that."

"That's the print I told you about at the morgue. The one hanging on Gretz's wall." Gurson laid the print, face up, on the table between them. "Kind of makes me think he was into something kinky."

"Bad investment, I'd say."

"Not quite. This one here's worth about twenty grand," said Gurson. "Limited edition."

"Really?" Collier laughed, sadly. "That will help pay his debts."

'By the way, who's the beneficiary?"

"No beneficiary, no benefits. Just outstanding debt."

"No insurance?"

"Nope." Collier shook his head. "Completely overmortgaged and overextended."

"You sound disappointed, Dr. Collier. Were you hoping to get a little something for all your trouble?"

"Are you implying—" Collier began, angrily.

"Mind telling me the real reason you and Gretz parted company?"

Collier glanced at the print disapprovingly, then up at Gurson. "As I said, I had an opportunity to buy an office of my own. We continued to be a strong referral base for one another. Of course, I was a bit old-fashioned, still am. Out of touch with the newfangled ways."

"Newfangled?"

"Prozac. Zoloft. Viagra . . . Chemical warfare," Isaac answered with a smile.

"Not your style?"

"I prefer the intimacy of dialogue."

"So Dr. Gretz was more interested in the power of psychopharmaceuticals?"

"It has its benefits, I'm sure."

"So Gretz medicated a lot of his patients, yes?"

Collier waved the air. "Why take twelve steps when you can take the elevator?"

Gurson looked at Collier's watch. Gold Rolex. "You work at a clinic downtown, don't you?"

Collier shook his shirtsleeve. The watch disappeared. "Yes, one day a week."

"Gretz worked there too, didn't he?"

"Yes." Collier shifted in his chair.

"Bit ironic for someone like you, isn't it? I mean, plugging addicts with experimental drugs to get them off drugs. Kind of contradicts what you were just saying before about your view on modern analytical methods, doesn't it?"

Collier said nothing.

"But you do drug them, don't you? Sometimes with pretty heavy stuff. Cutting edge, sometimes. Like guinea pigs, aren't they? Test cases. To help get FDA approval. A lot of money in all that. Drug companies, stock options."

Collier looked away.

Gurson fixed his eyes on the entrance door. "Methadone clinics, like the one you work at, are always under scrutiny. On the face of things, the place seems up front. But—"

"I'm not sure what you're getting at, Detective. My role at the clinic supports work that I believe in. I'm on board to counsel patients, not to keep them addicted, as I assume you're implying."

"I'm implying your story has holes in it." Gurson smiled widely. "Let's fill in a few, shall we?" He paused. "Would you say Gretz was a ladies' man?"

"A confirmed bachelor. Never wanted to marry or have children. I assumed it had something to do with his genetic situation."

Gurson rocked back in his chair. "Are you saying Gretz told you he had Huntington's disease?"

"A man's personal health is his own business."

"I see." Gurson didn't like his answers. "I called the support group for the disease; they told me you can't be a carrier if you don't have the disease yourself. Turns out you can have a test done. Autopsy indicated that Orrin didn't have it. Wasn't a carrier either. He was free and clear."

Collier kept quiet.

"Yep. All odds were in his favor. Lucky man."

"Perhaps he preferred not to know."

"Really. A doctor, for crissakes, you'd think he'd want to know." Gurson flipped open a small pad. "It's a troubling thing. I mean, if he took the test and he knew he was fine, then why would he kill himself?"

"I've no idea."

Gurson had Gretz's medical records. No mention of the test. No way to know for sure whether Gretz had taken the test. Gurson leaned forward and spoke softly. "Only a fool would be imprudent at a time like this. Man as smart as you, Dr. Collier, he knows that obstructing justice is a serious offense. See, I'm just trying to understand why a successful, perfectly healthy man decides to kill himself. Because if he didn't kill himself, somebody else killed him. That's how it works." Gurson continued. "The suicide note said he became accessible to consolation. You have any idea what he might have meant by that?"

Collier sat motionless in his chair, but the tiny beads of sweat forming on his brow tarnished the overall picture of composure.

Gurson placed a shot of Leone, charcoal broiled, in front of Collier.

Collier looked at the photograph. "Dear God . . . what. . . ."

"You think Gretz could have wanted to become accessible to consolation for doing something like this?"

Collier recoiled. He straightened his tie.

Gurson reached into the inside pocket of his coat and pulled out a small baggie. Inside were the pods he had gotten from Kane, officially tagged for effect. "Certain things tie him to the scene." Collier became attentive. Something about the seeds seemed to disturb him. Gurson sensed he wasn't telling all he knew. Gurson put the baggie back in his pocket. "I know you psychiatrists are good listeners; sometimes maybe you have a hard time talking yourselves. But you ought to give some more thought to helping me out, Dr. Collier. Before I start thinking you have reasons not to, you understand?"

Collier looked down at his hands, then up at Gurson. "I understand."

"Good." Gurson stood up to leave, taking a long look around him. "Yep, in places like this I guess you feel time has no meaning. But I tell you, Doc, you put some bars on the windows, you'd be surprised how fast time stands still."

EVERY YEAR, THE SAME FAMILY OF BIRDS MADE THEIR NEST OUTside Theodora's bedroom air-conditioner. She swore they were the same, their pale gray bellies, their melodious chirping. And even if they weren't exactly the same, she couldn't help thinking they were, coming back year after year, to have their babies on her windowsill. It was a good omen. Despite her barren nest, these little birds came to her; despite frigid snowy conditions, they sought comfort there, collecting twine and twigs, preparing to bring new life into her corner of the world. Heard them for the first time that morning, after yet another sleepless night.

A cry had awakened her again at dawn. A child calling for its mother.

Maaaaaaaa . . .

Was she dreaming?

Ren . . . calling out lost, weeping. Where is she? Yes . . . She can hear her . . . Ren . . . hurt . . . but where is she? The cry grows more intense, desperate. Must find her . . . help her . . .

The morning brought excruciating cramps, the onset of another cycle. Seven-thirty A.M. Tucker already up and gone. She fought the fatigue, got up, dressed, and watered her plants. Suddenly seemed so important. To make the dry earth moist. The warmth of her dog at her feet, leaning against her. Looking out the living room window, over the quiet street. Time to go. Run.

She entered the park on Seventy-ninth Street with her dog. Took off his leash and stretched her tight tendons and ligaments. And then they jogged past the playground. She imagined herself pushing a small child in a swing. Imagined looking into the child's face. A little girl with dark hair, green eyes. Like her, like Ren.

The morning air inside the park smelled sweet, unpolluted by the choke of automotive combustion. The sun rising in a nearly cloudless sky, a deep resilient blue. Minutes past seven, the footpaths of the park not yet clogged with human trespass.

He watched her lope across the green with her dog. He maintained a cool distance. Usually, she circled the reservoir a couple of times before heading back home, but today she was taking the high road. In long, strong strides she loped along the green periphery of the Rambles, then over the Bow Bridge, past the Bethesda Fountain and the Boathouse. He kept her in his sights but maintained his distance.

As usual, she cut west, past the Shakespeare Garden and the Delacorte Theatre. Straying off the footpaths, she and the dog seemed to be heading straight for the precinct. But then she shot left, slowed her gait to a walk along the edge of the Pinetum. Not to catch her breath, as he found himself trying to do, but rather, it seemed, to contemplate.

After a short while, she walked straight to where he thought he was well concealed.

"Not bad," she said, nonchalantly. "I thought I lost you."

He looked her over. Must have run some three miles, and she'd only worked up a light sweat. The well-toned body was hard won. The only thing she didn't have to work at all to maintain, he decided, was her sex appeal.

"You come here often?" Something changed in her face; her voice was warm and friendly.

"I work here." He wondered how long she'd known he'd been following her. He felt relieved, off the hook. He leaned against a tree.

"Still a trace of frost on the ground." She touched a low-lying branch. Then took a leash out of her pocket and tethered her dog to a nearby bench. The dog whimpered a while, then gave in and settled down to rest.

She returned back to him. "So, how long have you been following me?"

"Who said I was following you?"

Theodora stood, hands on her hips. "Either you've been following me or we just so happen to have been in all the same places at all the same times."

"Coincidence."

"Bullshit."

He brushed himself off, said nothing.

"You know, I don't mind that you've been following me."

"Oh?"

"Makes me feel safe, actually."

"Are you in some kind of danger?"

Theodora laughed. "We're all in some kind of danger, aren't we?"

"You play with words."

"Grown-up toys, I guess." She took a step toward him, reached out her hand. He half expected that she was reaching for his gun, making his first reaction one of defense. But then she pressed up against him, his back resting on the majestic pine. Her strong legs spread in a V, she locked him in, hip to hip. Then slowly, she dropped to her knees, unzipped his pants, took his cock in her mouth.

"Detective?"

The sound of Theodora's voice jolted Gurson back to reality. He sat up in the front seat of his Jeep and rolled the window down further. "I was just thinking about you." Gurson looked at his watch. Ten to nine. He'd been parked in front of her house for a half hour. She was dressed in sweats and sneakers. "Jogging in the park?" He opened his door and stepped out of the Jeep.

"Morning routine." Her hair was wet with sweat. She ran a hand through it. "What are you doing here?"

"Dreaming." Gurson stood on the sidewalk beside her.

"About falling?"

"In a matter of speaking, yeah."

She looked at him. "I suppose you want to come in?"

"You're a mind reader."

"A mind doctor," she corrected.

"Right." He smiled, following behind her now. "Read that article you gave me, thought we might talk about it." He spoke casually, as if they were old friends. "Of course, I'm not supposed to talk to you, am I?"

"Who told you that?" she said, laughing. "Let me guess. My husband."

"Indirectly."

"Are you afraid of my husband, Detective?"

"Should I be?" Gurson looked at her blankly.

"I'd think you're not afraid of anybody."

"Except you, maybe." His eyes followed her hands as she opened the front gate.

"Come on in," she waved him through. "I'll make coffee."

They stopped at the front door. Gurson watched as she pressed the code into the small box to open it. 3218. He filed the number. Old habit. She led him into the kitchen. Once settled in the large country kitchen on the first floor, she started making coffee.

Gurson opened the conversation. "I've been thinking. About what you said the other day about the severely neurotic. How they get confused about what's real."

"Happens to us all from time to time," she answered. "Sometimes our dreams seem so real we think we've done things we haven't. Conversely, there are times our waking moments feel so much like dreams we're left wondering if we've actually done anything at all."

His eyes traveled over her features, the slope of her brow, the corners of her mouth. "Give me an example."

"Well, let's assume we're talking about someone in a state of total denial about severe sadistic desires. The result of some deep internal conflict, let's say, or some past humiliation or unresolved pain. On the surface, these deviant impulses appear to be repressed. The person professes to feel nothing, shows no emotion. They experience a complete loss of memory of certain people, painful or shameful actions or events. In this way, they withdraw from their reality. Unconsciously, however, the pain of these experiences and their thoughts about them still thrive and threaten them."

"In their mind?" Gurson asked.

"Exactly. They disassociate from the truth."

"Which truth?" asked Gurson.

"That their sadistic desires still exist."

"So you're saying that they live in two worlds."

"Absolutely. Maintaining an invisible barrier between what is real and what's imagined. A defensive wall between the two worlds. But the anxiety and guilt only increase. Eventually the fantasy world that was created to suppress the turbulence begins to create more conflict. The unconscious becomes a dangerous place to be. It no longer assuages guilt or calms their traumatic fear of themselves or others."

"Nowhere to run, nowhere to hide."

"Precisely. They're trapped. Harboring their own death wish, or a wish to cause pain or the death of others." She hesitated, then went on. "The real world becomes the fantasy world. They release the tension to feel alive, acting out their aggressive impulses by hurting themselves or others. And then they have no memory of these actions. In effect, you could say, they cut out of both their real and fantasy worlds, existing on a narrow bridge that tenuously connects the two."

"Which is where?"

"Effectively, nowhere."

For a while they didn't speak. Theodora poured water over coffee grinds sitting in a cone-shaped cylinder. The smell of dark roast filled the air. Gurson watched the coffee drip into the glass carafe.

Theodora poured the coffee into two white mugs.

Gurson stirred his coffee with a spoon. Without looking up, he cut the silence and asked: "So who's V.?"

Theodora looked at him now. "You . . . me. Any one of us."

Gurson laughed. "I don't think so."

"Think again."

"You got some kind of rescue fantasy, maybe? You want to protect this lunatic's identity?" He paused. "Who protects this psycho's victims?"

"I thought that was your job, Detective."

Gurson reached into his jacket pocket. He held up the article she'd given him to read. "You talking about Cleary here?" He opened to a marked page and read out loud. " 'V. 's depression keeps him numb; controlling others keeps V. feeling alive.' "

"Do people often lie to you, Detective?"

"All the time."

"Why?"

"To stay out of trouble."

"So they lie out of fear."

"I suppose you could say that."

"People confide in you when they feel they can trust you . . . when you share something that shows you can empathize with their pain." Her voice was at once soothing and reassuring.

Gurson imagined she was real good at getting people to talk to her. "You should have been a cop." He smiled.

She looked at him quickly, then looked away. "Cops want someone to blame, someone to punish. Lock up in a cell. But what happens when they get out?"

Gurson leaned over toward her and whispered, "Who said anything about letting anybody out?" He grinned. "You got to help yourself in this life, Doc, don't you agree? I mean, maybe you think we should forget about Cleary and go lock up his old man. But then we find out his old man was an abused child too. So we go after the grandfather. But the grandfather's dead. So we excavate his grave, burn the bones, build a funeral pyre, and then what? Do we all jump on?"

"You're mocking me."

"Just doing my job."

"And I'm just doing mine." Her voice regained its authority. She looked at her watch. "Which reminds me." She stood up. "I've another workday to begin."

He stood up, feeling unsatisfied. Like one of her patients, he imagined, whose time was up before they were able to finish their last thought.

They walked silently to the door. And then, when he had nowhere to move, she asked him, "Have you ever killed anyone, Detective?"

He considered not answering the question and went to open the door, but it was stuck. He turned back to her. "In my mind or in reality, Dr. Weil?"

Knowing the door's weak spot, she unlocked it with a gentle tug.

He had one foot in the house now, one outside the door.

With a knowing smile that now unnerved him, she gave the answer he was thinking of himself: "I propose you're capable of either one."

[23]

Dealer's Choice

WEDNESDAY, APRIL 1

Tommy had warned Ren to stay out of the park. Unable to reach her high-priced, low-risk dealer, she ignored Tommy's advice. She cruised to the Rambles to cop. She stood under a streetlight at half past ten. A few guys passed her by, checked her out, kept walking. Gay guys mostly. On a good night, she could do a few off-duty cops, a couple of frustrated hubbies out walking the dog. Over on the hill she could see the lights of small butanes firing up, illuminating the faces of users. Her desire to get high was back. She was supposed to return to the clinic, for some follow-up. Be evaluated. But she hadn't bothered to go and now she was paying the price. She needed to fill her lungs with coke and nicotine. Magic sleep cure? Only worked if you were asleep.

The tall trees cast their shadows over the meandering walkways, their thick limbs shutting out the rest of the city, a natural boundary setting the mangy postwinter lawns apart from the city's artificial light and concrete. Weather had turned warm and clear. Spring was long overdue.

It was time for the park handover. Pedestrians and joggers taking their last laps, dealers and hookers moving in to take their place. She was hoping she could barter tonight. A vial for a quick blow job.

Ren chewed the life out of a piece of gum and walked down the wooded path to look for a dealer. Ren noticed a salesman. She flashed some money to pass Go. The dealer stepped all the way into the light. "Hey, baby, why dontcha put your money away."

"We can work it out." She put out her hand. "Over there." She pointed to a dark area, out of sight.

"Ooh-wee mama, take me wit-choo."

"First, the stuff." She put out her hand.

"Good as gone, baby. Good as gone. Everything is everything." The dealer smiled. "You give me a little something, a few bucks."

"Blow for blow." She smiled flirtatiously.

"I need some green, sugar."

She reached into her pocket, pulled out a ten. "All I got."

He considered, then took the money. "We got a deal." He handed her the vial.

Ren examined the take. Just enough to numb, come what may. "What say, we take a hit before we get started?" She was about to light up when she saw another figure emerge from the bushes. Hispanic, five eleven, 180 pounds.

Ren sniffed, wiped her nose clean, straightened up.

"You know a woman was killed in this park about a week ago," he said. "You're taking your chances out here, aren't you, sugar?"

"I'm not doing you both." Ren zipped up her leather jacket, backing away.

"Afraid we're going to have to haul you in."

"Haul me . . . where?" Ren was standing now, hands on her hips, off kilter.

"The vial you just bought. Dealer's choice."

Undercover. "Shit." Ren tried stuffing the vial in her mouth.

The cop intercepted the vial.

"Shit." Ren stomped and cursed. "Man, I trusted you."

"Didn't your mama tell you? Never trust strangers, honey. Let's go."

"Come on, it's the night shift. You for real? Where you taking me?"

"Mickey D's for a burger and fries, sweetheart, where you think we're going?" The first cop was laughing now. "Slow night at the CP precinct, darling. You're under arrest."

"Boys, wait up. I got a friend at the CP precinct," Ren started negotiating as they led her to their blue Ford.

"Oh yeah, and who might your friend be?" asked the cop up front.

The name hit the air like the tip of a match striking flint. "Detective Kane."

BIANCHI SAT AT HIS DESK LEAFING THROUGH A CATALOG. "I gotta get one of these." He showed Florio the picture of a robot dog. "Get a few dozen. Let them bark their goddamn heads off."

"Nah, you need this," Florio pointed to a white box in the left corner. "Makes white noise, birds chirping, the ocean and shit."

"Who wants the ocean and shit. I want to keep people out of my house."

"You hear about the guy who fell in love with a robot?" asked Florio. "Talked to it, took it out for walks. When it broke down, he buried it in the backyard. Neighbors saw him digging the hole, thought maybe he killed somebody."

The phone rang. Bianchi looked at it. "You answer it, Florio. If it's my wife, tell her I'll call her back."

Florio picked up the phone. He looked at Bianchi and mouthed, "Norville."

Bianchi rolled his eyes and took the phone. "Top of the morning,

Counselor." Bianchi listened with half an ear. Each time he attempted to cut in, Norville cut him off. "That's an interesting theory, Counselor." After a while, Bianchi started making notes. "Yes, I understand." When he hung up, the look on his face revealed to Florio that whatever Norville had to say wasn't good.

Florio ventured a guess, "Norville wondering if we got a confession from Kane yet?"

Bianchi answered him with an order. "Where the hell is Gurson? Find him now."

Florio disappeared and moments later returned to Bianchi with Gurson.

"Well, there he is now." Bianchi tapped his fingers on his desktop.

Gurson walked over to Bianchi's desk and rattled a piece of paper under his nose. "Found that link between Gretz and Leone." He looked over at Florio, who he wished weren't there. "Verdi reran both tissue samples. Found low traces of succinylcholine in Leone."

Bianchi tiptoed his fingers over to the edge of the sheet, lifted and read. "What about Gretz?"

"In small doses it's not the kind of thing you find unless you're looking for it."

"So he hasn't got any in him?"

"No."

"Sit down and don't get cocky." Bianchi set the paper aside. "Where are you going with this?"

"The shit's in the bird and it's in Leone." Gurson stood with his hands on his hips. "Cleary's still in Hoboken. I want a warrant for his shop before he decides to come back and clean the place up."

"The warrant's not a problem," Bianchi said. "But I got a bone to pick with you. You talk to Norville before you talked to his wife again?"

"Talk to Norville, what for?"

"He just called here. Says you went to his house . . . says you upset

his wife. Gave me an earful. I thought I told you to back off her."
Bianchi looked over at Florio, who was rubbing his hands together like a
fly. "Isn't there something else you ought to be doing?"

Florio examined his fingernails and decided to leave.

"What's with you?" asked Bianchi, now alone with Gurson. "You
and Norville got some private beef?"

Gurson thought, *My old man may not have seen this coming, but I got
eyes behind my head.* He put his hands up. "I don't know what you're talking about."

"Norville says you took a swing at him at Gretz's memorial. He's filed
a report against you with Internal Affairs." Bianchi glanced at the notes
on his desk. "He says you've been hassling his wife too."

"What the fuck?" Gurson barked sharply.

"He says you have a deep hatred for him, have had it for years. For
what you think he did to your father. Shall I go on?"

Gurson knew he couldn't stop Bianchi if he tried. "Go on."

"He says you've spent years thinking of a way to even the score.
He's shooting off his mouth about how Gretz was found the same way
your father was and now you're trying to set it up to look like one of
his wife's patients did it. Next thing, he says, you'll be dragging him
into it too. Says you're making it look like his wife is covering something up. He says you've been stalking his wife, trying to seduce her to
provoke him."

"And who's buying this crap?" Gurson asked sternly.

"He's made some interesting points."

"Such as?"

"Nobody with you when you found the guy in his car. Conveniently,
you left the scene with the guy's wallet and the suicide note. Then the
car conveniently gets sent to the pound. Only prints we find on the car
or the guy are yours."

"That's it?"

"He's digging deep, Gurson. He says you're a loose cannon. He knows you already have a record with IAB, says your wife complained you were following her around too. He says that since you were the one who requested the transfer to the Central Park precinct, it's suspicious. He's saying it makes it look like you've been planning something."

"Like what?"

"Like this . . . and Leone, maybe."

Gurson was puffing like a locomotive.

"You got to admit, it makes better sense than anything you've come up with so far. Everybody else was willing to accept the suicide. You're the only one pushing it the other way. I got to ask myself why." Bianchi said this without any hint that he believed Norville's theory lacked credibility.

An undercover narc poked his nose into Bianchi's office. "I got a broad here says she knows Kane. Picked her up on a buy-and-bust. Some of the guys say they've seen her hanging around the park before. What do you want me to do with her?"

Gurson and Bianchi exchanged glances. Bianchi said, "Show the lady the back room."

Gurson put his hands in front of him. "So, what now? You going to arrest me?"

"If Norville has his way," Bianchi began.

"I'll end up just like my old man," Gurson snapped. "He couldn't burn him, so now he's trying to burn me."

"I warned you to stay away from him."

Gurson closed his eyes and saw red.

"Right now, I need you to find out who the broad is," said Bianchi. "IAB's going to want to talk to you. I don't have to tell you how this looks. First Kane, now you. The shit's flying. You stay cool, I might be able to make some excuses; you lose it, you're on your own."

With his mind rolling and his stomach churning, Gurson followed Bianchi down the corridor. They looked through the two-way mirror.

"Who is she?" Bianchi asked the cop who booked her.

"Pross. Calls herself Ren," said the cop.

Gurson opened the door and entered the room. A small dingy space, a table and three chairs. Suitably uncomfortable.

"Ren. Interesting. What's it short for? Sur-ren-der?" Gurson engaged her in a seductive gaze.

"Just Ren."

"Ren. I like it. Like the little bird."

"Cute," said Ren, "but there's no W."

"I knew a girl once. Her name was Renata. We used to call her Renny."

"René." Ren offered out of the blue, "My name is René."

"René. You know what it means?"

She carried on the flirtatious volley. "Yeah, it means I give good head."

"Actually, in French it means 'reborn.'"

Ren looked around, bored. "You got anything to drink? Since I kicked, my mouth's dry as hell."

Gurson poured some soda into a paper cup and passed it to her. He watched her guzzle the soda and poured her more. Let her drink, soon she'd have to pee. "You kicked and you're buying. What's up with that?" Gurson asked.

"It's a free country. I come and go." Ren bit into one of her nails.

"You're working off some time, that right?"

"I try to help when I can."

"You one of Kane's informants?"

"Ask her."

He emptied the contents of her bag out on the table. Mace, spare change, tampon, lipstick, a prescription bottle and a .22 automatic. He held up the gun. "You got a license to carry this?"

Ren looked away.

Gurson put the gun down, picked up the bottle of pills and gave them a shake. He read the prescription. 5 mg. Xanax. Prescribed by Dr. Gretz. He put the bottle down.

"Where's Kane?" Ren demanded. "She'll vouch for me."

"When was the last time you saw Detective Kane?"

Ren shrugged. "About a month ago."

"Where?"

"In the park."

"What were you doing in the park?"

"I'm not talking to anybody but Kane."

"This prescription for Xanax," said Gurson, holding up the bottle, "says you got it from a Dr. Gretz. Who's he?"

"I don't remember."

"She don't remember. Isn't that convenient." Gurson looked up at the ceiling. "Who sent you there?"

"Nobody." Ren sucked on her thumb.

"Nobody, who," Gurson demanded.

"I got to pee."

Gurson shook his head. "Not yet. How do you know Gretz?"

Ren put her lips together.

Gurson picked up a plastic bag filled with vials and shook it around. "You want me to put you in the system? Four vials, you're a pred. You got something to help yourself out, don't bullshit me. You bullshit me, it's all over."

"Four vials, man, who had four vials? I didn't have four." She leaned back and gave him a look of disbelief. "You guys are all the same."

"Just trying to improve the quality of city life," Gurson smiled. "Clean up the streets."

"Quality of life," Ren snorted, "shit." She huffed and moaned. "I'm not talking to you. I don't know you. I want Kane. Or you can go and bust me. I need to pee."

Gurson went out and joined Bianchi on the other side of the wall. "We bust her, we lose her."

"Get Kane in here," Bianchi scowled.

Gurson lowered his eyes, containing a smile. He looked through the window at Ren, who was rocking in her chair. "What about the paperwork? Kane's restricted duty."

"Kane's still restricted, Gurson. And so are you. Restricted to duty inside these goddamn walls."

Kane arrived at the precinct within the hour. Gurson was waiting for her in the parking lot. "Leave your attitude at the door," he warned her.

"Long as you give me a claim check, so I can pick it up on the way out."

"Chick inside says she knows you," said Gurson. "Pross named Ren."

"Ren. No shit. I've been looking for her. Wondered when she'd turn up."

"You know her?"

"One of Leone's informants. What's she in for?"

"Buy-and-bust. She has a script for Xanax in her bag, prescribed by Gretz."

"No shit."

"There's more. Bird in Gretz's car was shot up with succinylcholine. Found traces of the same thing in Leone."

"They find anything in Gretz?"

"Nope. But the shit's hard to detect. Either he has none in him or I say it's too small an amount to pick up."

"Anything else?"

"Norville's filed a report at IAB."

Kane frowned. "What did I do now?"

"Not you, me." Gurson bit his bottom lip. "I took a swing at him at Gretz's memorial. He says I'm harassing him and his wife. Says maybe I'm setting him up to get even."

"He huffs and he puffs and brings the whole house down," said Kane.

"No joke. Bianchi's taking him seriously." Gurson opened the door to the precinct, letting Kane step through first.

"What's he got on you?" asked Kane.

"Twenty years," Gurson looked down at his hands. "And my prints. All over Gretz and the car."

Kane and Gurson stopped in Bianchi's office. He took one look at the two of them and reached for his Rolaids. "You're on, Kane. No crap this round."

"What about my status?" asked Kane.

"Like I told your partner, a little cooperation goes a long way."

"To where? I want full clearance." Kane looked Bianchi straight in the eyes.

"I can't make any guarantees. You've both been digging your own graves, dig yourselves out." Bianchi looked at the calendar on his bulletin board.

Gurson and Kane looked at each other.

Bianchi took out a handkerchief and blew his nose. "Now, who is this broad Ren?"

Kane didn't hesitate. "You could say Ren and Charlene got a little too familiar. She brought her home a couple of times, felt sorry for her."

"Did she sleep with her?" Bianchi asked directly.

"Yes." Kane's voice wavered.

"And you didn't mind?" asked Bianchi.

"Oh, I minded all right. I minded so much, I burned her up like a paper doll." She looked at Bianchi now, her eyes defiant. "That is what you're thinking, isn't it?"

"I'll get back to what I'm thinking in a minute, Kane. For now, you can just answer my questions. Politely, if you don't mind."

Kane looked at the door.

"Now . . . where was I?" Bianchi thought a moment. "This broad Ren, she trusts you?"

"She doesn't trust anybody," said Kane.

"So the two of you could be related," Bianchi said snidely.

Kane glowered.

"That's what they'll be saying, Kane. So you might as well hear it from me first. Like I told Gurson, you got to keep cool. If you handle this right, you'll get your clearance," said Bianchi. "If not, the three of us won't have a pot to piss in."

"The three of us?" Gurson asked, incredulous.

"I can't stop superiors from asking questions. Norville can hang you both if it works in his favor. I'm the one giving you a chance to prove him wrong. You don't, I'm in the trash with you." Bianchi paused. "Pretend this is the three four now. You're not working in a playground anymore."

Kane and Gurson left Bianchi's office without saying another word. Kane entered the room where Ren was being held. "Hey, girl. Mind if I sit down?"

"Kane." Ren gave her a warm smile.

"I've been looking for you."

"I read about Leone," Ren began. "I'm sorry."

"Are you?" Kane's tone turned cold.

"Of course I am," Ren insisted, "Me and Leone, we were friends."

"Leone's dead. She has no friends." Kane held up Ren's fanny pack. "They had a look through your bag. Four vials of crack."

"They planted that shit—"

"Let's forget about the blow for now. Let's talk about this." She held up the bottle of Xanax with Gretz's name on it. "Tell me how you know this Dr. Gretz."

"Just some shrink," Ren whined.

"Just some shrink that we found dead in the park."

"No shit." Ren pursed her lips, did her best to look surprised.

"Didn't hear about it?"

"I've been out of touch, I guess."

"You out of touch? Come on. You're the queen of touch, darling." Kane smiled.

"I want out of here."

"I know you do." Kane paused. "And you know information sets you free."

Ren looked at her nails; the lackluster red veneer was chipped. "I don't want any trouble. I told them I wouldn't talk to anybody but you. You're looking out for me, right?"

Ren was all artificial sweetness with her. Kane was aware of Ren's power to manipulate—the young woman had managed to con the street-smart Leone. Sitting there with her now, she understood why. Ren had a look of helpless innocence. Made you want to help her, straighten her out. She was a real chameleon. "They want to throw you in jail, Ren. I might be able to get them to give you a desk appearance ticket instead of an arrest, but you'd have to tell me how you know this Dr. Gretz."

Ren stretched her arms out before her and tapped the table.

"When was the last time you saw Gretz?"

Ren closed her eyes.

"Were you fucking him?" Kane asked.

Ren turned away.

"You were fucking Leone, I know all about that. High as Jesus, both of you." Kane stood up. "I ought to let them nail you to the cross."

Ren wiped the corner of her right eye. A gesture meant to get Kane's sympathy.

"You can turn off the waterworks, Ren. You know anything about a cop killing and you don't talk, there won't be a thing I can do to help you. You'll get some public defender fresh out of law school. I can hear the gavel coming down." Kane banged her fist on the table loudly.

Ren considered her options. The violent scene with the husband played through her mind. If she went whining to him about the cops now, what would he do? Might make her disappear permanently. When she'd been in trouble before, the wife always came through. But the trouble had never been this close to her front door. She'd have to do a lot of explaining. Out of habit, she took hold of the gold pendant hanging around her neck, rubbed the smooth disk between her fingers. Her lotus was sinking in this muck. Ren took a deep breath and looked at Kane. "What's this worth?"

"Depends. When was the last time you saw Leone?"

"Month ago, maybe two."

"Bullshit." Kane leaned in close. "When did you see her?"

Ren looked at a vein running down her arm. "Like two weeks ago."

"Before or after you saw Gretz?"

"Dunno."

Kane exhaled. "Nobody's coming here to bail you out, girlfriend. And personally, I'm already tired of you. How is it you go to this fancy doctor on Central Park West? Where'd you get the cash?"

Ren looked at the ceiling, then down at the floor. She looked at the door. She stalled. "What, now it's a crime to see a shrink and clean up?" Ren shook her head.

"I want names."

She could toss them a name, sure, and then what? Run like hell. Soon as they had what they wanted, she was expendable. "You got a cigarette? I need a cigarette."

Kane passed her the pack of Marlboros from her bag.

Ren licked her lips, put the cigarette between her teeth, and lit up. She took a deep inhale, then blew the smoke out in one long exhale. Her mind clicked along. "You know, there are plenty of guys out there into weird shit." She took another drag.

"We could talk about raising your status. You want to be a big fish?"

Ren turned her head sideways. "Big enough to swim away from the sharks. On the other side of that mirrored glass." She winked at the window.

"Talk and you walk." Kane snapped her fingers.

"You're shitting me. You're not letting me go." Ren gave Kane a dirty look. "Like a couple of years ago. Gave you guys a name, and what happened? Fifteen stitches in my head, that's what." She rubbed her scalp. "Who you got looking after me?"

"You're looking at her." Kane crossed her heart.

Ren put her hands on the table. "Maybe you should just put me in jail. I could use a little rest." She smiled at Kane. "Or maybe you could let me go . . . and I could help you."

"Let you go? How the hell does that help me?" asked Kane.

"You know how I work. You tell them how good I was to Leone. You tell them I got some connections. But I don't want anybody following me around. I need a couple of days. Then I come back. No bloodhounds, you understand."

Kane got up and left the room. She met Bianchi and Gurson on the other side of the door.

"She's full of shit," said Bianchi. "Give her a one-way ticket to hell."

"She already lives there. This one's been around, boss. She was one of Leone's best informants," said Kane. "I say we give her a day with surveillance. She tries to split, we book her."

"Wherever she lands, we can scoop her up," Gurson supported Kane's thinking.

"Famous last words." Bianchi shook his head.

"If she's willing to work with us, I say we give her some room to move." Kane waited for Bianchi's response, which was slow in coming.

Bianchi looked at Gurson, then over at Kane. "Okay. But you tell her she gets only twenty-four hours. If she doesn't cough up what we want, Satan's her next gatekeeper."

* * *

Kane reentered the room with the crime scene photo of Leone in her hands. She sat beside Ren and showed it to her. "You've got twenty-four hours."

"Twenty-four?" Ren balked.

Kane slid the photograph of Leone's defiled corpse into Ren's full view. "I want whoever did this. You help me find out and you'll fly with plenty of insurance. Try taking off *before* we get what we need, you'll crash and burn."

[24]

Transfer and Exchange

"What's your sign, Gurson?" Kane was back at her old desk, reading horoscopes from the *Post*.

"Virgo." Gurson was looking through his Rolodex, hoping some name would pop up at him, somebody he'd forgotten to call, some troll living under a park rock. He ran his hand over the rough stubble on his chin.

"'Domestic adjustment amicably settled. Earning power increases. Lucky number six.'" Kane folded the paper. "Might be a good day to call your ex-wife."

"Or ask for a raise." The phone rang. Gurson picked it up. "Gurson," he said into the receiver. "Number nine." He jotted something down on a piece of paper. "I could have told you that. A name. Right." He hung up.

"What's that about?" asked Kane.

"That photograph in Gretz's apartment. 'Woman Once a Bird.' Marked nine-slash-fifteen. Means it's number nine in a series of fifteen.

One of my snoops works for a big art dealer. Got him trying to find out who bought it."

"Nine," said Kane, "that's six inverted."

"My lucky number." Gurson was thinking of something Theodora Weil said about suicide. *"We're all the type, aren't we, Detective?"* Gurson rubbed his temples. "You got aspirin?"

Kane opened her top drawer and pulled out a bottle. She gave it a shake, listened to it rattle, then tossed the bottle to Gurson. He caught it midair, uncapped the top and nudged two tablets out, then washed them down with cold coffee.

Bianchi came along and planted the warrant for Cleary's place on Gurson's desk. "Carte blanche."

"His apartment and his shop?" asked Kane.

"One and the same," said Gurson. "He lives in the crawl space upstairs."

"Page the guys tailing Cleary," Gurson told Kane. "I want to know exactly where he is."

While Kane dialed, she kept talking. "Florio still on the pross?"

"I told him we don't want to lose her until we're ready to put her on a plane." Gurson took off his black leather jacket and hung it on a hook by the door.

Kane's phone rang. Hide-and-seek crew calling in. "Cleary's still in Hoboken," Kane called out to Gurson.

"Good," said Gurson.

"What are you really hoping to find?" Kane looked at Gurson.

"Old theory of transfer and exchange. We're looking for anything that links Cleary to the crime—the scene, the victim, any physical evidence. I'm working on a set of simple assumptions. Our killer's proud of his work. He's got to have saved something to help him reminisce on those cold, lonely nights."

*　*　*

After determining boundaries, they photographed and sketched the scene. Divided the two-story shop in squares and assigned an officer to each one of the eighteen sectors. They called in the Scientific Investigation Section. Since they were looking for dated evidence, over a year old if Cleary was responsible for the first arson killing, they spread Luminal all around. Luminal worked like magic. A chemical combination that lifted residual traces of blood, invisible to the naked eye—blood that perps thought they'd successfully cleaned up—and brought impressions to the surface. But blood degraded over time. There were no hard guarantees that they would pick up any impressions after so long. Still, it was known to happen and worth a try. They spread the Luminal and set their sights on finding more recent evidence from Leone's murder. When the Luminal picked up part of a footprint with a trace of blood behind an old MG, they refrained from premature rejoicing. Forensics would scour the area and analyze the scrapings. By early afternoon, they'd hauled six steel drums out of Cleary's shop and looked furtively at the old boiler in back. Decided to heave it the hell out of there. They'd only get one chance to do a thorough job.

Gurson was eyeing a blue '67 MGBGT at Cleary's shop when Kane paged him. Seemed Collier wanted to talk to Gurson, in person, as soon as possible.

"Call him back," instructed Gurson. "Tell him to meet me at the precinct. I'll be there within the hour."

Gurson signed off to the forensic squad, then made his way back uptown.

REN DECIDED TO TAKE HER CHANCES AND GET IN TOUCH WITH the wife. Maybe she would give her some money and a shoulder to cry her crocodile tears on. Ren planned to hook up with her in a public place, skate if things got ugly. Or if she sensed the cops were sniffing too close on her tail.

Fortunately, the wife was happy to hear from her, said she'd been paging Ren all week. How about the four-star on Fifth that afternoon? Date.

Ren made her way there cautiously. Moving in zigzags in the thick of the crowd. She figured the cops had somebody on her. She sat in the pale ocher lobby, hands in her lap, confident she'd lost whoever might have been following her. But everybody in the lobby looked suspicious. The world was full of spies. The guy holding the newspaper, for example, was most probably a slimeball moonlighting as the house dick.

She wasn't breaking any laws, sitting there, in their pretty lobby. And despite her chosen profession, she didn't look the part today. She was dressed respectably, wearing the blue skirt and wool jacket that the wife had given her. Her hair done, clean and neat. Besides, she was good at evading cops. Had years of practice. She planned it all so she'd arrive a half hour after the wife. Let her settle in. Had the room number on hand ahead of time. Knew how to play the elevator. Get off a few floors higher. Skip down the stairs the rest of the way. Confuse them.

She dug this hotel. The spacious lobby. Crystal chandeliers. Uncluttered oasis. Bustling with the animation of arrivals and departures. Easy money. Always had preferred the secret trysts alone with the wife. An arrangement that involved something you could hardly call sex really. A caring and tenderness that often moved the wife to tears. They had become friends, under unusual circumstances. That's how Ren saw it. Wife was maternal, looked out for her. Never had that kind of thing with anyone before. Definitely not with her own mother. She'd had something close with Leone. But Leone never let her forget who was in charge. With the wife it wasn't like that, not about the threat of lockup, or who worked for who. The wife was her best shot out of this mess. The wife cared about her. The only one left who she could count on for an ounce of sympathy. If push came to shove, she'd protect the wife. But first, she was protecting herself.

*   *   *

This bond they had made no real sense. But shit, the good in her life never did. It was just something that felt good for no damn reason. Didn't know who the hell her own mother was, but she'd imagined her. Imagined that if she met her, she'd be something like the wife. Smart, rich, beautiful. Someone who could teach her how to live the good life.

Maybe this kind of thinking was sick. Getting it on with someone who made you think *mother*. But it wasn't like that. The wife was just someone she would have wanted her own mother to have been like. Someone who she could turn to, to make things all right, take care of her. Somebody who loved her, unconditional.

Shit, she'd banged plenty of johns old enough to be her father. Nobody blinked an eye at that end of the stick. Sleeping with the wife wasn't nearly as revolting as banging the husband, whose idea of a good time was dressing up like a French maid. Or the other wrinkled old farts with their wallets bulging and their bellies hanging to the floor, into all sorts of crazy, lewd shit, buying her things and begging her to sit on their laps and call them Daddy. She'd take the wife's maternal trip over that any day of the week.

Father figures, mother figures. The world was one big extended family that basically fucked itself. She was just there to warm things up, make it happen. In the end, it really didn't matter. In five minutes, she'd go to room 1701, get herself some cash, and kiss New York and this Big Apple circus good-bye.

The door opened and the wife let her in. Picture of elegance, as usual, dressed in a black cashmere pantsuit, her hair loose. She closed the door, kissed Ren on the cheek. Ren noticed the flowers in a tall vase by the window. Exotic, tall stems, purple and orange. She walked over to the bouquet and inhaled. Closing her eyes, she envisioned a field of them. But then she came back to herself, to the reason she was there.

Theodora handed Ren a glass of chilled white wine. "I haven't stopped thinking of you. I've missed you."

Ren sniffed the wine, the way the wife always did, then took a sip. "Missed you too."

"I've been worried about you. Why did it take so long to call me back?"

"Some shit," Ren said, walking over to the window.

"Oh?" The wife invited Ren to come sit beside her on the plush down-filled couch.

"Friend of mine died," Ren said with a sigh.

"I'm sorry."

Ren sat down beside Theodora.

"What's his name?"

"*Her* name. Leone. You know, the one in the papers. The murdered cop. She was a friend."

"Friend? That's not what you told me." Theodora opened her purse and took out her cigarette case. "You said you were working off time to beat a prison rap for a bust."

Ren slipped a cigarette out of the case.

Theodora lit Ren's cigarette, and then her own, and picked up the conversation where they'd left off. "You said this Leone was feeding you drugs, making you have sex with her. That was how you were working off time. Not by helping her solve cases. You told me you were trapped, hated her, the whole thing." Theodora looked at Ren as though she wanted her to say something else. "You told me you were in trouble—"

"Well, I was, I mean am . . . now."

"*Now?*"

The wife's sarcastic tone surprised Ren.

"You told me Detective Leone was taking advantage of you. That she was using your bust to control you. Using you to get herself drugs, to get high. Making you do bad things, dangerous things." Theodora blew a stream of smoke high in the air. "In fact . . . I remember your saying you wished Detective Leone were dead."

"Well, maybe, you know . . . you were so concerned, like you wanted to feel sorry for me . . . maybe I exaggerated a little. I mean, made some shit up because . . ."

"Because why?"

"I don't know . . . guess it felt good to have you care so much."

Theodora sat back and laid her head against the sofa, staring up at the ceiling. Then she turned to Ren. "Didn't you tell me the police were going to send you away? That Leone was threatening to send you to jail? You said she was ruining your life. Making it impossible for you to stop hooking, to change." Theodora furrowed her brow. "Are you saying you've been lying to me?"

"Not lying exactly . . . I mean, you were so into it, I guess I kind of got into it too. You know, the whole sympathy trip."

"Sympathy trip?"

This meeting was not proceeding as Ren was hoping it might. "Please don't get all angry at me." Ren reached out her hand and rested it on Theodora's knee. "I need a friend. To listen."

Theodora methodically put out her cigarette. "I'm listening."

There was no good place to start. Ren took a last drag on her cigarette, and tried to begin at the beginning. Theodora took Ren's hand in hers to encourage Ren to continue. "With my record, I'm screwed."

"What are you talking about?" Theodora let go of Ren's hand.

"It was a small thing. Money on the side, you know. He hired me out, paid me to do a job."

"Who?" Theodora let go of Ren's hand.

"Your husband . . ."

Theodora stood up. "You've been fucking him when I'm not there?"

"No, it's not like that."

Theodora paced awhile. "You're making me nervous. Just tell me what's going on."

"Okay, okay." Ren took a deep breath.

Theodora sat down in a chair next to the couch.

"He saw me at this precinct . . . about a year ago. In the park. Cops were doing a sweep after the murder of some girl. Pulled me in. I was carrying some dope." Ren paused. "Your husband came along, you know, recognized me. Offered to help me out. Cut me a deal, got me out of there. He said now I owed him. Said I had to do a gig. He paid me."

"He paid you . . . to do what?" Theodora looked at Ren.

Ren sank into the sofa. "Your husband sent me to this shrink. To tell him stories. Wanted this doctor to fuck me . . . paid me to do it."

"My husband sent you . . . where?" Theodora stared at Ren's eyes, her focus narrowed.

Ren chewed her bottom lip.

Theodora stammered, something Ren couldn't quite make out. Something that sounded like "so help me God" and then something about cruel providence.

Ren cocked her head, unsure of the meaning of anything Theodora was saying. "What's that you're saying?"

Theodora's tone was caustic, angry. "What else would you have me believe my husband paid you to do?"

Ren looked at Theodora, still perplexed. "Beat the shit out of me last week. Told me not to see you alone anymore. Told me he'd kill me."

"So he knows we see each other alone."

Ren yammered on, Theodora's anger making her nervous. "He said he'd kill me. . . . And this doctor, you know . . . he's dead," Ren paused. "And the cops are asking who sent me there. Shit, it's not my fault."

At this, Theodora got up and walked over to the tall hotel window. She looked out over the city. A magnificent view of the park. She spoke softly, calmly. "Are you telling me the truth?"

Ren was thinking of the photo in her bag now. The night hubbie had stripped down to his garters. Did the wife know that she'd been meeting with him alone? Looking at the wife now, she realized if she pulled it out and asked for money, it could backfire. She'd pull away faster than a Formula One at the starting gate. If she was going to get what she needed from the wife now, it would have to come from the wife's sympathy for her, the way it had always been between them before. "I'm telling you the truth," she insisted.

"How do the police know you went to Dr. Gretz? I thought you just said you never told anyone."

"I didn't," Ren insisted. "I was in the park . . . cops picked me up the other night . . . had this script in my bag with his name on it. They wanted to know how I knew him, but I didn't tell them anything. Wanted to talk to you first."

"Did you ever tell your friend Leone that my husband was paying you to screw this Dr. Gretz?"

Ren thought a moment. "No."

"Are you sure?"

"I'm pretty sure."

"So you might have told her. When you were both getting high, maybe . . ." Theodora said, angrily. "Did you ever tell anybody else that you let Dr. Gretz . . . touch you . . ." She sounded disgusted.

Ren lifted her chin defiantly. "Hey, maybe you got some fancy romantic ideas about me. But that's what I do for a living. Remember?"

"How could you let my husband talk you into any of this . . ." Theodora's face was flushed. She put her arms around herself. "If it was about money, you should have spoken to me. I would have helped you. What do you expect me to do for you now?"

"I came here to tell you what's going down. The cops are on me. Asking questions. I think they think this doctor has something to do with Leone being murdered. Your husband's got me in the middle of something . . . I got nowhere to turn. When I couldn't get you on the phone, I went to your office—" Ren began.

"My office?" She returned to the couch, grabbed hold of Ren, and began to shake her by the shoulders.

"You're hurting me."

Theodora kept her hold on Ren. "You put that bloody bird's wing in my desk drawer, didn't you?"

"Jesus. What is this?" Ren shook herself free.

"You tell me," insisted Theodora, letting her go.

She looked up at Theodora, unsure what to say.

"Who put that box in my office?" Theodora demanded.

"I don't know what you're talking about."

Theodora refused to look at her. "This is the way you treat me. Coming here telling me lies. You and my husband . . . I should let you face the consequences. You think you can manipulate me, use me."

Ren shook her head, confused. "If there's anybody being used here, it's me. Supposed to say and do whatever you all want." She bopped from side to side, mechanically. "And then what? Cut me off, plant my ass in jail. No thank you." She huffed. "I'm here, aren't I? I could have split. But I called you 'cause I care about you . . . wanted to let you know what was going down."

"You called me because you need money." Theodora went for her coat.

Ren's fatigue was bearing down. She needed money now and the wife was her only ticket. She wanted to be long gone this time tomorrow. She had to play her right. She rushed after Theodora. "You're wrong," she sobbed, convincingly. "I'm scared. I need your help."

There was a long moment of silence.

Ren pleaded, "You told me you'd be there for me . . . told me no matter what . . . you and me were friends."

Theodora stopped and spoke her words emphatically. "You use the word so freely. *Friends*. Me, Leone, who else? Your pimp and dealer?" Theodora paused and stared at Ren. "You don't need any more *friends*," she stopped then blurted out, "you need a mother." She took Ren's hands in her own and said, "You have to swear you're telling me the truth now."

Ren bit her bottom lip. "I swear."

"You have to tell me if you've told the police anything. If you're working for my husband, you have to tell me."

"I'm not working for anybody. Nobody, nothing."

"You're sure?"

"I told them I needed some time . . . to get information . . . talk to people on the street. See what I could find out."

"People on the street. What does that mean?"

"People who'd never talk to the cops. People who would only talk to somebody like me."

"Have you spoken to any of these *people?*"

"No."

"Did anybody follow you here?" Theodora snapped.

"You're scaring me."

Theodora sat down, rested her head in her hands. "I'm not angry at you. Though God knows I should be." Theodora took her hand. "You're just a child, for godsakes . . ." her voice broke, odd and distant, ". . . caught in the middle. We have to think . . . we have to think how to get you out of this."

Ren moved closer to Theodora and sat on the coach. She rested her head on Theodora's shoulder. "I'm so tired," she sniffled.

Theodora gently stroked Ren's hair, over and over. They sat this way awhile. "It's all right," Theodora chanted, "everything will be all right."

Ren purred, relieved.

"You'll have to go away for a while," Theodora said aloud, to herself. "You'll need money . . . a place to go. Do you have someplace to go? Someplace safe?"

Without looking up, Ren sniffed, "Yeah."

"That's good." Theodora kissed the top of Ren's head. She reached into her handbag. "I brought something for you . . . something I've been saving."

Ren hoped it wasn't another bauble. She didn't have time to hock jewelry.

The wife took out her wallet. A lineup of the men she knew how to use. Straight from the U.S. Treasury. Twenty C notes.

Theodora watched Ren estimate the cache and tallied it for her. "Not all that much, but hopefully enough to get you going. Two thousand dollars."

Ren cautiously took the money, played the game. "I can't—" She offered the money back, without any real intention of returning it.

"You can and you will," Theodora advised.

Without speaking, Theodora helped Ren into her coat. Facing her, she noticed the mandala around Ren's neck. She set the chain right, her fingertips lightly brushing over Ren's warm skin.

"I won't be able to call you. . . ." Ren spoke softly, feeling the weight of the wife's concern. "Not for a while."

Theodora buttoned Ren's coat. "I know."

Ren bent to kiss her cheek.

Theodora put a gentle hand to Ren's mouth, then placed the same hand over her own heart. "Just promise me . . ."

"What? Anything."

"That you'll really go . . . that you'll start over somewhere . . . fresh . . . that you're not lying to me."

Some small part of Ren thought she might indeed be good if she ever reached the Sunshine State. "I promise."

In her mind, Ren was already gone. It was time to call Tommy. Get the hell out of this rotten city before they started reading her the *Miranda.* Or worse, her last rites.

[25]

Little Bird

THURSDAY, APRIL 2

Isaac Collier sat on an uncomfortable metal chair in the entrance hall of the Central Park police precinct. He kept his hands in his lap and his briefcase by his side. Felt out of place amid all the riffraff. His heavy-lidded, dark brown eyes explored the harsh surroundings. Police all about, mug shots hanging on bulletin boards, a drunk in a holding pen, cigarette butts scattered all over the dirty worn wood floors, fluorescent lights and dingy walls the dull beige of bureaucracy.

Gurson appeared and instructed Collier to follow him to a stark back room. Kane was sitting at a desk in the corner, under the room's single, small barred window. Gurson pulled up a chair for Collier then leaned against the edge of Kane's desk. Collier sat down and reluctantly placed his briefcase on the floor.

"Got to admit, Doc. Your timing's good." Gurson moved closer to him. "You here to confirm my suspicions? Your buddy Gretz, he racked up frequent flyer miles on the couch?"

Collier seemed uncharacteristically nervous, the way most men acted just before spilling beans. "There were certain complaints, construed as inappropriate. Not easy to prove, of course. Patient's word against the doctor's."

"So we're talking about sexual misconduct," Gurson suggested persuasively.

"Yes," Collier spoke in a cautious whisper.

"Any of these claims go into the trash because you're on the incident review board, Dr. Collier?"

Collier licked his lips. "If you are implying I was in collusion . . . absolutely not."

"You got names on these claims?" asked Gurson.

"Not even the Medical Board of Professional Conduct can give you those . . . legally," said Collier. "State law requires that all names be kept confidential."

Gurson stood up and walked behind Collier, laying a hand on his shoulder. "Then . . . off the record, what the hell are you here to tell us that we don't already know?"

Collier picked up his briefcase and placed it on his lap.

"From the beginning," said Kane.

Gurson brought him a cup of cool water.

Collier cleared his throat and took a drink. "That would be over twenty years ago. In Orrin Gretz's residency at Yale. As part of training, every psychiatrist undergoes a course of analysis. He was assigned to me. I expressed some concern about countertransference," said Collier.

"That's when a psychiatrist shifts his own unresolved life experience onto the patient," said Gurson. "Patient reminds him of someone, or something, that he himself hasn't worked through. All efforts then work on his own behalf rather than solely for his patient. Isn't that right, Dr. Collier?"

Collier looked surprised. "Yes. During his residency there was a particular case"—Isaac looked over at the file—"that caused more than a bit of concern. A young girl, about fourteen at the time." He paused. "Obese . . . but quite pretty and precocious . . . with severe libidinal cathexis—everyday images transformed into ghastly hallucinations. She'd been sent to our juvenile ward for treatment . . . became one of Dr. Gretz's first patients. She was remarkably bright. Emotionally damaged. She was brought to the clinic by local authorities. Claims of sexual abuse . . . relations with her father from a very early age. Nearly two months after she arrived, we discovered she was pregnant." He stopped, took another sip of water, then continued. "We assumed the child was conceived incestuously, before she was admitted to the hospital. Of course, no one in the family would admit to that. The girl was suffering from a case of hysterical paralysis. Her pain too acute to be tolerated. Memories, unless repressed, unbearable, terrifying. She refused to talk about any of it for quite some time."

"How long was she there?" asked Kane.

"About three years," said Collier.

"What happened to the baby?" asked Kane.

"Apparently, the young woman was greatly misled by the mother."

"How's that?" Gurson looked at Collier.

"The girl desperately wanted to keep the child. The mother told her she was going to be allowed to have and keep the baby. However, with us, the mother was vehement. Insisted the pregnancy be aborted. Of course, under the circumstances, we all agreed—she shouldn't have the child."

"So the pregnancy was terminated?" asked Gurson.

Collier dropped his head in a moment of sad reflection. "Yes."

"Did the girl understand what was going on?" asked Kane.

"Not really," said Collier. "There was no room in her head for such information. The procedure was performed under general anesthesia. She had no tangible memory of it."

Kane looked reproachfully at Collier.

"There were so many other issues to deal with," said Collier. "She was very fragile, not capable of making decisions for herself."

"Did you guys ever tell her about what really happened to the baby?" asked Kane.

"For a long time, she was convinced she'd given birth to the baby, that we had taken the baby away from her, sent it away."

"But you say the pregnancy was terminated," said Gurson.

"The young woman had severe neurotic dysfunction. She had tried to take her own life more than once. Initially, to belabor the point would have been detrimental. We hoped we might help her, eventually, to accept the truth," said Collier.

"What *was* the truth, Dr. Collier?" asked Kane.

Collier sat back and folded his hands on the table. "The pregnancy was terminated."

"So what's the catch?" asked Gurson.

"Unfortunately, a case of extreme countertransference had occurred. It seems doctor and patient became sexually fixated." Collier shook his head.

"You mean she and Gretz fell for each other?" asked Kane.

"Orrin insisted it was strictly one-sided. He'd spent years working to help the young woman. Extending compassion, gaining her trust, her confidence . . ." Collier paused. "Only natural that she might become fond of him. He insisted that her delusions were the result of anxiety, intensified because of suggestions that they terminate their analytic relationship. He said that this was the reason she was making her sudden claim."

"What claim?" asked Gurson.

"She raised a question regarding the paternity of the child," Collier said grimly. "After she left the clinic, she corresponded with me, long, accusatory letters. She insisted that the child we'd taken was Orrin's. That he had molested her when she first arrived in the clinic. She was convinced that there had never been any abortion. Believed that the child had been delivered alive . . . that Orrin was the father of this child."

"Was he?" asked Gurson.

"At the time, I brushed it off as delusional nonsense. I completely dismissed the possibility. But now, I'm compelled to wonder . . . perhaps she was telling the truth. Neither the gestation or paternity of the fetus was ever precisely determined."

"Did you ever discuss it with Gretz?" asked Kane.

"Of course, I discussed the matter with Orrin at the outset. Asked if he had taken advantage in any way. He denied all allegations." Collier paused. "Said the poor girl was severely deluded. That she had some bizarre notion that they were actually lovers. This was an ongoing fantasy of hers." Collier paused. "If he was guilty of anything, he claimed that it must be for spending too much time trying to help her."

"Did he help her?" asked Kane.

"In clinic, she certainly appeared to thrive. Gretz was hailed. I see now that they both may have effectively manipulated us all, in an effort to get her out of there."

"So you're saying Gretz may have abused her?" asked Kane.

"I'm not saying that," said Collier.

"Then what are you saying?" asked Gurson.

"I'm saying it was a complex dynamic," said Collier.

Kane tapped her fingers on the table. "Did you ever really tell her the truth about the baby?"

"We tried. But she spiraled in and out of delusions. On certain days, she believed her mother had the child. On other days, she believed that the child was still inside her. In the end, I think she merely pretended to believe us." Collier thought a moment. "In retrospect, I think the girl's mother contributed to the delusion by leading her daughter to believe that she had kept the baby for her, that she would care for it until her daughter was released." Collier stopped abruptly, reluctant to go on. He rubbed his forehead. "I'm afraid this is where the case grows even more complex."

"More complex?" said Kane, disbelieving, "How much more complex?"

"Six months after the abortion, the girl's parents were found dead."

"Dead how?" asked Gurson.

"Victims of an apparent homicide, suicide. According to investigators, the girl's mother shot the father in a rage over what he'd done to her daughter, and then she shot herself." Collier fiddled nervously with his tie.

"Never having told her daughter the truth about the abortion, I gather." Gurson crossed his arms.

"Unfortunately, that seems to be correct," Collier concurred.

"What happened to the girl?" asked Gurson.

"We were obliged to take charge of her. She stayed on at the clinic an additional two years, working through her trauma. Orrin personally supervised her education and welfare. The child was alone, no family to care for her. She was remarkably bright, as I said. She took a real interest in psychoanalysis. You could say it became her life. With Orrin's support, she went on to college, full scholarship at Yale."

"Real poster girl," Kane remarked.

"So you're saying Gretz became her mentor," said Gurson.

"In essence, yes. Under his tutelage she went on to become an analyst herself. Perhaps believing that in this capacity, if she worked hard enough, he might truly come to love her someday. Certainly has happened before," said Collier.

"You mean, before the law started protecting patients' rights," Gurson reminded Collier.

"So she goes off and becomes a shrink and that's the end of that?" asked Kane. "Deals with her neurosis by calling herself a doctor."

"Years passed, paths diverged. I heard she married. I forgot about it, really. Busy with my work," Collier rationalized. "Orrin went on to research post-oedipal realization."

"How ironic," Gurson said snidely, "the very thing he'd been accused of." He looked at Kane. "Acknowledging the arousal felt between analyst and patient. Totally deluded. Convinced he's actually helping people."

Collier looked away. "Of course, I cautioned him. But Orrin loved to test established boundaries, insisted they were only put into place to compromise the well-being of patients."

"What about the other complaints against Dr. Gretz regarding sexual misconduct?" asked Gurson.

Collier took a moment to contemplate. "Never enough proof. Claims were dropped. But then this last complaint came in, there was sufficient evidence. Disciplinary proceedings were to commence. I decided to contact Orrin directly. I'd known him for so many years. I felt he might confide in me." Collier hesitated.

"Did he?" asked Gurson.

"I told him that if any of it was true, he could lose his license, lose everything. He denied all allegations." Collier shook his head.

"And you believed him?" asked Gurson.

"He was despondent, said he felt he'd been entrapped. I acknowledged that possibility, but told him it might be best to arrange treatment for him, that if he were willing to work with the board, charges might be reduced to a reprimand." Collier hung his head. "Unfortunately, we never had the chance to help him. I assumed he'd taken his life . . . finally became accessible to consolation, as you said he wrote in his suicide note, because the allegations against him were true."

"You conveniently left all of this out at the morgue," said Gurson. "Why?"

Collier brushed off the question. "At the time, I didn't see the point. The allegations were as yet unproven, Orrin was dead and gone, why dredge up hearsay?"

Gurson gave Collier a firm look. "I say you didn't say anything because you didn't want us snooping around and finding out you turned

a blind eye. Maybe had some reasons of your own to want the good doctor out of the way."

"That's absurd," insisted Collier.

"Maybe. Or maybe you're just bringing this old story up to distract
us," said Kane. "Where is this old file you're blabbing about . . . where is
this woman?" Kane demanded.

Collier slowly opened his briefcase and took out a folder that he
handed to Gurson. The yellowed pages, scrawled with illegible nota-
tions, did little to educate Gurson.

"Translate this for me, will you, Dr. Collier."

"I called her to tell her about Orrin's passing away. We met briefly.
She asked for her old files, concerned they didn't get into the wrong
hands. I had held on to a copy . . . as a matter of course. Began to wonder if it wasn't all connected . . . if maybe something else wasn't
involved. . . ."

"This fat girl," Gurson said, taking hold of the file, "I assume she
ain't fat no more."

"No, she's not."

"Bet she's light as a bird," said Kane.

Gurson finished the thought. ". . . and still can't get herself off the
ground. . . ."

FLORIO SAT PARKED BY THE CURB PLAYING TAXI DRIVER, WAITING
for Ren to finish her business. He checked the time. Almost six o'clock.
She'd been in the hotel an hour and a half. Hotel security was keeping
an eye on her door. Informed him she'd hooked up with a woman in
room 1701. Gave him a description. Tall, slim, auburn.

When Norville's wife stepped out on the street, hotel security
flagged her for Florio. What the hell was she doing there . . . with Ren?

Moments later, Ren appeared carrying a small duffel. She hailed a
cab. Florio moved in, picked her up, and flicked his off-duty light on.

"Where to, miss?" Florio asked from the front of the cab.

Ren had already booked her flight. Terminal B. LaGuardia Airport.

"LaGuardia." Ren leaned back in her seat and closed her eyes.

Florio smiled to himself. Not flying today, honey. He pressed a button and all the doors locked. Next stop: Central Park police precinct.

Florio escorted Ren into the park precinct, with her kicking and screaming. He sat her in a holding pen and then had a brief talk with Gurson and Kane. He told them where she'd been and with who. Told them she was headed to LaGuardia. Hotel security said she was holed up with Norville's wife, who had checked in under the name Vogel. She was holding two thousand in cash and a rather disturbing four-color cameo of Norville.

Gurson held up the photo of Norville. "What do we do with this?"

"That's obvious," said Kane.

"Is it?" Gurson tucked the photo into a manila envelope.

"We blow it up and run it on the cover of the daily rags," Kane said, smirking.

"In a perfect world." Gurson put the contents of Ren's bag back into it. He carried the bag with him into the room where Ren sat waiting.

"You got exactly five seconds to talk before we ship you to Rikers, Ren." Kane walked in talking.

"You were heading to LaGuardia, with a hefty stash," snarled Gurson, flashing the wad of confiscated cash in Ren's face.

"Shit. I worked hard for that money," Ren insisted.

"And you're gonna work a helluva lot harder if you want it back," snapped Gurson. "Someone paying you off to go somewhere?"

"I was going to Starbucks. I like their coffee." Ren looked at her nails.

"Lock her up. I've had enough of her bullshit." Gurson turned to leave.

Kane took hold of Ren's arm and started lifting her out of her chair.

"You have the right . . ." Kane was reciting *Miranda*.

Ren was getting dizzy. "Wait." Ren's voice hovered between panic and protest.

"Possession . . ." Gurson joined the chorus. "Accessory to murder . . ."

Ren looked up sadly. "Murder? Whoa . . . wait."

"What are doing with this photograph?" asked Gurson. "Planning some blackmail?"

"You got it all backwards," Ren insisted.

"What the hell's going on, then? You working with Boyd Cleary?" Gurson barked. He held up a black-and-white of Cleary.

Ren stared at the photo, then looked away. "Don't know him."

"You sure about that?" asked Gurson.

Ren looked again. "I could have done him once. I could have done you once, too. But I don't remember."

"Oh, you'd remember Cleary," said Kane. "And you definitely wouldn't forget somebody like Detective Gurson, I'm sure."

"Then I guess I didn't do either of them," said Ren. "Did I, Detective?"

Gurson unfolded a piece of paper, pretending the Xerox of the take-out menu was filled with sensitive information. "What were you doing at the Morgan Hotel with Theodora Weil?"

They had tailed her, knew who she'd seen. "I don't know what you're talking about," said Ren, unconvincingly.

"Room 1701. You've been under surveillance, honey." Gurson emp-tied the contents of her bag on the table. The bizarre, candid photo of Norville in drag smiled up at them. "Our friend Ren here is going to tell us what she was doing with Theodora Weil. And she's going to tell us where she got this fine photograph of Tucker Norville. Or we've got a room for her at the Hotel Rikers."

Ren knew they could do that. Make it look like she killed somebody. They had ways of doing that shit. When they had nobody else to pin shit on, they settled on hookers, bums, anybody without a chance in hell of fighting charges. Ren looked at the door. No door had ever looked so closed. No room had ever felt so small. With each breath, it felt smaller. "I need air."

"You're going to need CPR when we're through if you don't get to it." Kane gripped the table.

Ren decided to start talking her way out. "It has nothing to do with her . . . it's him . . . her husband." She stopped short.

"You expect us to believe the A.D.A. has something to do with this?"

There was no more room to negotiate and Ren knew it. She decided to parcel out the truth. She put her elbows on the table and lightly banged her fists against her face. "He paid me to go to that shrink . . . Gretz . . . to tell him stories. Wanted me to tell him about my old man . . . how I screwed him in the woods."

"What's this got to do with Theodora Weil?" asked Gurson.

Their voices washed over her. Suddenly, she could only remember the wife's tenderness. The way the wife wanted to help, to protect her from all this.

"You planning to blackmail her with what you have on her husband?" asked Kane. "You sleeping with her too?"

Ren looked away.

"You ever see this photograph?" Gurson held up a copy of the Witkin print.

"No."

"This guy ever talk to you about birds?" Gurson held the photograph of Norville now.

Ren could see the wife sitting on that couch in the hotel room, looking lost and alone. But it wasn't the wife's pretty ass in the hot seat now, it was hers. Why shouldn't she tell them something? No one said she had to give it all up, not for nothing. Ren thought of the box the wife mentioned, something about bloody wings. "She said something about some bird's wings . . . thought I put them in her office. . . ."

Gurson looked at Kane. Kane started talking but Ren was only hearing part of what she was saying. ". . . everybody you've been fucking is winding up dead in the woods," Kane went on, "now's the time to talk, Ren. Body count's rising. You could be next."

This thought unsettled Ren; she moved uneasily in her chair.

"Norville know you have this pretty picture of him?" asked Gurson.

"No way," said Ren. "He was loaded."

"On what?" asked Kane.

"Pills and powder."

"You and Cleary setting him up?" demanded Gurson.

"What's my deal in all this?" Ren asked. "I tell you shit and then what?"

"You stay out of jail," Kane said.

"Why did Norville want you to do Gretz? Why?" demanded Gurson.

"I don't know why. Norville just wanted me to do the guy. Without his wife knowing."

"Is that what you were doing at the Morgan? Using this smut to blackmail the Norvilles? Is that what this money was given to you for? To keep your mouth shut?"

"I never showed her the picture," Ren insisted. "I just went there to tell her, you know, that her husband beat me up. If she paid me for the picture, I would have had to give it to her. She'd have taken it, would never have let me keep it."

Kane looked at Gurson. There seemed to be some logic in what Ren was saying. "So you go there, you tell her that her husband was sending you to Gretz to fuck him. What did she have to say about that?"

Ren had been Leone's informant for years. She knew how to play this game. Knew how to stall, twist things around. Give them a seed of the truth. Just enough to get them off and running. That was the way to buy time. See where the chips fell. Plan her next move. Ren crossed her arms and pouted. "She seemed surprised, upset."

"She ever say anything to you about a baby?" asked Gurson.

Ren shook her head. "She's just mixed up is all."

"Mixed up how, Ren?" asked Kane.

"Married to that creep. She just needs somebody to take care of, you know, she's okay, just wants somebody to love."

"Somebody to spend her money on, you mean," Kane barked, flashing the cash from Ren's bag.

"Somebody to treat like her own kid," suggested Gurson. "Somebody who might find that role convenient."

Kane finished his thought. "Somebody like you."

Ren looked away.

Gurson went on. "Is Boyd Cleary part of this circus?"

Ren wondered which answer would get her out of this dump. She decided to stick with the truth, as she knew it. She'd finger the man at the top of the garbage heap. Let Norville come and deny it. She figured she was fucked either way. She looked at Gurson with the eyes of a prisoner with nothing left to lose. "I'm telling you . . . all I know is, Norville said he wanted to set Gretz up . . . said he wanted his ass to fry."

"You got any proof that you and Gretz had sexual relations?" asked Gurson.

"Proof?" Ren took a moment to think. "Norville made me give him a pair of my panties . . . one afternoon right after I saw Gretz."

"Did you?" asked Gurson.

"What if I did?" Ren asked.

"We book you as an accessory to blackmail," said Gurson.

"Blackmail, shit. I just screwed the guy," Ren protested.

"Screwed him literally or figuratively, darling? Either way, he's dead now," said Gurson.

Gurson motioned to Kane. They left the room.

"She sure gets around." Gurson turned to Kane. "What do you think?"

"Let her chill in a pen. I say she's probably full of shit . . . or she's telling the truth." Kane fished in her pocket for a coin. "Heads or tails?"

"So you have no gut feeling for her, huh?"

"I have a gut feeling for her, sure. I feel like choking the life out of her."

"Because she was screwing with Leone or because she's screwing with you now?"

Kane looked at her shoes, then up at Gurson. "You ever find your wife in bed with someone else, Gurson?"

"That's one nightmare I've been spared." Gurson thought a moment. "If Norville took her undies, I figure he was probably planning to blackmail Gretz." Gurson reflected. "Makes me wonder if Collier conveniently forgot to tell us about getting any soiled panties along with that sexual misconduct complaint against Gretz." He called out for Florio. "Get Collier on the line. And what was the name you said Weil used at the Morgan?"

"Vogel," Florio yelled back.

"Sounds German," said Kane.

"We got any Krauts here?" Gurson called out. "Find out what 'Vogel' means."

"You feel like taking a drive in the woods?" asked Kane.

"What for?" asked Gurson.

"I want to go to the scene, where you found Gretz," said Kane. "Talk to the trees."

Gurson laughed. "You're serious?"

"Yeah. I want to walk around the scene again, feel it out." Kane started putting on her coat. "You coming?"

"I got Collier on line four," Florio said.

"Hold up, Kane. Two minutes." Gurson picked up the phone. "Yeah, Collier, tell me, you ever get a pair of soiled panties sent to you along with that complaint against Gretz?" Gurson cupped the receiver, shook his head no. "Yeah, well, should anything like that turn up, you'd be sure to let me know." He nodded, listened awhile, hung up. Gurson turned to Kane. "No panties."

"Or so he says now. You coming?" Kane was growing impatient.

Gurson grabbed the keys to the Jeep.

As they were heading out, Florio called out to Gurson. "Rudiger says Fogel means 'bird' in German." He pointed to a young cop sitting behind a desk.

"Old spelling was with a V. You could spell it with an F. Either way. Means 'bird.'" The cop flapped his arms.

Gurson opened the door for Kane. "After you talk to the trees, I think you ought to have a talk with the birds."

[26]

Ray of Light

Boyd sat in the front seat of the black sedan and fixed his gaze on the dash. Time to bring it all back to original. Blast the rockers. Dip the chassis in acid. Fix it all, the way it was before the rust crept in. The way it was meant to be. He left Jersey and turned onto the highway, could see the Manhattan skyline ahead. He shifted into fifth and smiled as the V8 engine hummed.

His keepsakes were in the glove compartment. A small yet significant collection that included poetry, a bird's wing, and a few photographs.

He released the glove compartment door and took hold of the box, set it down beside him on the passenger seat. He lifted the lid. It was good to have the sparrow's wing in his hands again, to feel the soft, smooth feathers, to receive the benefit of its magical powers.

Boyd thought back to his time alone with Theodora Weil. It was time to free her now . . . give her wings and watch her fly away.

The click of her tongue as it hit the edge of her teeth, her lips opening and closing. Secretly, he would tape their sessions. Alone, he would edit himself out. Then listen. Magnify the volume, let the air echo with the music of her voice. His name spoken over and over . . .

He could hear her calling him now. She needed him . . .

Boyd . . .

At night, alone, he deciphered the hidden meaning of her birdsong. The thought of being with her in physical space and time almost too much to bear.

He replayed the final act. With her last breath, she would say his name. In their dying embrace, he would be reborn. . . .

Boyd gripped the steering wheel. Refocused on the road ahead. All he could do to keep himself still. He checked himself out in the rearview. His thick, dark hair slicked back, his eyebrows, two bushy caterpillars arched over ebony eyes. He was almost good-looking, but the nose, broken one too many times, set the face off balance, and the thick lips stopped just short of sexy. He torched another fat joint, sucked hard, and coughed out a gust of thick Thai incense. Had a system for making the lights; that moment before yellow went red. Yeah, he was feeling lucky tonight. Radio on, quadraphonic rap, booming from the speakers. Lyrics, half shouted, half sung, inciting riot. He banged on the steering wheel and howled, making up the words as he went along.

As he drove on, he thought about her. How he'd so carefully shadowed her every move. Like he was invisible, with one of those magic cloaks that faggot cop talked about.

He looked for the cops in the rearview. Good as gone. Had he lost them? Yes . . . he could go to her now. He wondered if she'd found the little black box yet. Proud of his work, he smiled to himself. What must she be thinking if she had?

He'd hate to think she mistook the severed wing for anything less than the highest token of his esteem.

GURSON AND KANE DROVE DEEP INTO THE RAMBLES TO THE scene where he'd found Gretz in his Mercedes. Gurson parked the Jeep in the pitch black darkness, and they walked the scene once again. The Jeep's headlights provided the only beacon.

Kane stood in silence, meditative, as if waiting for a sign. Gurson leaned against the Jeep and looked up at the moon. Half full.

After a while, Gurson got back in the Jeep and waited for her. When she got back in, he asked her, "Gretz's ghost tell you anything out there?"

Gurson pulled out a pack of Marlboros.

"I thought you quit."

"I'm not lighting them. Yet." He put an unlit cigarette in his mouth.

"How many years you got on the force?" Kane asked.

"I stopped counting. Eight or nine, I think." He pretended to drag on the cigarette. "I was just sitting here thinking about all the years I've wasted, parked in the dark like this. Stakeouts, buy-and-busts, showdowns."

"How long you work undercover?"

"Few years. How about you?"

"About the same. Undercover's the fastest route to a shield and decent pay for a colored girl." Kane smirked.

Gurson looked out into the darkness, the dashboard lights illuminating the line of his jaw. "You remember your first stiff?"

Kane squinted her eyes. "Yeah. Some guy blown away on the street. Shot in the back. Big pool of blood. I kept thinking, his chest isn't moving . . . I think I even said that out loud. 'His chest isn't moving.' 'No shit, asshole,' someone says, 'he's dead.' I couldn't breathe. Like I had concrete in my lungs."

Gurson nodded. "I remember being fresh out of the academy. I was sent to help find this missing kid. Turned out she'd crawled into an abandoned refrigerator. Some schmuck had left the door on. I found her in there. Locked inside for a few days. She was just three years old." He paused. "I saw a refrigerator out on the street the other day, door still on it. Man, I went ballistic. Funny how certain things trigger . . ."

Kane finished the sentence, ". . . the past?"

Gurson felt around the dash. "I sure could use a match about now."

"This case is really getting you, isn't it?"

Instead of answering her question, he asked, "You believe any of what Ren said?"

"That Norville wanted to set Gretz up for sleeping with his wife? Shit yeah. The guy's a psychopath. He sends Ren to screw the doctor, then he nails him for misconduct. That's his trip. Set you up, knock you down."

"On the word of a whore?"

"He doesn't need her to testify. All he needs is an accusation."

"I say Weil went back to Gretz. All grown up. Thought she could win him back, on her own terms. The affair gets Norville pissed off. So he acts out. Figures he can blackmail Gretz, maybe enough to scare him off his wife," Gurson said. "Norville knows his wife is fond of Ren, protective of her. If he sends Ren to Gretz, he gets to blackmail Gretz . . . and at the same time he gets to mess with his wife's head. Plays both ends in. I figure Norville's playing private eye. Poking around in his wife's things. Reads some of her notes. She says she wasn't keeping any on Cleary, but say she got careless, you know, left something around the house. Cleary's name rings a heavy bell. Norville knows Cleary. Suspect for the first killing. Wife's notes confirm it. Norville sees an opportunity to use the guy to kill Gretz. Enlists him to do the real damage. Cleary's up for the challenge if he gets to throw Leone in for the bargain."

"Why?" asked Kane.

"Because he knows Leone is onto him for the first killing. High or not, she's a cop. A cop who won't let go."

"It fits," said Kane. "Norville's a cocky bastard. He feels omnipotent."

"That's the critical flaw in Norville's character," said Gurson. "Guy thinks he's God. Wants his wife's lover dead, wants it so bad he doesn't think about consequences. Hookers with peekaboo lenses or screwy patients who fall in love with his wife, he uses them all. Figures nobody will believe a whore or an ex-con over an A.D.A., not with his background and career."

Kane rolled down her window; a cool burst of air hit her face. "Or somebody's watching from the outside."

"What do you mean?"

"Somebody who hates Norville, for instance. Guy probably has plenty of enemies. Finds out who Norville's wife is banging, offs him, makes it look like Norville did it. We'd be looking at a real complex mind, of course, cunning. Somebody who plays out the scenario for a long time, pegs Norville and his motive. Cases the entire supporting cast, profiles all the players. Figures out the whole deal way before it ever goes down. Has everything neatly in place. It's a brilliant smear. Commit the crime Norville's dying to commit. Play Norville at his own game." Kane looked around her. The park drive was pitch dark, illuminated by his headlights and the occasional streetlamp. "Throws Leone in for the bargain, because she's getting too close." Her voice cracked. "Someone who knew how to get away with murder . . . and drive a car in here without being noticed."

Gurson tossed the unlit cigarette out the window. "I just did that, didn't I?"

"Yes, you did."

"Well, if you're right, you're sitting alone in the dark with a homicidal maniac."

For a long five minutes, silence dominated.

"And if I'm wrong?" asked Kane.

Gurson put the Jeep in drive. He turned to Kane. "How about we go talk to the Norvilles and find out."

THEODORA TOOK REFUGE IN THE BATHROOM, DOOR LOCKED. SHE turned the hot water on in the shower, letting the steam fill the room.

She sat on the edge of the tub and let her lungs fill with the moist vapor, clearing her head of all but one thought:

Who had placed the black box in her drawer?

Were those Boyd's handprints on her window? What did he want? Had he forgotten their oath of confidence, was he wondering what she intended to do?

Tell me about the woman in the park. . . .

She got up and took a bottle of Valium out of the medicine cabinet and thought of Ren as she swallowed the small blue pill, pale as a robin's egg.

Voices inside her head joined in a familiar chorus:

Be still . . . stop crying . . . there's nothing to cry about. . . .

Ren's stories about Leone untrue? No, Theodora had witnessed firsthand. Ren had been in trouble. She closed her eyes and saw the image of the photo Gurson had shown her. The disfigured remains of Charlene Leone.

The voices again, reprimanding and belittling her.

Stop crying . . . what are you crying about. . . .

Catching her reflection in the steamy mirror, she saw her father's face and found the reasons why. She had been only a child, an innocent victim of his drunken perversion and violent rage. She thought she had managed to escape from that past, rise above it, convert it into a questioned memory. But the past had repeated itself, over again.

She heard the phantom cry of a child she'd carried but never held.

Shhhh . . . don't be frightened . . . there's nothing to be frightened of. . . .

Theodora walked mechanically out of the bathroom and into the bedroom. She locked the door and walked to her closet to fetch the bottle of pills. Tucker had gone through his last liter of whiskey. A new bottle meant it was time for her to drop another dose of impotence. But the bottle of pills wasn't there. She looked again. Gone. Had Tucker found the bottle? Could he know what the pills were intended for? What else did he know?

Surely, he knew that she and Orrin had rekindled their old affair. How blind not to realize that it was Tucker who'd sent Ren to fuck Orrin. Surely he was not through with his sadistic revenge. She desperately wanted to reverse this imbalance of power. She walked over to Tucker's armoire and opened the mirrored door. The aluminum case sat on the top shelf. Its usual resting place. Where Tucker stored his Glock automatic, for their personal protection, and their occasional trips to a downtown shooting range. She reached up and took the case down and opened it. Her heart raced now as she found what she was least expecting. A xeroxed paper with the words: *I have become accessible to consolation. . . .*

A sudden chill ran through her. The line of verse painfully familiar.

She thought of the black box, the bird's wings.

She ran her hand along the written words.

Ptichka . . .

Surely, Tucker was out to drive her mad.

She carried the paper and the gun with her to bed. She laid the paper on her night table. Then carefully ran a hand over the gun's smooth nozzle. Opened the chamber and looked inside. Fully loaded. She closed the chamber, returned the now empty gun case to the shelf, and took the gun back with her to her side of the bed. Before placing the gun in the top drawer of her night table, she disengaged the safety.

She took another half of a Valium to calm her. Half asleep, the dog rested in the curve of her legs, and raised an unenthusiastic ear each time Theodora shifted her weight. She patted the dog's soft fur gently and grew sleepy herself, the line of verse meditatively playing in her head:

. . . become accessible to consolation . . .

She tried to fight sleep but the Valium dropped its velvet curtain, muffling the pulse of her gut-wrenching anxiety. A warm liquid wave pushed her further out to sea . . . *consolation* . . . The words in her head left her numb, yet still longing for a time in her life she could not place or name as real.

* * *

Tucker tried the door that adjoined the first floor of the townhouse to Theodora's office. Locked. He went to the key rack but there was no key. He grabbed a screwdriver and in a moment he was inside, quarter of a bottle of scotch in one hand, screwdriver in his pocket. He flicked on a light, took a swig from the bottle. The office was cold. He had snuck down here looking for a book. A book he'd seen before. A book that prick had given her.

He went to the bookshelves and scanned the spines. But he was too drunk to keep anything in focus. He pulled at the hardcovers, toppling them to the floor. Picking through the pile, he found what he was looking for. The book of poetry. He walked over to her desk now, turned on the desk light, tried the top drawer and was pleasantly surprised when it opened easily. He picked up the silver bookmarker. Could barely make out the inscription. For D? With affection, O. April 1979. He took another swig of whiskey and pocketed the bookmarker. He turned out the light and returned to the main floor, where he continued drinking in the den, until his bottle was empty.

He stood before the mantel and gazed into the dying fire. How long had they lived in these separate worlds pretending to be husband and wife? Years, the four walls answered.

Had she ever loved him?

No. She'd allowed him to love her while she used him. Never loved him, not the way she'd loved Orrin.

Tucker saw it plainly. She was a two-bit whore, a lying temptress who would continue to betray him. She was probably fucking the detective now, helping him compile evidence against him. He'd wanted to beat her to a pulp, force her into a confession, blast her about the pills when he'd first found them. But he knew from experience that her lies and denials would only make it a waste of time.

Before heading upstairs, he tossed the bottle of pills into the fireplace. He had kept them as some sort of evidence, force of habit, he supposed, though for what jury's eyes he couldn't say. He watched the plastic begin to curl and burn, and then, thinking better of it, reached a drunken hand into the fire and salvaged the curled plastic from the blaze. He shook his hand, the hairs singed, skin stinging.

Tonight, it was Orrin's shortcomings they would stay focused on.

He ascended the stairs to their bedroom, stopping briefly to fetch the baggie that he'd stashed in the hall closet containing the whore's black panties. Yes, tonight it was Orrin's shortcomings they would stay focused on . . .

"*There once was a woman named Dora who shrinked more than heads I assure ya. . . . She knew all her Freud and had a patient named Boyd . . .*" Tucker drunkenly sang. Amused by his limerick but unable to find the right words to finish it, he abandoned the effort and continued his climb.

OUT OF THE CORNER OF HIS EYE, BOYD NOTICED THE TWO GUYS in the black Ford. April fools. Rookie cops. Thought he'd lost them.

Fortunately, he had just the car for a quick getaway. One gently used police car, set free at auction with less than fifty thousand miles on the odometer. Repainted British racing green, this spanking V8 Ford sedan, with its rebuilt engine, cranked easily to 120. Pursuit speed and then some. Pumped up by the tune on the radio, Boyd put his foot to the floor.

Cops didn't have the horsepower to subdue this perp. Cleary treated the congested road like a race strip and kept the advantage. Backup? Well, looky here. Two additional cars joining the chase at the Lincoln Tunnel.

Fucking cops. Making him piss in their plastic cups. Messing with his DNA. Working up their *forensic* profiles.

Reason he'd had himself sterilized years ago. Sperm was definitely one thing a man like B.C. did not want to leave behind. Nuh-uh. Not anywhere. Devoid of sperm, hell, he didn't have to worry about getting entrapped by any goddamn whore. Crying rape, claiming some snot-nosed kid was his. Made it a fuck of a lot harder for the cops, too.

Sterility gave him power. Sterility was freedom.

Boyd tore off at top speed, disregarding lights that flickered yellow to red, his wheels spinning faster than a ray of light.

Orders to the squad: Proceed with caution. One of the drums in Mr. Cleary's shop was filled with bits of tooth and bone. Additional backup was on its way. This one was armed and dangerous.

[27]

Accessible to Consolation

In a deep sleep, Theodora didn't hear Tucker as he made his way upstairs. Didn't hear a thing as he turned the knob to find the bedroom door locked. He raised his voice an octave. "Locking me out of my own bedroom?" He pushed against the door with all his weight. But the door did not open. "Slut."

He fished out the screwdriver and, within minutes, pried the door open and let himself in.

Siegfried, hearing the commotion, raised a furry ear and began a low growl. But smelling Tucker, the dog calmed down. Theodora was roused but not fully awakened. Tucker came toward her. Looked at her lying there. Even now, he couldn't help but notice how her beauty had the power to enchant him. Remembering his purpose, he fought off such thoughts, went to his bureau and took out his gun.

Sleepily, Theodora looked up. "Tucker . . . ?"

"Whore . . ." Tucker drunkenly began.

Theodora opened her eyes, caught sight of Tucker's gun in hand, silencer neatly in place.

"Propranolol . . . hydrochloride . . ." he stuttered.

"What are you doing? Tucker . . . don't be a fool, put that gun away. . . ." She leaned back against the headboard, pulled her knees to her chest.

"God, how I loved you," he sighed, his tone oddly melancholy.

She was fully awake now. Adrenaline pumping. "You're going to hurt someone . . . put that gun away."

His laugh mocked her. "How could you go back to that pig?" Tucker said, disdainfully. "After the way he mistreated you . . . took advantage of you."

"You're drunk, Tucker. . . . We can talk about this tomorrow."

"Tomorrow and tomorrow and tomorrow . . ." Tucker waved the gun at her, his drama rising to a comic pitch. "You know your whore fucked him for less money than it costs to buy a pair of shoes." He reached into his pocket and pulled out the plastic bag with the black panties. He waved the bag at her. "Exhibit A. Your little darling's panties right here, smeared with your lover boy's semen."

This comment elicited the response he hoped it would. "For your dirty money. You used her . . . just a poor child. . . ."

"Child," Tucker cut her off, snidely. "Always going on about a child."

"Which you gave me and then defiled," she whispered to herself.

Tucker noticed the paper unfolded on the night table. He stepped closer. "I see you found your bedtime reading. Or were you looking for these . . ." He reached into his other pant pocket and threw the burned bottle of pills at her. "Trying to poison me . . . or content to simply render me impotent?"

"You're crazy, Tucker . . . you don't know what you're saying."

"You know perfectly well what I'm saying, you sonofabitch. And now you're fucking that detective. Planning to set me up." He uttered a macabre laugh. "Must admit, he's a fuck of a lot smarter than his old man was. Staging the suicide of your lover. I ought to thank him."

"That's ridiculous. You're drunk."

"And you're a fool, Theodora. Fell right for his little scheme. What was it, his blue eyes or his big dick?" Tucker was ranting, the gun in his hand waving at her. "Couldn't get me . . . so he went for my goddamned wife. He's under your skin now, isn't he, Theo? Knows everything about my sweet little bird," he went on maniacally. "Knows exactly what she will do . . ."

"Put down the gun . . . for godsakes, Tucker . . ."

"Time to become accessible to consolation, Theodora."

The dog began a low growl.

Steadily, Tucker cocked the trigger. For an instant, he considered turning the gun upon his wife, but instead passed a far more sadistic sentence and took aim at her dog. One shot, close range at Siegfried's head.

A PALE HALF-MOON ROSE IN THE DARK CLOUDLESS SKY AS GUR-son and Kane arrived at the Norvilles' doorstep. Gurson remembered the code . . . 3218 . . . pressed the numbers on the illuminated security box by the entrance to the townhouse. The heavy metal door clicked open and they entered a foyer.

Gurson could see another camera above the inside door, its red light flashing. He motioned to Kane. They ducked beneath it, creeping along the walls, wincing at each creak in the floorboards.

Gurson turned the knob very slowly and pressed the next door open. Darkness. Not a light on. Anybody there? Gurson could feel it. They weren't alone. He drew his gun. Kept it close and high. Checked the main floor. Nothing. He approached the den and listened as the pounding in his ears intensified. His own heart beating. The glow of street-lights vaguely lit dark corners.

Kane stayed back as Gurson made his way up the stairs. The plush carpeted landing muffled his footsteps.

At the top of the stairs, Gurson decided it was time to start talking.

"Norville, it's Gurson. How about turning some lights on. Not here to hurt anybody, just here to talk." Maybe he was talking to himself, maybe there wasn't anybody there. And if anybody was there, were they still alive?

Out of the darkness, he heard a woman crying. He followed the sound. It was coming from the room at the end of the hall.

Slowly, he entered. "Theodora . . . ?" Lights off, but he could see a silhouette standing beside the unmade bed. Silk quilt gathered in a dis-ordered pile. On the nightstand sat a digital clock, its green neon numbers ticking the seconds away. 10:46. 10:47. 10:48 . . .

"Stop . . . don't come any closer . . . don't move," she pleaded.

"Where's Tucker?" Gurson took a step toward her but stopped still in his tracks when he caught the gleam of a gun's barrel.

"He's killed my dog . . . Siggy . . . my baby. . . ." She spoke like a lost child, alone in the dark.

"Why did Tucker kill the dog?" Gurson asked. "Where's Tucker? Talk to me . . . tell me what happened, Theodora."

"Tucker . . . he came in here . . . crazed, screaming about Orrin. Making accusations, said I was sleeping with Orrin, sleeping with you. . . . He had a gun, he was going to kill me . . . he shot Siggy. . . ."

Gurson looked left and saw a large mass on the floor. A pool of blood. Cautiously, he inched closer and knelt down beside the lifeless body on the floor. No pulse. Gurson looked right. Was that another gun lying on the floor? "So you shot him?" He looked up at Theodora. Her naked shape visible beneath flimsy white cotton pajamas, stained crim-son. The gun in her hand still pointed at him.

"It happened so fast . . . I thought he was going to kill me . . ."

"Tucker think Gretz was getting in the way of your marriage? Was he jealous?"

She sobbed. "He sent her to Orrin . . . gave her money . . . she would never have done it otherwise . . . she's just a child . . ." Theodora rambled nonsensically. "Tucker was hurting her . . . going to hurt me. . . . He said you were setting him up . . . said you killed Orrin."

"He told you that? He tell you who killed Detective Leone?" Gurson asked.

"He said you'd been nursing your hatred for him for years . . . that you had something to do with it . . . that you were setting him up."

"But you know that's not true," said Gurson.

"I don't know what's true. . . ."

"Sure you do."

"No." She raised the gun.

"You planning to kill me?" asked Gurson.

"Why would I want to kill you, Detective?"

"Because I know the truth." He was thinking of how Norville had wanted to keep him away from Theodora so bad. Suddenly, it all fit and he knew why. He was thinking of what she had said about the truth. How someone in a state of total denial about severe sadistic desires could disassociate from the truth . . . live in two worlds. Because of some deep internal conflict, some humiliation, past pain. "Which world are you in now, Theodora? Fantasy or reality? Or are you on that narrow bridge in between?"

"You're quite cunning, Detective. But I'm afraid you're the one in denial." Theodora still held the gun at him. She was covered with blood. The dog's blood?

Gurson kept talking. "I want to help you—" He advanced toward her.

"Then drop your gun," she demanded, still aiming her gun at him.

Gurson raised a hand of surrender, tossed his gun to the floor. "Talk to me, Theodora. I want to help you."

"No . . . you just want to fuck me . . . like the rest of them."

"It isn't fair, is it," he spoke warmly to her, "when your parents are the big bad wolves and everyone you love and trust gets on the band-wagon right behind them. . . ."

"Don't analyze me," she yelled out.

Gurson was thinking on his feet. What was it she had said? *People confide in you when they trust you . . . when you show them you can empathize with their pain. . . .* "You and I were about the same age when our worlds fell apart, weren't we? We were just kids. It wasn't our fault. Men in authority misused their power . . . we felt abandoned. . . ." He paused. "They took your baby." He could hear her weeping now. "You could never forgive Orrin for that . . . and then he hurt Ren . . . used her the way he used you. . . ." Gurson laid one fact down and then another. In this dark room the picture was becoming clearer. "Gretz wanted to send Boyd Cleary to prison. . . . You didn't want that to happen, did you?" Gurson began.

"He was my patient. . . ." Her voice was childlike, as if she were try-ing to remember something important.

"More than just a patient . . . a wounded child."

"Yes."

"And you promised him that you would be his confidante . . . that you wouldn't let him come to harm."

"You don't understand."

"I think I do." Gurson watched her hands on the gun. She had him in range. "I know you bought Orrin that photograph—" Gurson was going on instinct—" 'Woman Once a Bird.' That's how you feel, isn't it? It's your perception of what Orrin did to you, isn't it?"

His self-assurance angered her. She was coming to the surface, her anger dissolving the shroud of denial. "A psychiatrist who fucks his patients is no better than a parent who fucks his children. Somebody had to stop him." She stepped away from the bed and into the light now, her ghostly voice carrying over the darkness.

Gurson could see the dog on the bed, the blood, the gun on the floor . . . and the outline of her face as she stood six feet from him. This is what he had to go on. This, and the story his mind was now piecing together. "After all you'd been through, Orrin was your hope and then he cut off your wings . . . denied you your deserved freedom . . . took away your precious child." Gurson paused just long enough to find the right words. "In your mind, Boyd and Ren have come to symbolize that lost child . . . haven't they?"

Theodora looked over at her husband lying dead on the floor. "You don't understand . . . I had to help them. . . ."

"What did Ren tell you? She tell you Leone was going to send her away . . . put her in jail?"

"Yes . . . giving her drugs to . . . keeping her high, on the street."

"And you couldn't let Leone get away with that, couldn't let Leone or Gretz take Ren or Cleary . . . you wanted to protect them . . . take care of them . . . like the children you never had." He kept talking, inching closer. "Ren needed someone to stand up for her . . . the way your mother stood up for you. . . ." He stepped one foot closer, but not yet close enough to subdue her.

"Mama kept the baby. . . ." She was crying softly now.

"Your mother, yes. But the pregnancy was aborted. . . . Collier said it was your father's child."

"No! Liars . . . bastards all of them. Covering it all up. Pretending it was my father's child."

"It was too painful to accept the truth. You needed to believe it was Orrin's child. The same way it's too painful now to believe that you killed him . . . that you killed Detective Leone."

Theodora's voice filled with sad resignation. "No . . . I can't . . . I can't remember. . . ."

"You can and you will. You shot Leone up with succinylcholine . . . paralyzed her, left her lying half dead in the snow. You let Cleary finish her off for you, didn't you?" Gurson paused. "Then he helped you stage Orrin's suicide."

"So cold . . . so much snow . . ." She was there now, back in the park, in the snowy woods.

"You have Cleary call Gretz into the park? Or did you call him your-self . . . entice him there. . . . tell him how you were warm inside his car . . . while you waited with the succinylcholine?"

Theodora was lost in the past now back in the park. "It's cold. . . ."

"Orrin humiliated you . . . shamed you . . . the way your father did." Gurson kept up a steady flow of reassurance. "Maybe you didn't want to hurt anybody. . . . Maybe you just wanted to gain a little control. By shooting Gretz and Leone with anesthesia, you could overpower them, reduce them to a condition resembling death . . . and then what . . . spare them with some final act of mercy?" He wanted to reach out and take hold of her, but she was still too far from him, still holding the gun.

"I only gave them a few cc's of the anesthetic." Her voice was flat, cold.

"You wanted them to feel the full extent of what was happening to them, was that it? Have Gretz and Leone powerless, the way you felt . . . the way you feel now?"

"Boyd . . ." she began, but then abruptly stopped.

"Got carried away, didn't he? Had to give the murders his own per-sonal touch. He signed off with the severed bird's wing and the slashes on Leone's back, didn't he?"

". . . wanted to do it myself . . ."

"But Boyd wouldn't let you do it alone . . . he had his own vendetta against Leone. She was onto him, wasn't she? For the first killing in the park."

". . . setting things right . . ." Theodora kept drifting off.

"That's how you rationalized the whole thing, isn't it? You were set-ting things right, the way no court of law ever would." Gurson tried to get her to focus. "Leone was a dirty cop who deserved to die and Orrin was no better than your father."

"I knew Orrin was betraying me for years." She seemed oddly proud of this admission.

"And yet you refused to acknowledge the situation. In a way you've contributed to your suffering."

"It was much safer to pretend," she said, laughing sadly.

"The truth caused you too much anxiety, Theodora, didn't it? That's why you offered yourself to Orrin again and again despite his abuse. Were you hoping he'd leave Ren alone, that he'd feel sorry for you? The way you offered yourself to your father to spare your mother the grief of his violent rage—hoping your mother would make it up to you somehow with the love and protection you so desperately craved?"

"I never offered myself to my father!"

"It wasn't so much your father's horrific abuses that made you suffer most, was it, Theodora? It was your mother's willingness to allow you to sacrifice your innocence for her own sake. You wanted a child to set things right. Needed to become the mother you never had. When the dam finally broke, murdering Orrin was the only viable solution, wasn't it, Theodora? The only way to love and protect yourself . . ."

"The only way to change things . . ." she began to weep.

"Ditto for Leone on Ren and Boyd's behalf, is that it? With Gretz and Leone dead and gone, you could all start fresh, one happy family. But eventually you'd have to acknowledge what you did, day after bloody day. You killed Orrin Gretz and Charlene Leone in cold blood."

Theodora's sobbing was unrestrained now, the heartbreaking cry of a wounded child.

"Tell me, Theodora . . . how do you become accessible to consolation?"

"I take you out of your misery, Detective . . ." For a moment she seemed to recover her anger. She aimed the gun at him, but then, once again she seemed faraway, lost. "Or you take me out of mine."

"I want to help you, Theodora . . ."

"I love the way you say my name, Detective . . . it sounds so sweet and kind." She turned the gun around and placed the barrel of the gun against her head.

"Put down the gun, Theodora . . . we both know suicide's no happy ending."

"There is no happy ending, Detective."

Gurson could hear her take a breath. She ran the nuzzle of the gun down the side of her head, and then between her breasts, directly aligned with her heart.

"I can't finish this myself. . . . Please, help me. . . ."

"Look at me, Theodora. I don't want to hurt you. Gretz and Leone are dead. Ren is safe. You can come with me. We can find a way to work this out. Get you the help you need. . . ." He could have sworn he had her. She was tired, ready to give in. But instead, in an instant, her energy shifted.

"Help me? How? By locking me up?" Theodora turned the gun back on him, her finger pulsed on the trigger. "To hell with you and your idea of justice . . ."

As Gurson lunged forward, leaping on top of Theodora, Kane clocked her target, took aim and fired. From above, the security camera caught what looked like a man and woman entangled in a lover's embrace. But in this frame, only one heart was still beating.

BY THE TIME BOYD PULLED UP TO THE NORVILLES' PLACE, IT WAS all over. He stepped out of the car, hands in the air. Didn't have much choice. An entourage of cops were behind him. Guns drawn, they emerged en masse to make a long-overdue arrest.

Bianchi, who'd been kept posted of Cleary's whereabouts, arrived on the scene. Kane appeared at the entrance of the townhouse. Bianchi called out to her, "Where's Gurson?"

"Alive and kicking. But we got two dead bodies in there. Three if you count the dog."

Bianchi joined Kane at the front door and followed her up to the master bedroom.

With all the lights on, it was a bloody mess.

Gurson was sitting on an upholstered armchair with an unlit cigarette dangling from his lips. "Hello, boss. Real shoot-out at the fantasy factory."

"Cleary led the cops here all the way from Hoboken," said Bianchi.

"Missed the grand finale." Gurson took a deep drag off the unlit cigarette, then broke it in half and set it down.

"Luminal picked up traces of Leone's blood in Cleary's shop. And they found a box of teeth . . . we're thinking they're probably from the first girl."

"Just like you thought, Gurson," said Kane.

"Moron's babbling like a brook. Wants to take full credit for the killings. Says we have to let his little bird go, says he killed Gretz and Leone, that she had nothing to do with it. Which makes me think she had something to do with it. He's down there giving the guys details, blow by blow. Has one of those bloody bird's wings you've been looking for in his car. A copy of that poem too, and that freaky photograph—"

"He doesn't get full credit on Leone or Gretz," said Gurson. "Weil was the brains. Cleary was her dupe, a willing pawn."

"I don't get it," said Bianchi.

Gurson stood up to explain. "Weil must have had it in her head that she was the mother of the walking wounded. In her twisted mind, Ren became like a daughter to her. Far as she was concerned, Leone and Gretz were out to hurt her kids."

"She must have felt that Cleary was another motherless child who'd been abandoned and abused—in need of her empathy and understanding, not another prison term," said Kane.

"Cleary must have confessed the first killing to her, must have told her how Leone was after him," said Gurson. "How much he wanted to kill her. Weil gets to thinking. With Cleary's help, she figures she can kill two birds with one stone. Get away with murder. You got to remember, Weil's not living in the real world all the time." Gurson put a finger to his head and twirled it.

"So you're saying Weil orchestrated the killings . . . enlisted Cleary's help?" asked Bianchi, following along.

"She claimed she didn't intend on killing anybody . . . just shoot them up and then who knows what she was thinking. She said Cleary got carried away, but more likely, I say they were in sync," said Gurson.

"What about the pross?" asked Bianchi.

"Doesn't appear she knew what was really going on. She was just screwing everybody and collecting her pay. I don't think Theodora knew that it was Tucker who was sending Ren to Gretz, probably figured it was one more of Gretz's manipulations. I figure Theodora was obsessed with Gretz, probably stalking him. I say when she found out Gretz was screwing her little girl Ren, it triggered her old rage. For a while, I'll bet Theodora tried to repress the pain, suppress all her sadistic desires. You know, pretend none of it was really happening. But the dam gave way. Once Leone and Gretz were dead, she must have completely cut off, disassociated from the reality of what she'd done. Actually convinced herself she had nothing to do with any of it."

"But Cleary remembered it all vividly," said Bianchi.

"Gets off on the remembering," said Kane. "Clips the bird's wings as souvenirs to help him remember. One for him, one for Theodora. Wants her to remember too. Imagines this sacrificial act connects them for life."

Bianchi looked on the floor to where Norville lay dead. "And what happened to Norville?"

"When we got here, Norville and the dog were history," said Gurson. "Looks like Tucker did the dog in to punish Theodora for betraying him. We'll probably never know the whole cat-and-mouse story between them. Found these by the bed. Sealed like some kind of evidence." Gurson held up the baggie with the black panties. "I'll have Forensics check them out, see if anything corroborates the pross's story."

"Theodora claimed he was enraged, said he shot the dog, thought he was going to kill her." Kane was looking at Norville on the floor. "Looks like he took a bullet in the chest and one in the head. I say she did him the same way her mother did her old man. Finally decided to let the sadistic bastard have it."

"And which one of you pulled the trigger on Weil?" asked Bianchi.

Gurson looked at Kane. Kane spoke. "Classic suicide by cop, boss. Weil wanted to kill herself but couldn't bring herself to do it. Set it up so Gurson would have no choice but to defend himself and go for her. I don't think she ever knew I was there."

"It was Weil or me, boss." Gurson saw the end play itself out again in his mind's eye. "Kane saved my ass."

Epilogue

ONE WEEK LATER . . .

Bags packed and checked, Ren sat next to Tommy on the 747. Airplanes made her blood race. The very idea of taking off. She looked over at Tommy. Cool as the other side of the pillow.

"I got a piece of this restaurant by the beach, baby, little gold mine."

Ren was busy looking at herself in her small compact mirror, applying a fresh coat of red gloss.

Tommy was musing, fantasies about the future. "Been thinking of keeping you with me. You can work the door. Dress up. Play hostess. No more outgoing calls." Tommy rolled a wooden toothpick between his teeth and gently laid a hand on her thigh.

The plane climbed to a higher altitude. The stewardess passed out packs of peanuts. Drinks were being served in the aisles. The screens filled with coming attractions. The fasten-your-seat-belt symbol disappeared.

Ren looked out the window, down at the ground below, rooftops small and distant. She closed her eyes and settled back in her seat. She changed the channels on her Walkman and opened her little bottle of

Smirnoff's. One deep swallow to cut the chill. She was headed due south, to a place where the sun always shined. Palm trees, coconuts, and swimming pools. Get dark as dirt, skinny like a boy. Strap on a string bikini, paint her nails sky blue.

She took hold of the mandala around her neck and thought about the wife. Kane said the poor woman really thought of Ren like a daughter. Had to admit, it had been nice to play that part. Never thought the wife would go so far as to kill anybody to protect her. Imagined herself standing by the wife's grave, laying down some lotus flowers maybe.

"You okay?" asked Tommy.

They hadn't given her back the money, but they'd given her something better. A ticket out of hell. She turned to look at Tommy, then looked past him, out the airplane window, at the blue sky and billowing clouds. "I'm in heaven."

He brushed her hair from her eyes. "Yeah. Maybe I should start calling you Angel, then."

Angel. She liked that.

THE GREAT LAWN WAS LITTERED WITH PEOPLE. ALL THE SNOW had melted days before, leaving the ground moist and ripe for spring. New Yorkers, out and about. Cooped up for months in their musty, stacked dwellings, they were re-staking their claim. A patch of city green.

Spring had sprung. Everyone was happy inside the walls, safe and sound beneath a sunny park sky. Tall trees in first bloom swayed in a tranquil breeze. Inside these walls, you could tell yourself you were anywhere. The city just a step away, bustling with all its choice and opportunity, but deep in this wood, life could get slow and quiet.

Gurson and Kane took a seat on a park bench. A red sun was going down in a cloudless sky, its splendor visible through the canyon formed by the twin towers of the San Remo.

"So, you think Theodora Weil has a kid floating around some-where?" Kane sat back and stretched her legs in front of her.

"Collier insists it's impossible, a total figment of Theodora's imagi-nation. Said Theodora was living in some kind of parallel universe." Gurson turned up the collar on his leather jacket. "He maintains the story of the abortion, though he's no longer denying Orrin could have fathered the child. Sounds like Gretz was a duplicitous bastard. And that story about Theodora's parents pretty much checked out. Records confirm that her mother shot and killed her father, then shot herself. She survived long enough to tell the cops what happened and why."

"So Weil played the same scene out again," Kane said.

"Only this time she extended the family circle."

"The past repeats itself," said Kane.

"Unfortunately. If you choose to live in it."

"You sound so damned sympathetic, Gurson."

"*Empathetic.*"

"That when you understand but don't really give a shit?" Kane teased.

"No, that's *pa-thetic*, Kane."

"I'll tell you what's pathetic," Kane went on, "Boyd Cleary. That sly motherfucker getting a vasectomy so we couldn't find his seed planted anywhere. Taking his victim's teeth and slicing those wings . . ."

"Can you believe that scuba suit they found stashed in his garage? Crawling around in Central Park like some goddamned amphibian," said Gurson.

"Makes me sick to my stomach thinking what he did to Charlene."

"Beyond my comprehension," said Gurson. "Guy needs to be rewired."

"Sit his ass in a chair with electric currents running through it." Kane shook her head. "I'm following the conditions of his confinement, believe me. If I have anything to say about it, that menace isn't going back to Wards, Gurson. Didn't do him no good the first time. This round, he's doing some real time."

Gurson looked at his watch. "Ren's about to touch down in Miami."

"Lucky girl."

"Damn lucky we didn't find a reason to book her," said Gurson. "Those black panties of hers for starters. Had her vaginal fluid and Gretz's semen all over the crotch. You got to wonder what Norville planned to do with them."

"You ever think it's possible Ren and Weil were the ones working this thing together against Gretz?"

"Doesn't jibe. Weil wouldn't put her up to something like that, not with the deluded way she felt about her," said Gurson. "I figure Ren was just hooking for Norville, like she said, manipulated by the lure of easy money."

"She's lucky she's alive," said Kane. "That child better wake up."

"Cops down there know where she's at." Gurson looked up into the sun.

"And so do I."

Gurson unwrapped two sticks of gum and folded them into his mouth.

Kane cracked a grin. "How can you chew that shit? Stuff rots your teeth."

"Better than nicotine." He folded the wrappers in small squares. "Besides, sugar helps me forget what a bitter place this world can be."

"Oh yeah? Gimme a piece."

"You gotta chew two." Gurson slipped Kane two sticks.

"I see what you mean." Kane worked the wad around in her mouth. "Know what Bianchi told me this morning? He pulls me aside and tells me he's sorry for all the inconvenience. *Inconvenience.* Tells me, despite everything, he thinks I'm a good cop. Lord have mercy."

"He's ready for the easy chair, Kane. Dreaming of his pension, wants to tie everything up with a pretty bow. This morning he started getting all religious on me . . . quoting the gospel, trying to tell me how the son need not revisit the sins of his father." Gurson looked off at a couple of kids and their dog playing with a Frisbee. An old guy was out on the green pushing a cart, making straight white lines on the grass. "Look at that," Gurson said to himself, "boys of summer . . ."

Kane gave him a gentle nudge in the ribs. "You still feeling guilty about Weil?"

Gurson tossed a stone, watched it bounce on the dirt. "Thought I could talk her down, get her to walk out with us. But then she cocked that freaking gun."

"You know she set you up, Gurson. Wasn't your fault. She wanted you to kill her. Classic suicide by cop."

"I thought maybe you believed her when she said I was setting Norville up. Thought maybe you bought the idea that I planned the whole thing. I figured you were aiming for me, but missed."

"It crossed my mind," she paused, "but then it took a left turn and kept going." She smiled. "I say Ms. Weil was hoping you'd fall in love with her, the way Cleary did. Thought you'd let her off the hook."

"She wasn't singing any sweet songs I could hear," said Gurson.

"You'd think these goddamn psychiatrists would have their shit together. Spending all their time trying to fix other people when they can't even help themselves."

The skyscrapers surrounding the park loomed like stone monuments, the lights in each window luminous orbs in the night sky. Streetlamps flickered on like clockwork. Gurson and Kane got up and walked awhile in silence, along a quiet footpath toward Central Park West.

Gurson tilted the brim of his Dodgers cap over his eyes. "By the way, thanks again for stepping in and saving my tail, Kane. I owe you."

"Yeah, come to think of it, you do. Two seedpods and a book of poetry."

Gurson picked up a stone and tossed it. "I hear there are a couple of prime cases waiting on us over at Manhattan North." He looked at her. "You aren't still thinking about that farm, are you?"

Kane stopped walking and looked back into the park. "Nah, put a few more years on before setting myself out to pasture." She smiled. "Hey, what did you end up doing with that shrink's cat?"

"Brought him home. My kid's crazy about him."

Kane punched Gurson's arm lightly. "You're okay, Gurson. For a funky white boy."

"You know, it's funny. I couldn't wait to get the hell out of this dump. And now, I don't know, I think I kind of like it here."

"Keep walking, man. Nice place for the little birds, but I say it's high time we hit the street."

8/0.3